Th

Enchantine

Book 2 of the 'Magic Fix' series

Also by Mark Montanaro

The Magic Fix

The Enchanting Tricks

Book 2 of the 'Magic Fix' series

Mark Montanaro

Elsewhen Press

The Enchanting Tricks
First published in Great Britain by Elsewhen Press, 2022
An imprint of Alnpete Limited

Elsewhen Press, PO Box 757, Dartford, Kent DA2 7TQ
www.elsewhen.press

British Library Cataloguing in Publication Data.
A catalogue record for this book is available from the British Library.
ISBN 978-1-915304-09-4 Print edition
ISBN 978-1-915304-19-3 eBook edition

Designed and formatted by Elsewhen Press

This book is a work of fiction. All names, characters, places,
territories, monarchies, governments and events are either a product
of the author's fertile imagination or are used fictitiously. Any
resemblance to actual events, feudal societies, anarcho-syndicalist
communes, royalty, places or people (living or dead – whether elf,
goblin, human, ogre, pixie or troll) is purely coincidental. No
unicorns were entrapped in the making of this book.

In 2009, I was waiting in a queue for a sandwich, when somebody took my hat and ran off with it. This book is dedicated to everyone except that guy.

Sir, if you ever read this, please return my hat.

Contents

The Known World

Chapter 1

It was another surprisingly cold night in Tygon Hollow. There had been a slight chill in the air of the Goblin realm ever since the death of their three kings. And that was nearly a week ago.

Some said it was a sign that the Gods were angry. Others said it was simply because autumn was over. A few even thought it was the ghosts of their leaders, haunting the tunnels of Nuberim and blowing cold air as they went. But that was just silly.

Warlord Sepping did not believe such hogwash: ghosts didn't exist, and autumn wouldn't be over for at least another few weeks. At any rate, it didn't matter. Goblins could handle the cold; they were built for it. Their green skin was thick and hard. They could withstand temperatures even Trolls couldn't handle. Back in the 12th Age, the great Goblin wizard, Gorbo the Magnificent, had managed to survive in a giant block of ice for over two weeks. Admittedly that was probably some sort of magic trick, but it was still very impressive.

Warlord Sepping's main concern was not the cold, but the risk of more people being killed. They had lost three kings. They were leaderless. Vulnerable. The other five civilisations of the Known World surely all knew this now. What would the Ogres plan next? And how about the Humans? He had no way of knowing.

"Have another drink," said Queen Afflech, who was sitting to his right.

It was just the two of them in a room, near the very centre of Tygon Hollow. Both had been staring into the space in front of them, barely saying a word.

"I feel like all I have done is drink recently," said Sepping.

"Hardly," replied the queen. "You have kept us all together during this difficult time."

Sepping shrugged.

"I mean it," she continued. "Outside these walls, people are farming and hunting, building and tunnelling. Their leaders have died, but they have gone back to work as normal. You and the other warlords deserve a lot of credit for that."

Queen Afflech was doing remarkably well herself considering the circumstances. She had seen her husband die, and both her sons killed within the space of a couple of weeks. That kind of thing does tend to bring you down a bit.

"You're too kind," was all the warlord said in return.

He looked down at his empty goblet and made his way across the room for a refill. There were four bottles of whiskey in the cabinet. He lifted the top off the nearest one and poured himself a generous helping.

"Can I ask you something?" he said to the queen as he sat back down again.

She nodded.

"If you had the option to take the throne yourself, would you do it?" said the warlord.

She laughed sarcastically. "It certainly would be nice to be given that option."

Queen Afflech was not fit to rule the Goblin realm, because she wasn't of royal blood. She had always known it. The warlords had always known it; even the peons would know it if they had bothered to pay attention at school when they were younger.

She had married King Grieber, which made her a queen. But she wasn't next in line to the throne. In fact, she wasn't anything in line to the throne.

"As it is, I've got nothing left," continued the queen. "My husband and two sons were killed. And on top of that, my title will soon be taken away from me."

"I understand. It's just another nail in the coffin," replied Warlord Sepping, before realising that probably wasn't the best metaphor to use right now.

The next in line to the throne was a woman. Lady Niella was King Grieber's niece. She was the only surviving child of his younger brother, who also happened to have died a few years earlier; he had poisoned himself trying to prove that a certain type of berry was not poisonous. He had proven everyone wrong, but then celebrated so much that he died of alcohol poisoning.

Queen Afflech took another sip from her glass, staring at the fireplace in front of her.

"Any more news about Niella's arrival?" she asked.

Sepping shook his head. "We don't even know whether she's left Khyan yet."

"How could she not have left? She must have heard from our messengers by now."

"Well yes, the messengers got there fine," began the warlord. "I understand she was excited by the possibility of becoming queen. But she became a bit less excited when she heard that the previous kings had all been killed."

Queen Afflech shrugged. "Well, she was never going to take the throne if they were still alive. It can't have been that much of a surprise!"

"Still, I think it made her a little nervous about accepting the position," said Sepping.

"Accepting the position?" said the queen. "It's her duty! It's not something she can just decide not to do. And even if she could, why in the name of the Gods would she refuse it?"

She lifted her glass to take another sip, realised it was empty but still waited until a final drop fell into her mouth.

"I don't understand the younger generation," she continued. "They are so sheltered, so naïve. Doesn't she know that most people would die for the chance to become a king or queen?"

"I expect so. After all, that is what a lot of them seem to be doing," replied the warlord.

Queen Afflech nodded slowly. "Well anyway, we need her here. We can't keep going on like this."

"She'll come to Nuberim soon, I'm sure of it," said Sepping.

It was a good six nights' travel from Khyan – although probably longer if they were being extra cautious about people killing them along the way.

The governor at Khyan had been instructed to ensure the future queen was always protected. The specific instructions were to 'wrap her in cotton wool'. It had taken her staff a few nights to prepare enough cotton or wool blankets and clothes for Niella to take with her. And they were all a little puzzled as frankly they didn't seem to offer her much protection. Although they did make her carriage extra comfy.

"When was the last time you met Lady Niella?" said the queen.

Warlord Sepping thought for a second. "It must be about five years," he replied. "She was only a child."

"She still is a child!" replied the queen. "She's only been in the Known World for seventeen years."

"True," replied Sepping. "When did you last see her?"

"About a year ago now," said the queen.

Sepping stared down at his goblet. It was empty already. He briefly contemplated getting another refill but decided against it. For the moment.

"What did you make of her, the last time you spoke?" he asked.

"We barely even did speak," replied Queen Afflech. "I was there to see her father really; I only had a brief chat with Niella."

The warlord nodded, even though she hadn't answered his question.

"I think it's crucial that we know where she stands on things," he began.

"Things?" replied the queen

"Yes, well everything," he continued. "What is her vision for the Goblin Realm? How do we deal with Higarth and the Ogres? What about the Humans?"

Now it was the queen's turn to nod her head.

"I agree," she said. "And I think there's a fair chance

she hasn't even formed an opinion on those things."

She turned to the warlord.

"She's going to need guidance. Moulding. Someone to teach her."

"Indeed," replied Sepping. He now decided enough time had passed that he warranted another drink. He grabbed the queen's glass too and walked over to the cabinet, stumbling slightly.

"And by someone, you mean us, I assume?" he continued.

"Yes," replied Queen Afflech. "In case you hadn't noticed, there aren't a lot of Goblin leaders left! So it pretty much falls to us, and Uoro."

Warlord Uoro was not with them in the room, but he and Sepping were the two most senior warlords in the Goblin kingdom. There were two others who were equally ranked, but they were younger and less experienced. So it was really an unwritten rule that Sepping and Uoro were the leaders among the warlords. They were a higher rank than the others in all but name and pay grade. And they could probably sort that out too, now they were practically in charge of the realm; they could give themselves more money if they wanted – maybe even fancier titles.

Warlord Sepping took a seat once again, handing Queen Afflech her glass.

"I think we should call ourselves 'Supreme Warlords' from now on," he said.

"What?" said the queen.

"Oh nothing," he replied. "But the real question is, what kind of a queen do we even want Niella to become? What do we mould her into, exactly?"

Queen Afflech took a sip from her rather full glass of whiskey.

"That's a very good question," she replied. "I suppose what you're really saying is, how do we teach her who to trust, when we don't even know ourselves?"

Warlord Sepping thought for a minute.

"I think that for the moment, we can't trust anyone," he

began. "We still can't be sure what was behind the deaths of King Grieber, or Prince Nutrec. But from the evidence we have, it looks quite possible that the Ogres were behind one of them, and the Humans behind the other. Both using dirty, underhand tactics to do so."

There had of course been three killings, but they knew what had caused Prince Grumio's death because they had both been involved in it. They had used the dirty, underhand tactic of stabbing him while he slept.

"I agree, we can't trust anyone," said the queen. "Both the Humans and the Ogres may have killed our kings. And then there are the other civilisations. The Pixies: our relationship with them has never been more than skin deep. The only trust I have in the Trolls is that eventually they will get angry and start wanting to kill each other again."

"And the Elves?"

"Well they're irrelevant really. Just annoying."

Warlord Sepping nodded once again. He used to think the only Elf that wasn't annoying would be a dead one. And even then, you would presumably have to carry their body and bury it somewhere, which would be quite annoying.

"We're alone," he said, looking down at his drink. "Completely alone."

Goblins were built for the cold. Their blood was warm; their skin was tough. Warlord Sepping had drunk half a bottle of whiskey. And yet despite all that, he still felt a sharp chill go through every bone in his body.

Chapter 2

The Known World was full of strange and puzzling things. There were sabre-toothed cats twice the size of any Human, which bizarrely ran away terrified whenever anyone came near them. There was an ancient tree in the Elf realm which could instantly send people to sleep if they touched it, but for some reason it only worked in the mornings.

And nobody had ever solved the mystery of the disappearing forest in the south of the Known World. No-one had ever entered it and come out alive on the other side. The real mystery was why people were still stupid enough to try, when it was just as easy to walk around it.

King Wyndham furrowed his brow. Right now, there were even more strange things going on than usual. There was a magic Pixie who could kill dragons with a flick of her wrist. She had the potential to change the whole of the Known World. And the rest of that world probably knew about it.

But the strangest news had come from a messenger only yesterday. He couldn't even comprehend it. Farthing had stood in front of the King, feeling both anxious and smug at the same time. He was just a messenger, but Wyndham trusted him – the man hadn't delivered a wrong message in his life. Except for one time where he had brought a declaration of war to the wrong Troll settlement, which caused a lot of confusion and unnecessary fighting. But everybody makes mistakes.

Now, as King Wyndham sat in his royal meeting room, he was relaying the news to his lords. All seven of them were gathered in the palace at Peria, the capital of the Human realm.

The royal meeting room was large and extravagant. Red curtains with gold lining were draped over the windows. Various historical artifacts were positioned across the walls. A huge portrait of King Wyndham hung on one side; it looked just like him, if he had been much younger and far better looking.

The lords were all staring at the King open mouthed. It still didn't make sense, even as he was saying it. He looked over at Elgin, the Lord of Peace. He was frowning.

"Didn't we send a messenger to the Goblin kingdom as a warning?" said Elgin. "You know, to warn him that he might be killed!"

"Yes, we did," replied Wyndham. "Apparently he couldn't act on the warning. Because he had already been killed."

Elgin sighed.

"Okay," he said. "But what you're saying is, that wasn't the only killing?"

"No. Prince Grumio, who would have become king, was also killed."

"Right," continued Elgin. "So that means Prince Nutrec was the next in line, so he became king."

"Briefly, yes," said King Wyndham. "Until he was killed."

Elgin closed his eyes. Wyndham surveyed the rest of the room. Most of his lords still seemed in shock.

"And finally, on top of everything else; the messenger said that it was two Humans who killed him? Two of our people?" continued Elgin.

"Yes, that's right," replied the King.

An uncomfortable silence followed. None of the lords had any idea what to say. The Lord of Health took a large gulp from his wine glass. The Lord of Religion took some bread from the table, hoping that if he kept eating, he wouldn't have to say anything. Eventually it was Elgin who spoke.

"Let's make sure we get our facts straight first, shall we?" he said. He turned to the King. "Is there anything the messenger told you?" he asked. "Did he know how these Goblins died? Are there any other suspects?"

King Wyndham shook his head. "Nothing I haven't already told you," he said. "Prince Nutrec was shot with an arrow. Prince Grumio was apparently stabbed, though the messenger wasn't sure on this. He just found out as he was leaving."

"Did he say who they think stabbed him?"

"They don't know. And they also don't know who killed King Grieber, or even how he died. Maybe it was just old age. But it could have been some sort of poison."

The lords nodded their heads. Grieber's death probably wasn't much of a mystery. The old Goblin king was a friend to the Humans, but he had a lot of enemies. Every Ogre in the East must have wanted him dead.

Wyndham stopped furrowing his brow and started scratching the back of his head instead. He also took a sip of wine, though he barely tasted it. The last year had been a particularly bad one for wine production, given the unusually cold weather. It hadn't affected the grapes, but people hadn't picked as many of them because their hands got cold.

"Grumio is the one that doesn't make sense to me," he continued. "He was nothing like his father. The Ogres liked him. They liked him because he didn't like us."

"What if they changed their minds?" said Elgin.

The King looked at him blankly.

"What I mean is, sire," he continued. "They could have had a disagreement about something."

"Rather a serious disagreement Elgin, I would have thought," replied the King, "if it ended with one of them getting stabbed to death."

"Well they *are* Ogres," responded the Lord of Peace softly.

Cecil, Lord of War, now piped up, turning to the King. "And you say they don't even have any suspects?"

"Not that we are aware of," replied Wyndham. "But then maybe they just wouldn't tell the messenger anything."

"Maybe indeed," said Elgin, adding absolutely nothing of value to the conversation.

"But what they do have," continued King Wyndham, "is a suspect for the murder of Prince Nutrec. Two suspects, both apparently Humans."

"What makes them suspects?" asked Cecil. "And for that matter, how do they know it was murder?"

"He was shot with an arrow from long range!" growled the King. "If it were suicide, it wouldn't be a particularly easy way to commit it!"

"Yes all right," continued Cecil. "But what about my first question? What makes them suspects?"

"They found the two Humans trying to flee from the citadel, moments after the arrow was fired," replied King Wyndham. "Apparently one of them had broken his leg, so they didn't manage to get very far."

The other lords agreed that kind of thing would probably hinder their progress.

"But that really is all we know, unfortunately," said Wyndham. "The messenger didn't see the Humans. He couldn't even find out their names."

Cecil took a breath, then also started to furrow his brow quite profusely. He was sure they hadn't authorised any secret missions to kill Goblin kings. Years ago, they used to have a 'secret operations team' who they would call on whenever they needed something done discreetly.

Unfortunately, the team became so secretive that they stopped even telling their plans to the Lord of War. So he had them disbanded for good. Although, of course, there was always a risk that they somehow still managed to exist. In secret.

He shook his head. Surely that wasn't the case. Whoever these two Humans were, they hadn't acted on behalf of him, or the realm.

"How old were they? What were they even doing there?" he asked.

"As I said Cecil, we really don't know anything else," snapped King Wyndham.

"What are they doing with them now?" asked Cecil.

Wyndham sighed. "We don't know," he replied.

"They have surely locked them up somewhere?"

"We don't know!" growled a few of the other lords at the same time.

"Now then," began the King. "I think only one question remains. What in the name of the Gods do we do now?"

Another silence fell. The Lord of Religion took another piece of bread and shoved it into his mouth. He always got nervous when someone mentioned the Gods – after all, that was supposed to be his area of expertise. Thankfully it was the Lord of War who filled the silence this time.

"The way I see it, sire, we have two options," Cecil began. "Option one: we do nothing. The problem with that is the Goblins might already think we had something to do with those two Humans killing one of their kings."

"That would dampen their trust and push them closer to the Ogres. It could lead to an all-out war between them and us!" interjected Elgin.

"Yes," continued Cecil. "Although the plus point about Option one is that it's the easy option. We're doing it right now in fact."

"Let's rule out Option one," snapped the King, staring down at the table in front of him.

"Right," said Cecil. "Option two, we send a message straight to Nuberim. We give our deepest sympathies and make absolutely clear that we had nothing to do with any of the killings, even if these two Humans were behind it."

"Deepest sympathies? Is that really going to be enough?" added the Lord of the People, who had been silent all this time.

"Well we could send some flowers as well," added Cecil.

"It's not enough," said Wyndham. "We can't just send a messenger and hope that they appreciate the gesture. They are hardly going to think 'ah well, they killed our king, but at least they sent us some nice flowers'."

"I agree," said Elgin. "I think you need to go there yourself, sire. It's the only way to show them that the whole of the Human Realm is on their side."

"Except, presumably, for the two Humans who killed their king," added the Lord of the People, unhelpfully.

King Wyndham cleared his throat. "I think you're right," he said, looking directly at Cecil. "I think I need to go there as soon as I can – before things escalate further – before the Ogres have a chance to poison the Goblins' minds."

"I'll come with you," said the Lord of Peace. "It's a diplomatic mission after all."

"And me," said the Lord of War. "With a small army, in case anything does happen."

"And me," added the Lord of Science.

Everyone else in the room suddenly turned to him. What was he talking about? It made sense for Elgin to come; to try and keep the peace. And it made sense for Cecil to come; in case he didn't.

But why did they need Wilfred? He was an old and wise man, but his areas of expertise were technology and research. His department had spent most of their time on ground-breaking experiments, like figuring out a way to ride unicorns without scaring them off. They hadn't managed it in hundreds of years, but were confident of a breakthrough any century now.

If they could figure it out, it would be very helpful. But surely the Lord of Science was better off staying here – he wasn't going to be of much help to the King on the other side of the Known World.

"I have been meaning to go to the Goblin Realm for some time," said Wilfred. "We have had some breakthroughs in transport mechanisms recently, which I think could help them immensely in the future. Why not share these with them now, almost as a gift during such difficult times?"

"Well is now really the right time to..." started the Lord of the People.

"It's as good a time as any," Wilfred interrupted. "Please sire, take me with you," he said to the King.

Wyndham kept his gaze on Wilfred. It may have been his imagination, but his Lord of Science looked rather red faced, almost quivering. Perhaps it was nothing, but he just didn't seem normal.

"Very well," he replied. "The four of us shall go. Theobold, you will take charge of the Realm while we are away."

The Lord of Gold nodded.

"Better send word out to the Goblins too, before we leave. Where are the messengers? Could someone get one of them to come in here?"

The Lord of Science sat back in his seat. He didn't have a plan. He didn't have an idea. He didn't even have any breakthroughs in transport mechanisms, but that wasn't important right now.

But he did know he had to go with the King. He knew who those two Humans were; they were called Ridley and Fulton. He knew that because he had sent them there. He had done it with the best of intentions – he couldn't have known they would kill the wrong king!

And now, he had to fix things, but he had no idea how.

Chapter 3

The full moon shone brightly above Orthica, the capital of the Ogre realm. In the highest room of the tallest tower in the city, the six most powerful Ogres in the land were sitting.

Beams of moonlight penetrated the room, putting the candles on the walls to shame. They lit up the crocodile skull which rested on the centre of the table. Ideally it would have been a dragon skull, but those were nearly impossible to get hold of.

Lord Protector Higarth and his generals were feasting on roasted mutton, discussing important business in between mouthfuls.

"I don't understand why we came back at all," bellowed General Lang.

"Do not question the Lord Protector," snapped General Chandimer, before turning to the Lord Protector and asking: "why did we come back, again?"

Higarth looked down at his shoes. He needed new ones. That was about the only thing he was sure of right now.

"We had to leave," he replied. "It's what the Goblins wanted; they needed some time to deal with this situation they have somehow found themselves in."

General Chandimer nodded furiously, agreeing with everything his leader was saying.

"Besides, we have more to do than look after the Goblins," continued Higarth. "I can't be away from the Ogre realm indefinitely. Orthica doesn't just sit back and wait for us to return. I need to be here for my people."

He turned to General Litmus. "What's been going on since we've been away?"

"Nothing much," replied the general.

The glare he got from his Lord Protector encouraged him to expand on this a little further.

"Reports are that our food production is strong, with meat and vegetable outputs likely to be the highest in years," he continued.

"Well good," replied Higarth. "And the morale amongst the peons?"

"Again, all fine as far as we can tell," said Litmus.

"I see," said Higarth. "Thank you. Now then, I think we can get back to the issue at hand."

Higarth did not like to concern himself with domestic affairs any more than necessary. Of course, he was the leader of all the Ogres, and that meant he was responsible for their welfare.

But it was hard to even keep track of peoples' welfare. They did occasionally send out surveys to every Ogre in the realm; but the response rate was always very low, particularly among those who couldn't read or write.

Besides, the Ogres were a proud people, and the way to help their wellbeing was not by feeding them and clothing them. It was by crushing their enemies – by defeating anyone who may oppose them.

So all that really mattered was that the other civilisations knew their place. And right now, the Goblins presumably still didn't. They had just lost three kings in a row. The only issue of any importance was what to do about them.

"Let me be absolutely clear," he continued. "We need to return to the Goblin Realm. We can't let those puny little creatures try to get out of this mess on their own."

General Lang nodded. It was an angry 'yes I already knew that' sort of nod – the distinct 'we should never have left the Goblin Realm in the first place' nod that you don't see very often.

"We need to think about how we do it though. We can't just walk back there as if nothing has changed," said General Litmus.

"Indeed," added General Chandimer. "We would not be welcome. The Goblins still suspect that we might have had something to do with the deaths of their kings."

"Which we did," added Litmus.

"Yes but that's not the point. The point is that right now they don't trust us in Nuberim."

"Who said anything about going to Nuberim?" said the Lord Protector, with a sly smile which revealed his unwashed set of extra yellow teeth.

His five generals all looked at him with wide eyes.

"They don't trust us there right now; they simply wouldn't be friendly to a surprise visit," he continued. "So how about, we go to a place where they are a lot friendlier. I was going to propose that we make our way to Siglitz."

If you asked a child at school to draw a map of the Known World, they would probably draw something that resembled a circle. The Elves, Humans and Pixies would be on the left-hand side (or the 'West' if the child's education was a bit more advanced). And the Trolls, Ogres and Goblins would be to the East.

If you then asked the child to mark out the Goblin realm, they would shade the bottom right corner of the circle. Presumably the child hadn't quite mastered shapes yet.

But apart from that the map would be pretty much right. The Goblins lived in the south-eastern part of the Known World. The realm of the Ogres was just above that.

Siglitz was to the North of the Goblin realm. In fact, it was their northernmost settlement of any significant size. Tens of thousands of people lived there, spending their nights working, trading and socialising. Many of these people were Ogres.

"Interesting," said General Hurgen, the first one to break the silence. "So what you're saying is, we should start somewhere closer to home. Somewhere we know they are on our side."

"Exactly," replied the Lord Protector.

"And what exactly are you proposing we do there?" asked General Gorac.

Higarth looked down at his general. They were sitting at a round table – it signified that all the generals were equally important. But Higarth's chair was higher up than theirs, because he was more important.

"I'm proposing that we pay them a visit," he said. "To make sure they know that we are on their side; that we are their true friends; that the Humans should have no place in the Goblin realm. From now on, it should be Ogres and Goblins, side by side once again. The way it always used to be."

"Who should go?"

"Just us," replied Higarth. "And a couple of hundred soldiers."

Gorac smiled and nodded. "To keep the peace," he added.

"Exactly," said Higarth again.

"But what about the Goblin army? They must have soldiers at Siglitz?" interrupted General Lang. "Surely they won't let us just overrun the city with our soldiers?"

"They will if they know what's good for them!" bellowed General Gorac. "Besides, I expect they will be friendly towards us. Many of them will have been to our realm before. They will understand that we're doing this to help them."

"And if they don't?" replied Chandimer.

"Well then we may have to chop a few heads off, in order to keep the peace."

Lord Protector Higarth nodded, still smiling. General Litmus started to breathe slowly as he surveyed the room. It had suddenly just got darker; two torches seemed to have simultaneously burnt out. His Lord Protector and the other generals didn't even seem to notice.

"I think that perhaps..." he stammered, "we should consult with the Overseers of Night and Day?"

Higarth sighed and sat back in his chair.

Since the dawn of civilisation the Ogres had only ever worshipped two Gods. One would help them thrive during the dark nights; to grow and conquer others while they were at their strongest. The other would help protect them during the day; to keep them safe from the scorching sun.

These were the Overseers of Night and Day. They had other names once, but these had been lost in ages past. There was a time when it was considered highly blasphemous to speak their real names, or to write them down. This meant, quite predictably, that people eventually forgot them. Although the positive point from this was that nobody would ever blaspheme again.

"Do you really think that's necessary?" replied Higarth.

It was a fair question. The Gods had rather gone out of fashion in the Ogre realm over the last few hundred years. Forgetting their names can have that effect. People still believed in them of course, but it was hard to find many temples or monuments left to them at all. Most Ogres preferred to worship them in their own way, which generally didn't involve building expensive structures.

"Well we shouldn't anger them," said General Litmus. "Besides they can help us. Perhaps if we had had the Gods on our side in Nuberim, we wouldn't have ended up in this mess."

"The Gods are always on our side," replied Higarth. "At least, they had better be if they know what's good for them!"

"Yes, but nevertheless I think we should be safe," added the general, slightly worried that his lord protector had just threatened the Gods. That was probably frowned upon in religious circles.

"I agree," added General Hurgen.

"Very well," said Higarth. "Everybody close your eyes."

The Lord Protector and his five generals all bowed their heads, with their eyes firmly shut.

"Overseer of Night, and Overseer of Day," began Higarth. "These are dire times we find ourselves in. The Goblins need us, now more than ever. Please help us show them the right path, so that they can be at our side once again."

Litmus nodded, keeping his eyes firmly shut.

"Please help us to do what we know needs to be done. If you do not agree with our plans, please give us a sign."

There was a long pause. Complete silence. All anyone could hear was breathing and the occasional cough.

"Right," said Higarth, as he opened his eyes.

His generals all followed. As General Litmus looked around the room, he could have sworn it looked lighter than it had before. Had those dead torches suddenly caught fire again? Was that a sign from the Overseers that they should go ahead? Or not go ahead?

Maybe someone had snuck in while they had their eyes closed, to light them up again. Or maybe it was just natural for a room to seem lighter after closing your eyes for a while.

If only the Gods made their signs a bit more obvious. Perhaps provide them with a key to explain whether something meant 'yes' or 'no'. It would also be helpful if they just said something every now and again.

"Well?" said Higarth, looking directly at General Litmus. "Are you satisfied?"

"I think so, my lord," replied General Litmus. "Although perhaps we should make a sacrifice, just to be on the safe side?"

"What were you thinking?"

"Well a goat would be the obvious choice, my Lord Protector," said the general.

"Fine," replied Higarth. "But only a small one. And an old one. We don't want to waste any of the good goats."

"I expect there are a few dead goats at the butcher's down the road – ones that can't be eaten because they're spoiled," added General Lang. "Why don't we just use one of them, rather than sacrificing one that's actually useful to us."

"Perfect," said Higarth.

"Yes, my Lord Protector," replied General Litmus, without suggesting that this seemed to be missing the point of a sacrifice.

Chapter 4

"Is there anything else I can do for you, Miss Petra?" asked the maid.

"No, nothing at all thank you," she replied.

She felt a little uncomfortable having someone cleaning her room and attending to her every need. She had never experienced anything like this back home in the realm of Pixies.

"I suppose if you wanted anything else cleaned, you could just magic it yourself?" said the maid.

Petra feigned a smile. It had only been a few days since her act of heroism from the balcony. Destroying that dragon had saved lives, perhaps thousands of them. And it had instantly made her into a celebrity; she couldn't walk down the street without people spotting her and wanting to say hello.

Of course, since she was a Pixie in a city of Humans it was difficult to remain inconspicuous. She was at least a foot shorter than most of them, and her bright green eyes could have been seen a mile away.

Saving the city of Peria had been an unbelievable experience. Killing that dragon had given her the kind of rush that couldn't be beaten. But she didn't much care for the fame and admiration that came with it. It was fun at first, seeing everyone's faces and signing autographs. But it didn't take her long to get tired of it: the constant pointing, whispering, the requests from people to turn their friends into frogs.

They tended to get a bit disappointed when they realised she couldn't do that sort of magic. She could create flames, and that was about it. And setting their friends on fire was probably a bit much for most people.

"I'll be going then, for now," said the maid.

"Yes, thank you," said Petra. She nodded to the maid as she left the room.

"Oh, Miss Petra?" called the maid, opening the door again from the outside.

"Yes?" she replied. She half expected this to be a cheeky request for an autograph.

"I think the King is coming this way; I can see him down the corridor," said the maid, before closing the door behind her.

'Ah' thought Petra. She had gotten to know King Wyndham fairly well since she had been in the city. And despite being ruler of an entire realm, she had found him to be very approachable. It said something about the King's character that he was happy to come and speak to her directly, rather than summoning her to one of the great halls or meeting rooms.

Sure enough, she heard a knock on her door, and she called for him to come in.

King Wyndham entered. He was not alone. By now Petra had become acquainted with the King's inner circle, so she knew the names of all three of his companions.

First came Cecil, the Lord of War, with his dark hair and pale complexion. He would have almost looked like a Pixie himself, had he not been so tall and Human like. Then came an older Human, his greying hair beginning to match the light robe he was wearing. This of course was Elgin, the Lord of Peace.

Finally came the oldest and greyest of all of them: the Human who seemed to carry a pipe wherever he went, just to make him look intelligent; Wilfred, the Lord of Science.

"Good morning, sire," said Petra. She attempted a little bow, still not quite sure of the right way to greet the King. She acknowledged the lords afterwards.

"Good morning," replied King Wyndham. He made his way across the bedroom and stood by the cupboard. His lords, in the absence of any chairs, did the same.

"You may have heard rumours about the Goblins," continued Wyndham.

Petra shook her head. "What about them?" she said.

"Ah. Well a couple of days ago we received a messenger from Nuberim."

"The Goblin capital," added Elgin, patronisingly.

"Yes. And he didn't come with good news. In fact, it was rather bad news," continued King Wyndham. "Or even, rather weird news. It seems that three Goblin kings have been killed!"

"Three? Goblin kings? Killed?" said Petra, so startled that she basically just repeated the whole sentence.

"Yes, that's pretty much exactly what I said," replied Wyndham.

"But I thought the Goblins only had one king?"

"They do," he replied. "He got killed. And the prince who was first in line to the throne also got killed. So the crown then passed to his other son, the second in line to the throne."

"And what happened to him?"

"He got killed," replied the King. "He was shot with an arrow during the Dernbach festival."

"Ah they must have succeeded!" said Petra.

This was surely Fulton and Ridley. It must have been. She had met them back in the Pixie Realm. The two Humans were on their way to the Goblin capital, carrying their bows and arrows. They had told them their plan; surely this meant they had done it. Unless there were two other Humans who had the same plan.

"What do you mean 'succeeded'?" asked Wyndham in surprise.

"Well," replied Petra.

Then she stopped for a second. What had she just said? She wasn't supposed to say anything! Fulton and Ridley's plan was a secret. Top secret, presumably. But then, this was the King of Humans she was talking to, and three of his lords of the realm. Surely they were in on the plan? The King must have been the one who sent them to do it! Wasn't he?

"King Wyndham," said Petra, before pausing again. "My lords… do you know what I know?"

23

"About what?" replied Wyndham.

"About... you know?" said Petra.

"What?"

"Well about the Goblin king..." said Petra, careful not to say too much.

"I just told you about the Goblin king!" snapped King Wyndham, getting slightly annoyed. "So if you're asking whether I know the thing I just told you, which you now know, the answer is yes I know it."

Petra felt herself going slightly red. Even so, she held her ground. She wasn't going to give anything away.

"Listen here," said Elgin, "if you know something we don't, then keeping it to yourself will not help anything."

The young Pixie nodded. But she didn't agree; keeping it to herself could stop Ridley and Fulton getting caught for a start. They would probably find that quite helpful.

"Do they have any idea who has done the killing?" asked Petra.

King Wyndham looked her in the eyes. "Yes, they do," he replied. For the first time in a long time, he felt that he couldn't trust this Pixie. She was hiding something.

"Who is it?" said Petra. This almost felt like a game. A staring contest. And she wasn't going to be the first to blink.

"They have a couple of suspects," replied Wyndham, without blinking. He kept his gaze firmly on the young Pixie. "Nothing more than that."

"Do they think it's Ogres? Trolls? Humans?" she said.

"Why would they think it's Humans?" said the King, keeping his eyes wide open.

"Well presumably because of the two Humans they caught at the scene," added Cecil, blinking heavily. "Even though they were nothing to do with us, whoever they are."

Petra breathed. "So it was two Humans, and they caught them?"

King Wyndham closed his eyes for a second to compose himself. "Yes, that's what we've been told. They think the two Humans were involved."

"I think we've answered enough of your questions," added Elgin. "But you haven't answered ours. You said they must have succeeded. That means you knew about this. How?"

"You have to tell us everything," said Wyndham. "Don't you see how important this is? The fate of the Known World could depend upon it!"

Petra looked up at each of the four Humans in turn: possibly the most important four Humans in the kingdom. They were only a couple of feet taller than her, but right know they seemed like giants.

And then it struck her. The Goblins had captured Fulton and Ridley. They were in trouble. Big trouble.

She might as well tell the King everything now; it surely couldn't do them any more harm. Maybe the Humans could even help them escape.

She breathed again. It almost felt like a relief. It was terrible news of course, and she couldn't bear to think about what might be happening to them right now. But at least it made her little dilemma a bit easier. Every cloud.

"It was in Lupa Green; that's where Samorus and I used to work," she began. "It was where we made healing potion. On the outskirts of Madesco."

"The Pixie Realm," said Cecil, to no-one in particular.

"Yes," Petra continued. "It was actually just before we left to come here. Two Humans knocked on the door one day. We had no idea who they were."

"What did they want?" asked Wyndham.

"Healing potion," said Petra. "At first they said they were merchants, on their way to Nuberim. But they had a bow, and arrows."

She kept her focus on the King but could feel the gaze of all three lords as they stood like a stone wall surrounding her.

"It's a bit of a blur, to be honest," she continued. "But one thing led to another, and in the end they told us the truth."

"Which was?" said the King.

"They weren't merchants at all," she said. "They were on a mission to kill the Goblin king."

The King and the lords all looked at each other. The young Pixie had certainly got straight to the point!

"Which Goblin king?" asked Cecil.

"Well, I thought there was only one. Presumably they did too?" said Petra.

"Why were they going to kill the Goblin king? What reason did they give?" asked Wyndham.

Petra paused for a moment. "They didn't say."

"Did they say who sent them?" asked Wilfred.

"No," said Petra, beginning to feel slightly stupid.

They probably should have asked the Humans these questions when they had the chance. Instead, they had just let them go. In fairness though, she hardly could have imagined she would have to explain this to the king of all Humans a few weeks later. After she had just killed a dragon.

King Wyndham put his hand through his thick, white hair. "Well what else can you tell us about them?" he asked.

Petra cleared her throat. "One was older; dark haired, I would say about 40 years old. He was called Ridley. The other was younger; fair haired. His name was Fulton," she said, smiling slightly.

The lords all seemed taken aback. Or at least the King did.

"They told you their names?" asked Wyndham.

"Do you think they were their real names?" asked Elgin.

The young Pixie thought for a minute. "I think so," she said. "They told us the truth about their plan. Why wouldn't they tell us their real names too?"

King Wyndham thought for a second. "Maybe this is something we can check. They may have had friends or family; we can see if anyone has been reported missing."

He turned to the Lord of War. "Cecil, they must have got that bow and arrow from somewhere. Maybe they were even our archers. Have there been any who have deserted recently?"

"Oh yes, plenty," replied Cecil. "But I'll have to check whether there are any with those names."

The King nodded. "Please do so, quickly. We want to know as much as we can before we leave."

"Leave?" said Petra. "Where are you going?"

"We're going to the Goblin Realm!" replied the King. "We need to try and sort this mess out. We need to make sure that the Goblins are still on our side."

"It's actually the reason we came to your room in the first place," said Elgin.

"Yes," continued Wyndham. "We came to see whether you wanted to join us. Along with Prince Vardie, and Samorus."

"And your answer, of course, is yes," added King Wyndham, before she had a chance to reply.

Petra smiled. "Samorus won't come," she replied.

"I know," said Wyndham. "That's the only reason I'm inviting him. Although he can come with us for half the journey, on his way home."

"How do you know I don't just want to go home too?" said Petra.

"You're a little too important now to go back to making healing potion" replied the King.

Petra nodded. She didn't want to go home anyway. She knew she had an amazing gift, and she wanted to use it to help people.

The King and his lords turned to leave the room.

"Wait, just before we go..." said the Lord of War, turning to Petra. "Is there any chance I could get an autograph? It's just my niece is a big fan."

Chapter 5

It must have been a week now, maybe two. It's hard to keep track of time when you're sitting in a prison cell, so deep underground that you don't know whether it's night or day. And it's also very boring.

Ridley and Fulton spent a lot of the time sitting in silence. They talked to each other every now and then, but after a week or two of being stuck in the same cell with each other, you tend to run out of things to talk about. And of course, the other person starts to drive you mad.

Ridley had learnt a lot about his cell mate by now. Fulton liked to snore. He also liked to clear his throat, cough, and make pretty much every noise imaginable. After a couple of days, peoples' annoying habits become infuriating habits. And after a couple more days, they become almost criminal habits. Ridley would sometimes close his eyes and imagine his companion being tried and sentenced for breathing too heavily, getting his mouth forcibly shut as punishment. It helped.

In a way though, he was glad to be sharing a cell. He was slowly going crazy, of course, but if he were on his own it would surely be happening twice as quickly. At least he had someone to share his pain, his boredom, and his exasperation with.

They were stuck in a Goblin prison, about as far away from home as they could possibly get. The cell was uncomfortably small. They could only just about stand or lie down. And of course, they didn't have beds. Their bed was the floor of the cell. Their pillow was the floor of the cell. Their chamber pot, luckily, wasn't the floor of the cell. The guards let them out to go, as well as to stretch their legs and wash every now and again.

Stretching their legs involved walking up and down the

29

dark corridor outside the cell, accompanied by a Goblin Guard. Washing involved that same Goblin guard covering you with cold water.

In truth, it could have been a lot worse. At least they got to leave the cell occasionally. They also got fed a wide variety of exciting foods. It wasn't always potatoes and fish heads – sometimes they gave them the tails as well.

The quality of the food didn't matter. Well that wasn't strictly true: it did matter, because it was revolting. But it was better than nothing. Clearly these Goblins wanted to keep their prisoners alive. Ridley and Fulton had assassinated their king, or at least one of their kings. The Goblins could have left the two Humans to starve, or had them instantly killed.

But the Goblins hadn't done that. Ridley and Fulton were still useful; they could provide information or be used as a bargaining tool. They were far more useful alive to their captors, who probably still didn't understand what had happened – or who to trust.

They were also a source of fascination to the Goblins who guarded them. There were usually two or three of them at any one time, changing their shifts every so often. The guards were tall, green and fully plated in dark metal armour. The light from their torches would flicker from time to time, revealing their dark eyes and sharp white teeth. But after a while, they didn't seem so intimidating; they just seemed like ordinary people who were just as bored as their prisoners.

The guards would stare at them, sometimes whispering something to each other and then laughing. Over time, they started to taunt the two Humans, ask them questions, and giggle at their silly answers and funny accents.

"Oi, Human," one of the guards would say. "What do you call this thing?" whilst holding up a jug.

"A jug?" Ridley or Fulton would reply, to more cackles of laughter.

"It's called a flagon you idiot," the guard would reply, and then turn back to his co-workers. "Stupid Humans and their funny words. Look at his small hands; I bet he couldn't even open a door with those things."

The two Humans didn't mind. It was one of their few sources of entertainment. And they were reassured that the guards were becoming less fierce; they were relaxed, almost friendly at times. They seemed to talk more loudly to each other, paying little attention to the fact that Ridley and Fulton were there.

Ridley looked over at his companion. The torches in the corridor just about gave enough light to make him out. Right now, Fulton wasn't making any noise. He also didn't seem to be moving. But he wasn't asleep. He was just staring into the darkness.

The poor guy. He couldn't help but feel pity for his younger partner in crime; Ridley missed home, and he missed his wife. To an extent. But he felt like an old man; he had lived a decent life.

Fulton was only in his twenties. He had always been so full of hope and energy. He had so much of his life left to live – he had never had a proper job, never been in love, never even learnt how to sleep without snoring.

Ridley wondered what the poor guy was thinking as he sat there motionless. Sometimes, if not all the time, he felt like he needed to look after the young man.

"Is everything okay?" said Ridley.

Fulton turned his head slightly.

"I'm okay," he replied. "I was just wondering what would happen if a human and a centaur had a baby."

Ridley coughed. "What?" he said.

"Well, you know how centaurs are half horse and half Human. So presumably they came about by a horse and a Human getting together long ago."

"Um," replied Ridley.

"So what would happen if a Human got together with a centaur instead?" continued the young man. "Would it only be a quarter horse? And how would that even work? Arms as well as hooves? And how many? What about Human legs?"

Ridley took a deep breath. "I'm not sure that's how it

works," he said. "I mean for starters, do centaurs even exist? I'm pretty sure they're just a myth."

"No they're real", replied Fulton. "My grandad said he had a friend who saw one."

"Where? In Peria?"

"Obviously not," said Fulton. "It was in Blackthearn forest."

"Blackthearn?" retorted Ridley. "The forest where the trees grow tall, and the branches are so thick that they form a solid roof; so impenetrable that even light itself cannot get through?"

"Yes," said Fulton.

"Meaning that the forest is always in total darkness?" said Ridley.

"Yes," replied Fulton, indignantly. "That's where he saw it."

"But if it's total darkness, how did he... never mind" said Ridley. "Well regardless, I'm still pretty sure it doesn't work like that. Even if centaurs do exist, you can't just make a half Human, half centaur creature. It's not possible."

He looked at the young man, whose face now looked a little sullen. Weeks in a Goblin prison cell didn't hurt him, but questioning the possibility of Human-centaur hybrids apparently did.

"But cross-breeding is possible, isn't it," continued Fulton. "I mean, it happens all the time. Well, some of the time. Humans mating with Elves. Or even Pixies?"

"Pixies?" Ridley rolled his eyes. *Here we go again*, he thought to himself.

"Yes, Pixies," replied Fulton.

Ridley sighed. He was thinking about the Pixie girl again; the one they had met on their journey through Madesco. She seemed to have magic powers – she could somehow create fire with her bare hands. She could also somehow make Fulton fall in love with her after knowing each other for less than a day.

"I know you don't understand it," said Fulton, "but I miss her. I really do."

"You don't even know her," replied Ridley. "There's nothing to miss."

It was Fulton's turn to sigh. "You don't understand it," he said again.

"Okay then," said his cell mate. "Explain it to me. We've talked about this a hundred times since we've been here, but you're right, I still don't get it. So please explain how you're so in love with someone you barely know. Someone of a different species, who is less than five feet tall; who you would have to crouch down to hug. And just to top it off, who could probably burn you in flames by accident if you ended up having a fight."

"She wouldn't burn me in flames, she's not like that!" said Fulton indignantly.

"You've clearly never been married," he replied. "I'm just saying you would have to be careful if she got annoyed. Arguments happen."

"Yes all right," said Fulton. "But you still don't get it. I don't care about that stuff. I only care about, well, her."

Another sigh.

"Can I ask you something?" said Fulton.

"As long as it's not about where baby centaurs come from," said Ridley.

"What's getting you through this?" his companion asked, ignoring him. "When you're sat in this dark, unforgiving place, and time seems to stand still, what are you thinking about? What's giving you the strength to keep going?

Ridley thought for a moment. He ran his hand through his hair; it was so thick now that it was almost a challenge.

"You think about your wife, don't you?" continued Fulton.

"Yes," he said. "Well, sometimes. A lot of the time I think about trees, and rivers, and juicy rib eye steaks dripping in tomato sauce."

"Right," replied Fulton. "Well I miss those things too. But most of the time, I think about Petra. I see those beautiful green eyes, and that long, dark hair. I see her smiling at me and telling me it's going to be okay. I realise I barely know her, but I don't care. She's what's getting me through this."

Ridley looked out the cell bars for a second, and then down at his feet. They were barely visible given how little light they had in the cell.

"Okay, I'm sorry," he said. "You hold onto that feeling. If it helps you, then it must be a good thing. And who knows, maybe you'll even see her again someday."

Fulton nodded. "Maybe," he said.

"You could write her a letter," Ridley joked. "Ask one of the prison guards to deliver it to the Pixie realm. Look for a dark-haired girl stood somewhere near a bonfire."

The young man smiled. "Maybe I should. Or how about a poem?"

Ridley laughed.

"Petra, I'm so glad we metra. And I'll never forgetra, the way we…"

"Watched the sun setra?"

"Something like that," said Fulton. "Although technically we never watched the sun set together."

"You've never spent more than two minutes together," replied Ridley. "There are trees which have had longer conversations than you two. But… maybe one day you will get to watch the sun set together. You never know."

Chapter 6

"Lord Preventor," said the Ogre messenger, loudly.

"Protector!" replied Higarth. "You've been reporting to me for over ten years, what's wrong with you?"

"Sorry, Lord Protector," he replied.

"Hmmm, actually I quite like 'preventer'. It sounds authoritative. You can call me that for the rest of the night."

"Er okay. Yes, Lord Protector. Preventer," said the messenger.

"What is it, Pulch?" said Higarth.

He was standing in Techney barracks, on the outskirts of Orthica. They had been preparing to leave for the Goblin realm for six nights now, and Higarth was getting impatient.

The messenger looked up at his Lord Protector. Pulch was short for an Ogre – barely over six feet tall. His hair was grey, and his eyes a rather dark red. Even after all this time, he still spoke with a quiver whenever addressing his taller, fiercer looking chief.

"It's news, my Lord Protector. From the Human realm," began Pulch.

Higarth turned to him. "The Human realm?" he repeated.

The Ogres tried to keep track of everything that was going on throughout the Known World. Ideally, they would have spies in each realm who could live there, build the trust of the locals and feed all the information back to the Ogres. Actually, in an ideal world there would be no other civilisations except Ogres, but this would be the next best thing.

Unfortunately having a network of spies was extremely difficult for one simple reason: everybody looks so different. You couldn't just send an Ogre into Peria

35

dressed in Human armour and ask them to blend in, saying 'Hello there chaps, lovely day to be a Human isn't it? Oh don't mind the red eyes and dark green skin, I'm just feeling slightly tired. Also, the sun makes me dizzy so I wondered if we could do all our business at night from now on. Anyway, who wants to tell me about the secret plans that we mustn't let the Ogres see?'

Since they couldn't do that, the next best thing was to use the locals themselves. And that was also very difficult; it meant finding people you could trust to betray their own kind. This was easy enough with Goblins, or Trolls, since they were often on the Ogres' side. But it was hard to find a Human, an Elf or a Pixie who you could trust not to run away from you, let alone help you.

All this meant that their intelligence generally came from three sources: capturing people, bribing people, and hiding Ogres in dark corners where nobody could see them. Using any of these sources was risky, as there was always a significant chance of getting caught.

As a result, they rarely did use them, meaning information from the western realms was often hard to come by. So when a messenger came with news from the Humans, Higarth would generally take notice.

"It's news from Peria," started Pulch. "Terrifying news!"

"Terrifying?" said Higarth. This word wasn't used very often in the Ogre realm. Ogres don't get terrified. They make terror, but they don't feel it themselves.

Pulch looked around the room. It was decorated the way you would expect from an Ogre military base. Long swords and axes hung from the walls, most of them embellished with a silver skull at the top of the handle. A huge grey shield was propped up by the door.

"Yes, Lord Protector. Terrifying and unbelievable," continued the messenger. "Firstly, a dragon came to their realm. I saw it myself at one point."

"In Peria?"

"Yes. Well, I saw it from a distance, as I was a lot further east. But apparently it was flying right above the city. An adult, full-sized one!"

"I find that hard to believe. What are the chances of that happening?" said Higarth. "You barely ever see dragons these days, let alone in the middle of cities."

Pulch nodded.

"I hope it did a lot of damage to the city?" said Higarth, looking quite excited. His red eyes were flashing, his yellow teeth showing through his smile.

"Well actually, quite the opposite," murmured the messenger. "You see, a little Pixie killed it."

Higarth frowned.

"You what?"

"It's true, Lord Protector."

"A Pixie. One Pixie?" said Higarth. "One of those pathetic four-foot-tall creatures who hide in the grass, and try to avoid fighting at all costs?"

"That's right," replied Pulch.

"Killed a full-sized dragon?"

"Burnt the dragon to flames with her own bare hands apparently."

Higarth continued to frown.

"You're quite sure it wasn't the other way round? To state the obvious, it's usually the dragon that does the setting on fire."

"No, my Lord Protector."

"And you haven't been drinking?"

"No, my Lord Protector."

"Well did you see it for yourself?"

"No," admitted Pulch. "But I heard it from multiple sources. A young, female Pixie. She just stood on the balcony, and fire came out of her hands. Like…magic!"

Higarth shook his head. This was all getting beyond ridiculous.

"And what, according to your sources, happened next?" he said, almost sarcastically.

"Well it died, and then the Pixie went back inside."

"Of course."

"Lord Protector, I realise how this sounds," said the messenger.

"I'm sure you do," replied Higarth. The Lord Protector

was already on his feet, but now he started to walk slowly across the room. "Pulch, are you familiar with how rumours start?"

The messenger looked at him blankly.

"Somebody sees something, and then tells someone else. But they exaggerate slightly. Then that person tells a third person, and they exaggerate further. Maybe they misremember some of the details as well. And this happens again, and again, and again."

"Yes, my Lord Protector," said Pulch.

"And before you know it, the story is nothing like what actually happened," continued Higarth. He turned back to his messenger. "So with that in mind, do you think it's possible that a Pixie just started a bonfire and accidentally killed a cat or something? And then over time it escalated into this ridiculous story which bears no resemblance to the truth?"

Pulch paused for a second, trying to choose his words carefully.

"Yes, my Lord Protector. I think that's possible," he replied. "But I did hear it from multiple sources. I'm just telling you what I heard."

"Okay," said Higarth. "Thank you. Please wait outside."

Pulch nodded and duly obliged. He was glad to be out of this intimidating room, and away from his equally intimidating leader.

Higarth stared at the wall. He reached out and grabbed a large axe, which was hanging up in front of him, roughly at eye level.

He clenched it with both hands, and the weight of it took him off balance slightly. He steadied himself and stared at the blade. It looked sharp but slightly dented. It had seen action in the past – in fact every weapon in this room had once been used in battle.

Higarth shook his head as he thought about his messenger's ridiculous story. He had never slain a dragon himself of course; it was rare enough to see one, let alone come close enough to fight it.

But there were plenty of tales of heroic Ogres in past ages, who bravely fought and killed the beasts. The great reptiles would swoop down, beating their wings, covering the land with fire. But then, just when all hope seemed lost, a blade or an arrow would pierce their skin. The dragon would fall to the ground, defeated, while the Ogre would stand there, looking triumphant and presumably quite smug.

The weapons in the tales would vary, from small stones to giant blades. But in every case, one thing was certain – you needed strength and brute force. You couldn't kill one of those things with magic.

'Magic'. The Lord Protector even hated the word. There were some Ogres who still practised it, but most considered it a complete waste of time. It generally consisted of turning things funny shapes or strange colours. Occasionally people might manage to kill something with magic, but it most cases it would take so long the creatures would have died of old age anyway.

So magic was at best inefficient, and at worst completely pointless. That's why the Ogres tended to leave it to other civilisations who had more time for it, like the Pixies or Goblins.

Higarth frowned. Maybe there was more to magic than people thought. Perhaps there were some undiscovered tricks that had some uses, or some wizards in the Known World who had real powers.

But Higarth didn't believe it. And he didn't believe this ridiculous story of a Pixie killing a dragon. But just in case it was true (which of course it wasn't), he would send some more scouts across the Human and Pixie realms to look for her. And bring her back to the Ogre realm.

Someone who did believe this story (which of course he didn't), would probably send more soldiers to the Goblin realm too. There was a risk the Humans were going there, and the Ogres shouldn't get caught with too few soldiers; especially if the Humans had a magic Pixie with them (which of course they didn't).

"Gorac!" shouted Higarth. His general was next door. "I think we need to bring a thousand more soldiers to Siglitz."

He thought for a minute.

"And let's send a few scouts to the Human Realm. And the Pixie Realm," he added. "Armed with weapons."

Just in case. If a dangerous magic Pixie was out there, it was probably best they found out. And ideally had them 'dealt with' quickly, before they caused any problems.

Chapter 7

You wouldn't have known it was a coronation. There were so few people there.

Generally when a Goblin king or queen was officially crowned, there would be thousands attending the event. The citadel would be full of noise and celebration – it was a lot like the Dernbach festival, except with a little less booze (it was a coronation after all, not a party, so you couldn't go quite as mad).

People would come from all corners of the Goblin realm to celebrate together, cheer their new Monarch and drink responsibly.

This time was different. Lindric Hall might have been considered a large place to have a meeting, or even a banquet; it was the grandest room in the whole of Tygon Hollow. But for crowning a new queen, it was incredibly small.

There was a reason for this. Three Goblin kings had recently been killed in quick succession, which meant that Goblin monarchs were now something of an endangered species.

This meant the celebrations would have to be small, the cheers would have to be quiet, and the drinking would have to be even more responsible than usual.

Warlord Sepping surveyed the room. He was dressed in his military suit: a purple tunic, with plated metal over his shoulders. His chest was embellished with medals. The only thing missing was his sword; he had been asked to remove it before entering.

There were about fifty Goblins in the room, all of them dressed smartly. They were some of the most important people in the realm.

He could see the High Missionaire standing near the fruit buffet, talking to a couple of old Barons. She was the spiritual leader of all the Goblins, and it was her job to place the crown on the new queen's head. Sepping hadn't seen her for several years, and she seemed to have aged a lot.

The warlord turned his gaze to the other side of the room. The future queen was standing there, looking like a nervous child. Well to be fair, she basically *was* a nervous child. She was seventeen years old, and about to take on the greatest responsibility in the entire realm.

It was surely the most dangerous job in existence, apart from possibly dragon taming or shark wrestling. And nobody had ever successfully done either of those things, so they didn't really count.

Being leader of the Goblins on the other hand was a very real job. This would be hard enough in peaceful times. But right now, nobody felt safe – least of all someone whose three predecessors were all killed. So Lady Niella's trembling lip and wide eyes were quite understandable. It would have been strange if she wasn't afraid.

She did look the part though. Her long, silver hair had been pulled back, revealing two diamond earrings. She wore a traditional purple robe which almost reached her feet. And for some reason she had a blanket around her shoulders, which looked like it was made of soft cotton or wool. Apparently someone had wrapped it around her to 'keep her extra safe'.

A loud voice bellowed across the room.

"Oh great warriors, civilians and members of the Goblin realm. Please take your seats. The coronation will begin shortly."

Sepping looked round the room. He hadn't even noticed the chairs before. They were metal, covered in a yellow velvet, and positioned in rows facing the standing area. He followed the crowd as everyone gradually moved to their seats.

The first row was saved for the most important people, which meant Queen Afflech and a few civil lords. The warlord apparently wasn't important enough, so took a seat in the second row. Warlord Uoro came and sat beside him, looking equally well dressed, and equally annoyed at not getting a seat in the front row.

Only Lady Niella and the High Missionaire were still standing. Everyone else in Lindric Hall was now seated and the general chatter began to die down.

The throne was behind the two standing Goblins: a large, padded chair with a raised base. It was the same throne they had used for every previous coronation since the 11th age, except for Princes Grumio and Nutrec. Those two hadn't lasted long enough to have a coronation.

There was obviously a question as to whether either of them were kings at all. Neither were officially crowned, and Prince Grumio was technically dead before it was his turn. The scholars had debated this endlessly. Some felt they deserved to be remembered as rulers of the realm, even Grumio. Other scholars thought this was ridiculous, but eventually agreed to it. King Grumio would be recorded as the king whose reign lasted less than zero nights – a record nobody would ever be able to break.

Two long haired Goblins stood up and joined the High Missionaire and Niella at the front. Both wore long, purple robes and were holding wooden lutes. They began to play softly.

Warlord Sepping closed his eyes. He wondered whether it was really necessary to have musicians here. Surely even they were a security risk? He opened his eyes again and tried to study their instruments, just in case there was a knife hidden in one of them. He convinced himself that was highly unlikely.

"Good night, everyone," began the High Missionaire, as the lute players left the stage. "Thank you all for coming here to witness the coronation of our new queen."

There was an awkward round of applause.

"I know these are not ideal circumstances, and I would also like to thank everyone for understanding why we needed to go without the large crowds and open space. And nearly all the wine."

43

There was an awkward laugh among the audience.

"But that does not make this night any less important. Tonight we mark a new era for the Goblin realm. We do not look back at the terrible times we have faced. Tonight, we look forward, at the terrible times ahead."

She cleared her throat. "The peaceful and prosperous times ahead," she said, correcting herself.

There was an even more awkward laugh.

"Not the best start," whispered Warlord Uoro in Sepping's ear.

His fellow warlord nodded, still looking ahead at the High Missionaire.

"Lady Niella, please take your seat upon the throne," bellowed the High Missionaire.

The new queen did as she was told. She looked pale; even her hair looked whiter than before.

The High Missionaire walked over to a table to her right, where a rather large book had been carefully placed. It was covered in dust. The pages looked tattered and worn down. This was the sacred text: the holy document which every Goblin followed religiously. It was the book of the Gods. It dated back to long ages past, presumably. Nobody knew for sure.

She picked up the book with care and carried it over the future queen.

"Please place your hand on the sacred text," she said.

"The sacred text," repeated the audience. It was tradition. If someone mentioned the sacred text, you repeated it. Otherwise, it was bad luck.

"Do you solemnly vow to lead the Goblin Realm, from now until the night of your death?" continued the High Missionaire.

"I do," said Niella, nodding at the same time.

"Do you vow to protect all Goblins, and to put the welfare of your people before all else, from now until the night of your death?"

"I do," said Niella.

Sepping wondered if they really needed to keep repeating the part about 'death'.

The High Missionaire suddenly lost her grip on the book. She watched in mild shock as it fell to the floor.

"Be careful!" shouted Queen Afflech from the front row. "Do not damage the sacred text!"

"The sacred text," repeated the audience.

The High Missionare breathed heavily. "Okay, everybody please calm down," she said.

Very slowly, she reached down and carefully picked the book from the floor. It seemed okay; the pages were still intact.

"Everything is okay. I have not caused any harm to the sacred text."

"The sacred text," said the audience again.

The High Missionaire shuddered. She composed herself and got back to the ceremony at hand. She faced Lady Niella again.

"Do you vow to remain honest and true to the five almighty Gods, from now until the night of your death?" she continued.

"I do," said Niella again.

"Thank you," said the High Missionaire.

There was a pause.

"Thank you!" she repeated loudly. An embarrassed civil lord rose from the front row and handed her the crown.

"In the name of the Gods: Agach, Gorblech, Tinha, Logen and Lun," she continued. "I declare you Queen Niella, leader of the Goblin realm."

She placed the crown on the new leader's head.

"Please, be upstanding".

The audience of fifty Goblins stood up and started clapping. There were even a few cheers.

"Poor thing," muttered Warlord Sepping. "This is the easiest part of the job. Right now, all she has to do is sit there. And that seems to be difficult enough."

"True," replied Uoro, as the clapping was still going on. "Although technically she's already lasted longer than her last two predecessors. So that's something!"

Sepping nodded. "She's going to need us by her side every step of the way," he continued.

"Definitely," replied Uoro.

"I say we leave her tonight. Let her enjoy the coronation as much as she can," said Sepping. The clapping was still loud, but they kept their voices low.

"She should have at least one night of peace," said Uoro. "But tomorrow, we tell her everything that's happened. We warn her of the perils that could come next."

The lute players came back to the front and started playing the same tune as before. It was a soft rendition of 'Our Land and Our People: Everything We Owe to the Gods' – a classic Goblin song from ages passed.

The lyrics were known to be a little confusing; they included a lot of discussion about whether it actually was 'their land', or if it was the Gods' land since they owed everything to them. It ended by being clear that regardless of the situation, the land certainly wasn't owned by Ogres, Pixies, Humans or anyone else.

Despite the lyrics, the tune was very moving, so most of the time the Goblins just played it with instruments and didn't bother singing it.

The two warlords joined the forming queue, as everyone started making their way to the front of the room to hail their new queen.

"What worries me most is how little we know about her," whispered Uoro. "What if we do need to fight the Humans or even the Ogres in battle? How do we know if Niella will be capable of making that decision?"

"She only needs to make one decision," replied Sepping. "She needs to decide to let us make all the decisions for her."

Warlord Uoro smiled. "Hopefully that will be an easy decision for her to make," he replied.

Chapter 8

King Wyndham was flying. Although he was sitting at the same time. Something strange was going on. He looked down and saw he was on a white horse with wings.

Of course! He was riding a unicorn. It was night-time, but the stars were out. There was enough light for him to see the animal clearly. Everything made sense.

But he didn't remember how he had got here. *Why* was he riding a unicorn? He didn't usually ride them. In fact, nobody had ever ridden one in the history of the Known World. It was almost impossible to get close to a unicorn, let alone try to ride one.

He looked out to his right. Was that a blue dragon in the sky? It certainly looked like one – a huge, winged creature covered in scales. But was it smiling? He could have sworn it was giving him a big, toothy grin. The dragon then winked at him. That was odd – dragons didn't usually wink.

Come to think of it, dragons didn't smile either. And blue dragons didn't exist. He changed his mind about everything making sense. In fact, nothing made sense at all.

"Ah, it's a dream!" he shouted.

The King had finally cracked it. He was asleep; none of this was real. He felt rather proud of himself for figuring it out. It must be a sign of royalty – surely the average person wouldn't realise when they were in their own dream.

Then he thought for a moment. This was still unusual; Wyndham didn't usually dream at all, and when he did, they weren't this vivid. It must mean something. It could be a window into his subconscious. Maybe he secretly wanted to ride a unicorn? Or have a blue dragon smile at him?

That seemed unlikely. Didn't he generally wish for peace or prosperity for Humankind? Or to have multiple wives?

King Wyndham looked down to the ground. They were clearly very high up. He beckoned the unicorn to go lower. He wasn't sure how he did it, but the animal seemed to comply.

As the ground below him grew closer, he started to make out features of the landscape. There were snow-capped mountains in the distance. And was that a river?

The unicorn flew lower still. The mountains had disappeared now, and all he could see below him was grassland. It looked dry and lifeless – almost grey, as if the grass had forgotten it was supposed to be green.

Things came more into focus. He started to make out some buildings on the ground. There weren't many, but something about them seemed strange. They were all fairly small and spread out from each other; in fact, they seemed to be completely evenly spaced.

As he stared, he began to realise the buildings were all exactly the same. There were six of them, arranged in two rows of three. They were grey buildings, probably made of stone. They could have been town halls or churches. But they were identical to every last detail.

Suddenly, one of the buildings seemed to catch fire. How did that happen? It had seemed perfectly fine, and then within an instant it was up in flames. Maybe the smiling blue dragon had paid them a visit. But he didn't see anything; it seemed to spontaneously combust.

The building next to it caught fire. Very strange. Even from his height, he could see a clear gap between the buildings. Surely the fire couldn't have just spread from one to another. But then, he was riding a unicorn; anything could happen right now.

Another one set alight. And then another. Finally, the last two buildings caught fire. King Wyndham watched as the flames consumed every one of the stone structures, eating away at them until they were nothing but clumps of ash.

It seemed strange that stone buildings could burn that quickly. Or indeed at all. But again, he was riding a unicorn.

And then, suddenly, he wasn't. He had leant too far as he gazed at the buildings and now felt himself slipping down the right side of the creature. He reached out his hand to try and grab on to the wing, but it was too late. He was falling, hurtling to the ground like a thunderbolt. The King closed his eyes and held his breath, waiting for the inevitable end.

He woke up with a jolt. Thank the Gods! It was all a dream. Although he had known that all along, he thought to himself smugly.

"Is everything all right, sire?"

Wyndham was puzzled for a moment. It wasn't normal for his wife to call him sire. Or to sound like a man. Another dream?

"Sire…is everything all right?"

He saw the Lord of War's face at the door to his tent. His dark hair was gelled back, and he was wearing a rather oversized grey robe.

Now things were back to normal. King Wyndham remembered it all. He had left the queen two days ago, as they set off for Nuberim.

A few of his lords had come with him. So had Petra, along with her two companions: Prince Vardie of the Pixie realm, and Samorus, her elderly mentor. He had also brought an army of two hundred people. And some servants.

The King questioned his decision on that again. Why had they needed to bring so many soldiers? This was a diplomatic visit. They were just guards. They weren't going to do any actual fighting.

But then, these were dangerous times in the Goblin realm. The whole of the land was in disarray. And they didn't trust Humans right now – humans had shot an arrow at one of the Goblin kings.

This meant that if Goblins saw them, they might not think the Humans were there on an official diplomatic mission. They might think they were there to cause trouble. So they needed more soldiers, to reinforce the point that it was an official diplomatic mission. It had definitely made sense when Cecil explained it to him. Definitely.

Wyndham paused. He couldn't get that dream out of his head. He had seen six identical buildings catch fire, one after the other. Why? It had to mean something, didn't it?

"I'm fine thank you Cecil," replied the King eventually.

"Glad to hear it sire. Should we prepare to set off for the day?"

"Yes, shortly," replied Wyndham. "Cecil, do we have any seers among our party?" he added.

"Seers?" asked Cecil. "You mean... people who see things?"

"I mean people who can see into people's minds," replied the King indignantly. "You know, seers?"

"Ah," replied Cecil. "We don't tend to use that term any more sire. It is considered offensive."

"What? To who?"

"Well... people who can't see," replied the lord. "These days, we tend to use the word 'reader'".

"Reader?"

"Yes, as in mind reader."

"But isn't that offensive to people who can't read?" replied Wyndham.

"Ah well people can always learn to read. But they can't learn to see."

Wyndham took a breath. "Cecil, who's the king?" he said.

"You are sire," replied Cecil.

"Yes. And as king, I will use whatever word I want. And in fact, if anyone gets offended by my use of the word 'seer', then I order them to stop."

"Yes, sire," said Cecil, nodding. "I believe one of the captains is a... seer. I'll go summon her."

"Thank you," replied the King.

Seers were people who studied the ancient art of mind

reading. Some people in the military considered it a useful skill. Most of course considered it complete and utter nonsense. But they didn't tell the seers that, so the seers never knew.

Seers didn't generally believe they could fully see into someone else's mind. It was more about spotting people's behaviours – their mannerisms and their responses; anything to get an insight into their subconscious. And one of the best ways of doing that was through their dreams.

"Sire?"

A middle-aged woman showed her face at the door of King Wyndham's tent. She had white hair and bushy eyebrows.

"Captain Soder, at your service. You sent for me?"

"Are you the seer?" asked King Wyndham.

"The reader sire, yes," replied the captain. "How can I help?"

"It's about a dream," replied Wyndham.

Captain Soder sat down, and the King told her everything. The captain stayed silent, nodding.

"What do you think it means?" Wyndham said finally.

"Well firstly I'm no expert," said Captain Soder. "But the six buildings probably represent something."

"Like what?"

The captain thought for a minute.

"Well, maybe you secretly desire to have six different wives, but you're worried that they would all find out about each other. And the fire represents each one getting very angry at…"

She saw the glare coming from the King.

"Or maybe the buildings represent the six civilisations of the Known World?" she continued, stuttering slightly. "Perhaps their burning up in flames represents a fear you have, that one by one every civilisation will fall."

Wyndham was taken aback. That actually made sense.

"And of course," continued Soder, "dreams can sometimes mean more than that. Maybe it's not just your fear; maybe it's a vision for the future."

King Wyndham paused. "You really think that's possible?"

"Maybe," shrugged the captain. "Many of the ancient scrolls talk about people who had such visions. They say that oracles have been around since the dawn of time. Or at least since the Third Age. Before that, nothing much happened so there wasn't really anything to predict."

Wyndham frowned. "But I saw them burn. I saw all six of them burn. If that's a vision, then I just saw the end of the Known World!"

Captain Soder shrugged again. "Personally sire, I believe that no matter what we see, we always have the power to change our future."

Wyndham nodded, still frowning. "But what about the blue dragon. And the unicorn?" he asked.

"Well maybe deep down you've just always wanted to ride a unicorn. Or befriend a dragon. Or maybe it's showing you that even if the people of the Known World ended, magical creatures would still survive."

This brought a smile back to the King's face. "Maybe," he said. Then he thought for a second. "The six buildings, burning to ash one after another...you don't think that could have something to do with Petra, do you?"

"You mean the magic Pixie that can burn anything to ashes in seconds?" replied the captain. "No, I'm sure that's just a coincidence."

Chapter 9

Siglitz. The city that sometimes slept, but not very often. It was in the north of the Goblin realm, and was certainly a moderately interesting place. It was widely known for being one of the largest cities in the realm, although not the largest. And one of the liveliest cities, but not the liveliest.

It definitely had its place in history. It was where they invented the double-wind cork, which kept wine bottles in a slightly better condition than the single wind cork. And of course, it was where the famous Goblin wizard Jagra Velt once stayed, when he was on his way to visit somewhere more exciting.

Lord Protector Higarth wasn't here for the history. He hadn't brought an army of nearly two thousand soldiers to visit the museum of cork-winding. He could go another time. Right now, he was here for one reason alone: to get the Goblin people on his side.

Siglitz was the nearest big city to the Ogre realm. It had many high buildings and its tunnels were full of torches – all very similar designs to those in the Ogre realm. More importantly though, plenty of Ogres actually lived there. They were bigger and stronger than their Goblin friends, and could make good money in construction, security or weightlifting competitions. So many of them had made the trip across the hills and found a new home.

All this meant the people of Siglitz were very receptive to the Lord Protector of the Ogres. When he showed up with thousands of soldiers, they probably didn't even feel threatened. They must have assumed he was just passing through or helping the city with extra security.

The governor of Siglitz had welcomed them warmly. She had opened the city gates straight away, to save them having to climb over the wall.

Well, having to step over it anyway – another interesting fact about Siglitz was it arguably had the smallest walls of any city. They were made of stone, but time had eroded them into nothing but old-looking obstacles. They frankly offered no extra protection, except to make potential attackers slightly more tired by having to hurdle over them. Residents of the Elven city of Alshmar claimed to have an even smaller wall. But it was so small, nobody had ever managed to see it.

The governor knew Higarth and his soldiers were coming. She didn't know there would be quite so many of them, but just saw it as an extra-large celebration. Two thousand soldiers coming to visit. Wonderful.

She was called Jonash, or 'Governor Jonash' to anyone less important than her. Which was nearly everyone. She was tall for a Goblin, her hair white and drooping down below her pointed chin. She had ruled the city for over ten years and was well known across the Goblin realm.

She was also well acquainted with the Ogres. She had been to their lands many times to build relationships, marvel at the Ogres' tall buildings, and laugh at their relatively shallow tunnels.

She was a friend to their people – that much was obvious. She had put on a wonderful feast for the visitors. Well it would have been a feast if there weren't so many people, which meant the food had to be spread quite thinly.

But there was more than enough for the Lord Protector and his generals. They were enjoying their own meal in a private room; it was underground but fairly close to the surface.

"Have some more chicken, Higarth," said Jonash.

"If you insist," replied the Lord Protector.

He reached over and stuck his fork into the slab of meat, bringing it back to his plate. The chicken wasn't bad. Neither were the potatoes. They were almost as good as the Ogres would cook.

"More wine?"

"Of course," said Higarth.

The governor topped up his goblet. There were no waiters in the room – they had brought the food and then left. Higarth didn't mind that though. It meant they had privacy. Just his generals: Lang and Chandimer, the governor and her two deputies.

"So when did you last come to Siglitz?" asked the governor.

"It's been a while," replied Higarth, taking another sip of red wine. "We took a different route last time, when we went to Nuberim. So we didn't come through this city."

"It must be great to be back," said the governor.

"So great," replied Higarth. "Such an exciting place. I hear they have added a new exhibit to the double wind cork museum?"

"They have indeed," said Jonash, her white eyes lighting up. "So tell me about your last visit to Nuberim. Must have been a terrible time to be there?"

"Oh yes," replied Higarth. "Such a tragedy."

"So what do you make of it?" asked the governor. "Three kings. Killed! None of it seemed to make any sense."

"We know the Humans killed Nutrec," added General Lang.

"Two Humans did, anyway," said the governor. "We don't know why though. From what I've heard, they were just a couple of looneys. Unlikely that the leaders actually ordered them to do it."

"Pfff," retorted Higarth. "I wouldn't be so sure. If I had to guess, I would say that the Humans were behind every one of the killings."

"Interesting," said Jonash. "But they were all so different. One was stabbed to death, one poisoned and one shot with an arrow!"

Higarth nodded. "Yes. But they wouldn't want them to look connected, would they? Humans aren't stupid. Well, not all of them anyway. Not all the time."

The governor took a sip from her drink. "But why though?" she asked. "King Grieber and Wyndham were friends. Why would he want to kill him?"

Higarth shrugged. "Maybe he changed his mind. Humans can be so fickle."

The governor smiled. "And how could they even have done it? There weren't any Humans near King Grieber at the time. He had been at a private dinner. Only Goblins there and…you guys," she added in a low voice.

"Governor Jonash, I hope you're not implying that we…"

"No, not at all!" replied the governor hastily. "I just don't understand how it could have happened."

Higarth sat back in his seat. "Maybe we'll never know," he said.

He finished off the last of the chicken on his plate. The governor decided to change the subject. "So have you heard the rumours from Peria?" she asked.

"What rumours? Have the Humans managed to ride a unicorn?" asked Higarth.

It was common knowledge that they had been trying for years, but so far hadn't even managed to sit on one. Or even catch one. Or have one look at them in a friendly manner.

"No, not that," said Jonash. "I mean the magic Pixie."

Higarth stopped and put his fork down.

"You mean the Pixie that can make fire?" he asked.

"Yes. Well more than that. A young girl. Apparently she killed a dragon, just by shooting fire from her hands!"

Higarth looked around. His generals had stopped eating too and were staring intently at the governor.

"I had heard something," he replied. "It sounded preposterous though. Most likely just a silly rumour."

"Maybe," replied Jonash. "But what if it's true? What if the Humans use this Pixie to attack the Eastern realms?"

"Just a rumour, I'm sure," said the Lord Protector, shaking his head.

He didn't mention that he had sent out soldiers to look for her. Quite a few soldiers. He had sent them out in groups of five, so they covered a wide area between them. He had said that whoever caught her and brought her back would be rewarded with a thousand silvers. Or maybe a hundred, depending on how generous he was feeling.

Higarth still didn't believe the rumours. But if they were true, the Humans would know the Pixie was in danger. They wouldn't keep her in Peria. They would escort her to safety somewhere else. Most likely she would be in the west of the Human realm, or maybe back near her home. But wherever she went, they would find her.

"So tell me, Higarth," said the governor. "If it's nothing to do with this magic Pixie, why have you come to Siglitz? And with a large party of soldiers?"

Higarth paused. "We've come to keep the peace," he said.

Governor Jonash was a little taken aback. "But it's quite peaceful here. No real problems at all, despite everything that's happened."

"Yes, but what about in Nuberim?" replied Higarth.

"Same story, I would say," replied the governor. "Everyone's still in mourning obviously. It's been such a tough time. But we're getting on with it. No riots, no fighting. Just back to work. Everything does feel at peace."

Higarth looked visibly frustrated. "Well then we'll make everyone even more at peace!" he bellowed.

"And support the Goblin leaders during this difficult time," added General Litmus. "That's why we're here – to offer support. The Ogres are always there to help the Goblins in their time of need. Always."

"Okay," said Jonash, quietly. "And how long will you be staying here?"

"As long as we want," replied Higarth, grinning. "By which I mean, as long as you need us here, obviously."

The governor didn't respond.

Chapter 10

Petra held her palm out vertically and sent out a burst of flame. It hit the pile of logs on the ground in front of her. They turned to charcoal in an instant. No fire remained, just a few black ashes.

"Sorry, but I did say," said the young Pixie, looking at the disappointed faces around her. "Do you want me to help you collect some more firewood?"

The group of soldiers around her were silent. It had been another long day of travelling. They must have been looking forward to a fire, and the opportunity to get some food cooking.

They could have just used oil like everyone else. But no, they saw the magic Pixie walk by and just had to ask her for a favour. She tried to explain it didn't work like that. She could make fire, but not in the normal sense. Her flames turned things to dust in an instant – not much help when it comes to lighting a campfire.

"That's okay, we have more wood here," said one of the soldiers, starting to smile. "Thanks anyway. It was still pretty cool to see."

Petra laughed. "No worries," she said, turning away.

She headed back to Samorus and Prince Vardie. The three of them had their own tent. It was very spacious – you could probably have fitted ten Humans in there.

This was the third day they had been travelling with the Humans, on their way to the Goblins. Right now they were still in the Human realm, but Petra had never been this way before. The journey had been good so far; the land was full of grassy hills, which were easy enough to climb and gave nice views of the area around them.

Yesterday they had come across the forbidden fountain, which Petra had previously only heard about in stories. They used to say that if you drank from it, terrible harm would come to you. Although they found out in the 9th Age that an eastern baron had started that rumour, so he could purchase the fountain cheaply and be the only one who got to drink from it. The seller then got rather annoyed, so he hired an assassin who killed the baron. Which meant technically the baron had been right all along.

Now, they were camped near a forest. Petra took a moment to stare into the trees on her way. She didn't know what forest this was, or if it even had a name. She wondered what amazing creatures were living inside it – maybe there were griffins, or even centaurs.

She stopped as she heard a rustle in a nearby tree. Something shot up into the bushes above. Just a squirrel. But quite a large squirrel – definitely larger than normal. That counted as an amazing creature.

Petra kept walking towards her tent. It wasn't far now. The tents were relatively spaced out, but there were only about a hundred of them. So it didn't take too long to walk from one end to the other, even for a four foot tall Pixie.

"Excuse me! Magic Pixie!"

It was a soldier shouting from nearby. Another group standing in a circle. Surely they didn't want her to…

"Could you help us light a fire?"

Petra sighed. She stopped in her tracks and started walking towards the group. There were six of them standing round a pile of logs.

"Listen, it's not what you think," she said.

"You are the Pixie, aren't you?"

She sighed. "Yes," she said, "but I can't do what…"

Petra stopped suddenly. Something had brushed past her ear, missing her by a whisker. It struck one of the soldiers in the chest, who started crying out in pain.

Was it a knife? She turned round instantly. It came from the trees in front of her. Something was moving. This time, it was definitely bigger than a squirrel.

She held out her hand and let out a flame without even thinking. Whatever was in those trees had surely thrown the knife. The fire burnt the first tree in sight to the ground. The poor tree had presumably not thrown the knife, but there were always casualties in battle.

It seemed to work though. Whoever or whatever it was seemed to turn and flee.

"Hey!" shouted one of the Human soldiers.

A group of them ran into the forest in pursuit. She heard shouts and cries, which gradually died down as the soldiers disappeared among the trees.

Then she heard a sudden blast of noise. It must have been a horn or trumpet. It was hard to explain, but it didn't sound normal. Certainly not like anything she had heard from the Humans, or the Pixies. It was different.

It sounded again, a little softer. And maybe a couple more times. It was hard to tell now. Pretty soon everything was silent, and she saw no movement in the trees.

The soldiers didn't reappear. Whatever they were chasing, it was probably doing a good job at running away.

Petra caught her breath. She then turned to the poor Human who had been struck. He was lying on the ground. A couple of others were crouched around him, including one who was attending to his chest. He was blocking her view, so she couldn't see how the wounded guy was doing. But he wasn't crying out in pain anymore, which probably wasn't a good sign.

She walked over to him. As she got closer, she could see he was already gone – the knife had hit him right in the chest. No amount of healing potion could have helped with that. Even if healing potion actually worked.

"I'm so sorry," she said to the soldiers, breathing hard. "Is there anything I can do?"

One of them looked up. His face was red and his eyes were watering.

"Don't blame yourself," he said solemnly.

"What? Why would I blame myself?" replied Petra. "I meant I'm sorry it happened. It wasn't my fault was it?"

"Well no," replied the soldier. "But didn't you see how close that knife came to your head?"

Petra paused. "You think it was meant for me," she said slowly.

He nodded. "Look around," he said. "There were no other attacks. It was one person, throwing a knife. Do you think it's a coincidence that it came right by your face?"

Petra frowned. "Just after someone shouted 'Magic Pixie'," she said.

"Yeah, they probably shouldn't have said that," replied the soldier.

She took another deep breath. She just realised how close she had come to getting killed. By someone who meant to do it. A wave of guilt flowed over her too, as she looked once more at the dead soldier. He seemed quite young – probably not far off her own age. That made it even worse.

"What was his name?" she asked. "Jenrick," replied the soldier. "And my name is Syland, not that you asked for it."

Petra was silent. The soldier looked down at his companion again, and then back up to the Pixie.

"He was a good man," he said.

"A great man, I'm sure," replied Petra. "A real hero. He didn't deserve this. Nobody could have deserved this!" she started to well up herself. "Did he have a family?"

The soldier shook his head. Petra leaned over and kissed Jenrick on the forehead.

"I'm so sorry," she said again. "Be at peace now. May the Gods be with you in your resting place."

She wasn't a big believer in the Gods herself. And Humans worshipped different Gods to Pixies. But that didn't matter. It was still the right thing to say.

As she brought her head up, she got a close look at the knife in his chest. It was a dull silver colour, and absolutely huge. She probably couldn't have grasped her whole hand around it.

"What's that on the handle?" she asked.

It was a skull, carved into the metal. A little worn, but still clearly visible.

"Ogres," said Syland. "It's a symbol they use. I would bet anything they were behind it."

"Ogres? Around here?" said Petra. "But we're still in the Human realm. Isn't it a bit unusual for Ogres to travel this far?"

"Well not really," he replied. "You get them wandering around these parts sometimes. They're usually up to no good. An Ogre wouldn't come to the Human realm unless they wanted to cause trouble."

Petra wiped the tears from her eyes.

"Think about it," continued Syland, or whatever his name was. "You're a threat to them. You're the most powerful weapon we have. The most powerful weapon… anyone has."

Petra felt a chill down her spine. Were there really Ogres after her? And not just a couple, but the whole of the Ogre realm? And what about Goblins? Or even Trolls?

She shook her head. Enough questions. She couldn't know anything right now, so there was no point speculating. Hopefully the Humans would catch whoever did it and bring them back to camp.

She started to turn back to her tent. She had to see Samorus and Prince Vardie, and tell them what had happened. They wouldn't be able to help, but at least she would feel relatively safer with them. And a little less guilty that someone may have just been killed because of her.

"Wait," said the soldier.

Petra stopped. "What is it?" she asked.

"Before you go," he added. "Would you mind using your magic powers to light that campfire?"

Chapter 11

If you challenged a Goblin to a digging contest, you wouldn't win. Unless of course you happened to challenge one of the Cult of the Underground, who opposed digging in all its forms. They would never even make a dent in the land if they could help it, let alone dig a hole. It meant they lived entirely above ground, unlike other Goblins. They probably could have come up with a better name.

The Cult of the Underground believed that the Sacred Text of the Goblin Gods strictly banned digging in all its forms. It didn't, but their belief was so strong that they never needed to check.

All the other Goblins, however, were natural born diggers. They dug with their hands; they dug with their feet; they would have dug with their heads if it didn't look so silly.

Of course, digging competitions already existed in the Goblin realm. The annual contest at Dagmah was a celebrated tradition. People would come from all over the realm to watch the hopeful competitors dig as deep as they possibly could.

The winner was the one who dug the deepest hole. They were given a trophy, once they had climbed back out. Which generally took a while.

The holes then formed the start of new mines, tunnels and villages. Some saw it as a truly great competition. Others as a cheeky source of free labour for the Goblin civil lords.

All these reasons meant that Goblin settlements went deep. While Ogres were proud of their high towers, Goblins were proud of their deep holes. They had the deepest and darkest dwellings in the whole of the Known World.

It was hard to find anywhere deeper or darker than a

dungeon, and that's where two Humans still found themselves. Ridley and Fulton had been in the prison at Nuberim for ages. Well not literally ages of course, as an age lasted for a hundred years. It was more like one thousandth of an age. But when you're stuck in a jail cell, that's a very long time.

The novelty had definitely worn off.

Ridley sat against the wall and looked through the bars of the cell. There was a Goblin soldier sitting in the corridor. Just the one. That was unusual.

"Hey," said Ridley in a low voice.

Fulton stirred and gave him a look. It still felt dangerous to talk to the guards. The Goblins sometimes asked them questions and even came across as quite friendly. But they were often cold and aggressive with the prisoners, depending on their mood.

"Be quiet," snapped the guard. He looked very young, like a child dressed in his dad's armour. His hair was white and fairly short. His luminous eyes glared at Ridley across the dark corridor.

"Sorry," replied Ridley. "Just thought you might want to talk, that's all. How's your night going?"

"Don't talk to me," said the guard, gruffly. "I don't speak to you prisoners."

"You're not allowed?"

"No I'm allowed, I just don't want to."

"Because we're criminals?" asked Fulton.

"No, because you're Humans," replied the guard, turning his head. "Yes I know it's the 14th Age, and these days many Goblins consider Humans as our friends. But I don't. You're inferior to us in every way."

Ridley almost smiled. He didn't really mind the insults; it was nice just to be having a conversation with someone new.

"What makes us inferior?" he asked.

"Everything," said the Goblin guard. "Let's face it. Goblins are stronger, more intelligent, better diggers, we can see in the dark. And we're funnier," he added.

"Oh really?" Ridley retorted.

"Yes. You Humans with your so called 'jesters' who

wear stupid hats with bells on. What's funny about that?"

"He's got us there," admitted Fulton to his cell mate.

"Whatever," said Ridley. "Tell us a joke then, mister funny Goblin, sir."

The guard rolled his eyes. "Fine," he said. "Did you hear the one about the person who had no ears? No? Neither did he."

There was a short silence.

"Because he had no ears, he couldn't hear it. It's a joke within a joke you see, very clever. You Humans wouldn't understand it."

"Yes, I find the best jokes are the ones you have to explain why they're funny," said Ridley sarcastically.

The guard rolled his eyes once more.

"How come you're on your own here?" asked Fulton. "Usually there's always two or three guards."

"People can take time off, can't they?" snapped the Goblin guard. He took a breath. "It's the annual digging competition at Dagmah next week. A few of the guards are on their way to watch it."

"The digging competition? Ah yes, I reckon a Human might win it this year," said Fulton, just to wind him up.

"Don't be ridiculous," said the guard. "Only Goblins are allowed to enter. Besides, a Human couldn't dig a hole deep enough to plant a potato."

Another funny joke. Although Fulton sniggered quietly at this one.

"Now, enough questions," said the guard. "And let me get back to work."

He sat in silence, staring at the cell. That, of course, was his work.

"Can I just ask one more question?" said Ridley.

"Fine," snapped the guard, who apparently talked to Humans quite a lot now.

"What's been happening in the outside world? We've been stuck down here for weeks now, deep below the surface. We know absolutely nothing."

"You know nothing because you're Humans," replied the guard, hilariously.

Ridley nodded. "Seriously though, is there anything you can tell us?"

The guard sighed. "If I were you, I would be less worried about what's been happening in the outside world, and more concerned about what's going to happen to you!"

Ridley took a moment. "What do you mean by that?" he said.

"Well firstly, your impending death," said the guard, without flinching.

The two Humans looked at each other. Ridley frowned, and took a moment to breathe.

"This really comes as a surprise to you?" said the guard, almost sniggering. "Surely you didn't think you could kill our king and get away with it; just spend a little time in prison and then get sent home?"

"Well no," said Ridley. "Obviously. But nobody had said you were going to kill us. I guess we assumed if you wanted to, you would have done it by now."

The guard let out sarcastic laugh. "Stupid Humans. Of course we're going to kill you!"

Fulton felt his pulse start to race. He swallowed hard.

"Cheer up Humans," continued the guard. "Dying isn't something to be afraid of. It's actually quite easy – everybody manages it eventually. But before we kill you, we're going to do something much, much worse."

The Goblin cackled. He refused to answer any more of the prisoners' questions. He just let them sit in the dark, trying not to imagine the horrors they might soon have to face. What could possibly be much, much worse than death?

Ridley put his hand on Fulton's shoulder. He could feel it shaking. The longer they had sat in this cell, the safer they had felt. It wasn't pretty, but at least they were being kept alive. A part of him had always believed that they could just wait it out; sit in this cell until the disagreements with the Humans and the Ogres were over. And maybe then, just maybe, they would get released.

All those hopes had just been shattered, like a Lothian broadsword trying to cut through armour. Those swords really were rubbish.

Chapter 12

King Wyndham surveyed the landscape around him. They had passed through the woods and managed the difficult task of getting every soldier over the Turner River. And every horse.

They were still in his own realm, but everything felt a bit different now that they were east of the water. The terrain seemed more unforgiving. Thorn bushes and ferns crept across the ground, making it harder to travel.

Very few people lived in this side of the realm. Its proximity to the Ogres made it undesirable to any Human. It was often neglected by the people in power. Occasionally the Lord of Gold would announce an initiative to bring wealth and prosperity to the east of the realm. But it usually dwindled out when he remembered how dangerous it was to go there. Of course, equality was important. But safety was even more important, especially his own.

Wyndham had been sitting on his horse all day. But even that was tiring. He sympathised with the soldiers who had to travel on foot this whole time. They were probably more tired than he was.

The sun was now beginning to set. It was soon time to set up camp for the night. They had to be careful; after the incident with Petra he was more alert than before. That poor soldier who had been killed. He had spoken to the Pixie about it at great length; she was convinced that they had meant to kill her.

If only they had caught the scoundrels who did it. How had they managed to escape? In some ways it didn't matter. It was Ogres, he was sure of that. And more than likely they had been ordered by their Lord Protector to catch Petra.

It was a chilling thought. But this wasn't the first threatening situation the King had been in. He wasn't afraid, just alert. He knew what to do. He had ordered guards to ride with Petra on all sides. At night, twice as many soldiers would take the watch while the others slept. Nobody would come near his secret weapon. Well, Petra was more than that. She was his friend.

Most importantly, Wyndham had changed their plans. They were no longer going to Nuberim. Not yet. It was too dangerous – there could be Ogres everywhere. He didn't want to risk a bloody battle which they weren't prepared for.

No. They were on their way to Lancha, a city in the south of the Goblin realm. It was safer, and more receptive to Humans than the settlements further north. They would stay there for a short while and recuperate. Get a feel for the situation. And only venture to Nuberim when they were ready.

He had also sent a messenger back home to ask for more soldiers. They didn't have enough. They had sword fighters, and a few spears. No archers. They needed more of everything.

Wyndham suddenly stopped. His horse let out a grunt. He'd heard a noise. Was it screaming? There was some commotion up ahead. He looked around, everyone near him had now come to a halt. There was shouting. He saw a cloud of dust. People had started gathering round something, or someone.

King Wyndham got down from his horse and ran towards the crowd. His chainmail was weighing him down, so he found this quite a challenge.

He was panting heavily by the time he arrived at the scene. There were a lot of people there now. And there was still a lot of shouting.

"What…what happened?" asked King Wyndham, between breaths.

"Sire!" cried Cecil. He walked up to the King, clearly in a state. "She's gone sire. They took her!"

"Who? Who did they take?" Wyndham knew the answer, even as he was saying it. They had female soldiers, but there was only one person in real danger. Only one person on the King's mind.

"Petra!" replied Cecil.

King Wyndham closed his eyes. "Who took her?" he shouted, dismayed.

"We don't know," said his lord. "It all happened so quickly. Some rider came galloping through and snatched her from behind. I didn't see a thing. Apparently they were covered in a dark hood."

"You couldn't see their face," added one of the soldiers standing nearby.

The King put his head in his hands. "How did this happen?" He bellowed, red faced. "I told you to put guards on all sides!"

"We did," replied the Lord of War. "But not behind her."

"That's one of the sides!" exclaimed King Wyndham angrily.

"Is it? We thought you just meant left and right. Front and back aren't really sides are they? They're more…"

"Enough!" growled the King. "I'll deal with you later, Cecil. We need to act quickly. Did anyone chase after them?"

"Yes, lots," replied the Lord of War, slightly relieved. "Longfield galloped straight after him, along with a few of his trusted sword fighters."

Wyndham let out a breath. He looked at the crowd around him. He saw Samorus on one side, still sitting on his small horse. He was in tears. Petra's horse was next to him, without a rider, presumably confused.

One of his soldiers was consoling Samorus. It wasn't helping. The crowd stood there in uncomfortable silence. It seemed to last a long time. Eventually, the King sent a few more riders out to look for Petra.

"We'll set up camp here tonight," said Wyndham, when the riders had left. "There's no point in travelling any further today."

There were a few nods amongst the crowd.

"And Cecil," he added, turning to his Lord of War. "Make sure that you order all soldiers to take shifts guarding the camp. On ALL SIDES."

When they had set up his tent, King Wyndham went

and sat inside it. He invited Samorus and Prince Vardie to join him. The three of them simply sat there in silence, feeling like parents who had lost their child.

"I wish we had just stayed in my hovel in Madesco," said Samorus at last. "She would have been safe."

"We'll get her back," said Wyndham, solemnly. "We will."

Another silence. But not for long this time. Charlon came to the door of the tent. He was one of the King's royal guard. In fact, he was one of the people who Wyndham had ordered to ride out and see if he could see any sign of Petra.

Charlon was still clad in armour, but he had taken off his helmet. He looked dejected and in pain. Whatever had happened, it was not good news.

"What happened? Did you find her?" said King Wyndham, hurriedly.

Charlon shook his head. "We found Longfield and his men. They were...they were dead," he said slowly.

The King let out a shriek, without thinking. He had only been considering the possibility of his soldiers returning empty handed. It hadn't even occurred to him that they wouldn't return at all. Whatever was out there, it was far more dangerous than he had thought.

"All of them?" he said eventually.

"All of them," replied Charlon. Sweat was running down his brown. "Longfield had an arrow through his heart. So did Samuels and Jakubs. The others seemed to have been stabbed."

The guard put his head down. He wasn't enjoying this conversation.

"What do you think happened?" asked Wyndham, still trying to comprehend it.

"There was a dead Ogre there too," continued Charlon. "We think they must have been attacked by a group of them."

"What about Petra?" blurted our Samorus.

The guard shook his head. "Her body wasn't there," he replied.

Samorus breathed. They all did. Breathing was rather important right now. Or indeed at any time.

"So as far as you know, she's still alive?" asked Samorus.

"Yes," sighed the guard. "I expect whoever took her is keeping her captive. Maybe Longfield and his soldiers found her, but the Ogres fought them off."

"And killed them," added King Wyndham.

"Yes," said Charlon. It didn't need repeating.

The old Pixie didn't know what to think. He believed she was still alive; he had to. But she had been abducted, most likely taken prisoner. And the people who were trying to rescue her had been killed. She was lost. And they had no way of finding her.

Samorus couldn't help but feel a little responsible for all this. He had been her mentor. He had been the one who had found out her powers, and gone with her to the Human realm in the first place. If it wasn't for him, Petra would probably still be in Madesco living a normal life. And so would he.

There was no chance of that now. The old Pixie wondered if he would ever see his home again. He hadn't even told his customers that he was going away – he couldn't have known he would be away this long. They were probably wondering where their healing potion was.

He imagined them knocking politely on the door of his hovel. Then when he didn't answer, knocking again, slightly less politely. And finally, less politely still, kicking the door down and breaking into his home.

When they found he wasn't there, that would probably be the end of his healing potion business. They would assume he had died. Or magically disappeared. Either way, he didn't really care.

Petra's disappearance would have caused more of a stir. She didn't have particularly close family, but she had some good friends.

She would see them again. Samorus vowed that to himself. Even though he had no idea how he could make that happen.

Chapter 13

It had all begun with the First Age. Everybody agreed that was a sensible place to start.

But nobody could agree on what came before it. Many people thought nothing existed, until the Gods created the whole of the Known World in one go. Even then, they couldn't agree on which Gods, since every civilisation worshipped different ones. So there was plenty of fighting about it.

The High Elf of Lanthyn once tried to bring about peace, by suggesting that maybe each civilisation was created by their own Gods. That sounded great, until the Humans asked who created the land, or the rivers, or the animals. The High Elf didn't have an answer. So there was plenty of fighting about it.

Some people believed the Known World had existed well before the First Age, but they just hadn't started counting yet. Legend had it that a wise old Goblin queen wanted to know how long she had been alive, so she started keeping a record of each year that passed. Of course since she was alive when she started counting, she never could figure it out. But at least everyone born after her would never have that problem.

It was a great theory, except that the Ogres were fairly sure it was a wise old Ogre who started the system. And strangely enough, the Humans seemed to think it was a wise old Human. And so on. There was plenty of fighting about it.

As time passed, records got better, and there was less to be uncertain about. Everybody knew that the Second Age came after the First Age; people had written it down. But all the civilisations disagreed as to when the next age should start. Some questioned why they needed a new age when the old one was working perfectly well.

Eventually, once everyone had done plenty more fighting, the whole of the Known World started using the same system. Of course their records of events were still very different. For example, the Humans had a record of the invasion of Fretsina, when thousands of Goblins overran the Elf city and brutally murdered everyone who lived there.

Elf records called it a massacre. Goblin records called it a successful peace mission. Ogre records said the Ogres heroically rescued the Goblins from their failed peace mission and turned it into a success. But at least they could all agree it happened in the 54th year of the Fourth Age.

With one fewer thing to fight about, the six civilisations of the Known World could turn their attention to all the other things to fight about. The most popular ones were land, gold, and of course which civilisation was the best. They hadn't settled that one yet.

As Warlord Sepping sat in the Royal Hall at Nuberim, he didn't really know what to fight about anymore. In truth, he didn't want to fight at all. But he knew a fight was coming. And he had no idea how his new queen was going to handle it.

It was only the four of them in the room: Sepping, Uoro, Queen Niella and Lady Afflech. The 17-year-old queen was now in charge, even though she had never overseen so much as a homework assignment before in her life.

She must have been overwhelmed, and even a bit frightened. It was only her second night as queen. She looked as if she was trying not to show it. Or at least, she looked as if she was trying to look as if she was trying not to show it.

She was still wearing her crown. She also wore a silver necklace and diamond earrings. It was a good idea to look the part, even if she didn't feel it. She still had the thick cotton or wool blanket wrapped around her shoulders, which apparently kept her safe.

"Firstly, your Majesty," began Warlord Sepping. "Congratulations on becoming our queen, and the leader of the whole of the Goblin Realm."

"Indeed," said Warlord Uoro, "And may I just add how well you have done so far."

"It's only my second night as queen," replied Niella.

"Yes but the first night went very well," replied Uoro.

"Absolutely," added Sepping.

The queen looked at them both in turn. "So why are we here?" she asked.

"Ah well," said Sepping, "we're here firstly to introduce ourselves as Warlords of the realm."

"I know who you are already," replied Queen Niella.

"Of course," added Uoro. "But we wanted to make it a proper introduction. Tell you about what we do, understand how you would like to work with us…"

"I'd like for you to get to the point," said Niella sharply.

The warlords were taken aback.

"Okay," said Sepping. "I'll be blunt. We're at war."

Niella frowned.

"Well, we're not technically at war right now," replied Sepping. "But there's a real risk of it happening, and we need to be prepared."

"As you know," began Uoro, "the last three Goblin kings were all killed. The Humans killed one, and we don't know who killed the other. But it might have been the Ogres."

"You mean Grieber? Didn't he die in his sleep?"

"After a dinner with the Ogres," said Uoro.

"Right," replied Niella.

"So now," said Sepping. "The question is what comes next. What are the Humans planning? And the Ogres?"

"We have had messengers saying that Lord Protector Higarth has come to Siglitz," said Uoro. "With about two thousand soldiers."

The queen raised her eyebrows. "What are they doing there?"

"Just visiting apparently," said Sepping. "We think they're on their way to somewhere else. Possibly here."

"Here?" asked Queen Niella. "You mean they're going to attack Nuberim?"

"No of course not," said Sepping. "More likely they'll call it a friendly visit. To give us more soldiers to fight the Humans."

"To make sure we're on their side?" asked Niella.

"Exactly," replied Sepping.

"Well maybe that's not a problem?" she asked. "If they are just here to see if they can help, and then return home?"

"Yes," added Sepping. "But two thousand is quite a lot of soldiers for a routine visit. And it's more worrying when you consider what's happening further south."

"What?"

"Word has it that the Humans are coming to Lancha," said Uoro.

"Why?" asked Niella. "Don't tell me, a…"

"Friendly visit," said Sepping. "To give us more soldiers to fight the Ogres."

"It's not a great sign," added Uoro. "Our realm is basically becoming a battleground for the Ogres and Humans."

The queen nodded. "So what are you planning on doing about it?"

The two warlords looked at each other.

"Actually, that's really for you to decide," said Sepping. "You're the queen."

Niella paused. Her face went even paler.

"Ah. Well any chance of a bit of guidance? What do you advise?"

"Well," began Uoro. "We could ask them both to leave. But I can't see that happening. I doubt there's anything we could do to convince them to back down, without somehow controlling their minds…"

Mind control was a dangerous thing. At least, it would be if it worked. Back in the 12th age, the Goblins had spent years testing various potions and hypnotic techniques on people, trying to control their thoughts. Some were told they weren't allowed to leave until their minds were fully controlled. That seemed to work: people confirmed they were definitely mind controlled. Then they left and refused to come back.

"We could attack them," continued the warlord. "Or just sit and wait, and hope for the best."

"Let's not forget," added Sepping. "That the Humans were behind the death of one of our kings, and the Ogres might be too. We can't trust either of them."

The queen looked at her two warlords in frustration.

"Umm any chance of some actual advice? All you've done is state the obvious. Maybe tell me what you would do if you were me?"

"I'd take the crown off for a start," said Uoro. "It must be very heavy."

"And?" snapped the queen. "What then!"

"I would send out messengers," added Sepping. "Ask both Higarth and Wyndham to leave. Really, really nicely."

"And if they don't?"

"We tell them if they don't leave, we'll consider it an act of war."

"Isn't that a little extreme?" asked the queen. "Then we'll be facing a war on both fronts! Can we afford to do that?"

"No. We don't have the resources. Or the soldiers. It would be a gamble. We'd be hoping they accept and leave."

"So what could we do?" asked the queen.

"We could tell them if they don't leave, we won't consider it an act of war. But we will be really, really disappointed in them," replied Uoro.

The queen put her hand over her face.

"Haven't they both killed one of our kings?" she asked. "Isn't that already an act of war?"

"Only if we think we can beat them," replied Sepping. "But the thing is, we don't actually have proof that either of them were involved in the killings. We caught two Humans, but they weren't necessarily sent on King Wyndham's orders."

"Right," said Queen Niella. "So we can't fight them. And the messages would likely do nothing."

"Isn't there another option?" came a voice. The three of

them looked round. It came from Lady Afflech. They had forgotten she was even there. She was apparently less noticeable now that she no longer wore a crown.

"If we can't fight both the Ogres and the Humans," she continued. "Why don't we join forces with one of them, to fight the other?"

The two warlords glanced at her, and then at each other.

"That could work," said Warlord Uoro. "But we don't completely trust either of them. How could we pick a side?"

There was a silence, as they all took a moment to think.

"We could see who has the most soldiers?" suggested Uoro.

"How about we consult the Gods?" added Sepping.

"Or," said Lady Afflech. "We side with the civilisation we trust the most. Or distrust the least. Humans killed one of our kings. Ogres might have killed another. So on balance, we should side with the Ogres."

"That makes sense, I suppose," said Warlord Uoro.

"Yes. And if I had to bet, I'd say the Ogres will have brought more soldiers," said Queen Niella.

"So we're in agreement?" added Sepping. "We send a messenger to the Ogres and invite them to come to Nuberim. When the Humans come too, we'll be ready for them should a battle break out."

"We should fortify the city as well," added Lady Afflech.

There were plenty of entrances into Nuberim, which was great for when you wanted people to come and visit. Not so great when you didn't.

"Agreed," said Sepping. "Oh sorry," he added. "Queen Niella, do you agree."

"Yes," said Queen Niella, rolling her eyes. "But a war with the Humans should be our last resort. Do not forget that."

The warlords and Lady Afflech looked at each other. For a seventeen-year-old in her second night on the job, the queen seemed to be doing rather well.

Chapter 14

Petra woke up. She couldn't see a thing. Was she blindfolded? Probably. She could feel something around her face. It was very uncomfortable. It also smelt disgusting – like burnt cow dung, or the clothes of a pipe smoker.

Her hands were tied behind her back. They were tight and rather uncomfortable. The rope was cutting her wrists.

She could also feel the wind against her cheeks. She was moving. If she had to guess, she was probably on a horse. Being forcibly transported somewhere. Probably not somewhere good.

"It's going to get light soon, shall we find somewhere to rest?" said a voice from nearby. It was deep and cracked. Petra shuddered just hearing it.

"Oh great idea," said another voice. "We just find some Goblin inn nearby and ask to spend the day there. And also ask them to ignore the tied-up Pixie we're carrying with us. Moron."

"I didn't mean a public place," replied the first voice. "We could find a cave or something. Or just set up camp."

"We're not stopping to rest," bellowed a voice from just behind Petra.

She realised she must be riding this horse with someone else. Someone who was keeping her tied up. That was when she noticed something tugging at the collar of her top. One of these people was holding onto her.

"Who made you the leader, Gagan?" said the first voice.

"Well, I'm the one who caught her, aren't I?" replied the voice behind her. "I'm carrying our reward right here.

And I'm taking all the risks. If she suddenly breaks free and conjures up some flames, I'm the one who gets burned to death."

"She's tied up, you idiot," replied one of the voices. "And besides, we don't even know she's the one the Lord Protector is looking for. Maybe she's just a random harmless Pixie who couldn't magic up some bread from a pile of flour!"

"She's the one, trust me," said the voice behind her. "But we need to keep going. If we ride quickly we could be in Siglitz in a couple of nights. And there are Humans everywhere. We can't risk stopping."

"Since when were you afraid of Humans?" said another voice.

"I'm not, you fool," said the one behind her. "But there's only four of us. If a hundred Humans attacked, we would be in trouble."

"Speak for yourself," said the voice. "I could kill a thousand Humans with my bare hands if I needed to."

"Well maybe you should go and do that then, Portac," replied the person behind her. "The Lord Protector would probably reward you for that too."

"Whatever," replied the voice, presumably of Portac.

Petra tried to remain calm. She was taking in everything she had just heard. They were Ogres. That much was obvious. The way they talked about Humans was enough of a giveaway, but she also knew they called their leader 'the lord protector'.

And they were going to Siglitz. Wasn't that a Goblin city? She wondered why they were taking her there. It was probably best not to think about it.

Instead, she thought about her options. Her mouth wasn't tied – she could talk to these Ogres. Ask them to let her go? Maybe threaten that there was an army of Humans nearby, and they were sure to be killed if they didn't release her? She couldn't see that working. It seemed like that would only make them laugh, and ride faster.

She tugged gently at the rope around her wrists. It was

no good. She needed her hands – there was no way of creating magic without them. She had tried of course, many times. How cool would it have been if she could create flames from her mouth, like a dragon? Or from her nose, like a confused dragon who was still learning how to do it.

But she couldn't. Without her hands she was useless. She had no weapon against these people.

She felt a couple of drops of water on her head. And then a few more. It was starting to rain. Within a few minutes it was pouring down. She thought she heard some thunder too.

"Dammit," said the voice behind her. "This is too much. I can barely see in front of me right now. And the muddy ground is not good for the horses."

"Surely you're not suggesting that we stop, Gagan?" came a sarcastic voice from nearby.

Petra heard a loud sigh. "Fine!" he said. "If we find a safe place with no-one around, we can take shelter. Just until the rain dies down."

"Great," replied another voice. "How about over there? You see the pile of boulders to the right?"

"Where?" said another voice.

"Follow me you idiot."

Petra could feel the horse slow down. She could hear the loud splatter of the hooves against the mud. She was also soaked through, and imagined the Ogres were too.

She could hear noises all around as the horse came to a stop. Then, alarmingly, she could feel herself getting picked up and thrown off the animal. She felt a thud as she landed into the arms of another Ogre. He placed her firmly on the ground, on her knees, and then began to tie up her ankles.

Was that really necessary? It wasn't like she was going to try running away while blindfolded, with her hands tied behind her back. She wouldn't make it ten yards.

"Wow, what are the chances of finding this place?" said one of the voices. She couldn't tell them apart – they all sounded so similar.

83

"There are lots of hills round here," said another voice. "I bet there are a number of these caves too."

"I think you mean, well done Potrac for finding it," said a third voice.

"Fine, whatever," came a response. "I'm completely drenched, can we get a fire going?"

"We shouldn't draw attention to ourselves."

"Who is going to find us here," said another voice. "It's raining so hard you can barely see out of the cave. Nobody can see us."

"Okay, we can make a fire. But first we need to check every inch of this cave. You never know where a Goblin may be hiding."

"Don't tell me you're afraid of Goblins now too?"

"Be quiet!"

Petra stayed knelt down in a very uncomfortable position. The ground was hard, and it was causing her pain in both knees. But she didn't move. She couldn't move, really.

Before long, she could hear the sound of cracking wood, and felt a little heat nearby. They must have managed to get a fire going. She thought it would be a struggle given all the rain. Maybe there was some dry stuff to burn in this cave.

"How about cooking some food?" said one of the voices.

"As long as you're quick," said another.

"What do we even have? Any meat?"

"No. Not unless you want to go catch something. Got some mushrooms though."

"That'll do."

Petra was famished. But she thought better of asking for some food herself.

"Wait, what?"

Petra suddenly heard noises all around her. She had no idea what was happening.

"Who are you?" said a voice. It was softer and higher than the others she had heard. This one was new.

There was a silence. Then from what Petra could tell,

one of the Ogres started laughing. The others joined in.

"What are those, slingshots? What are you going to do with them?"

"Don't move!" came the higher voice. "Tell us who you are. Why have you come here?"

"Put those things away!" said one of the Ogres. "You may have noticed that we're all carrying actual weapons."

"I said not to move!"

"Enough of this!" came a lower voice.

There was a flurry of noise. Shouting. Swearing. Shuffling. Knocking. Petra just stayed kneeling down, unable to do anything.

And then silence, once again. Petra froze, trying not to breathe too loudly.

"What's your name?" came another high voice. "You, the little one kneeling down. What's your name?"

"Pet... Petrunia," said Petra. She had realised a bit late that she shouldn't have said her real name. At least she didn't quite do that.

"Petrunia?" replied the voice. "Are you a Pixie? Why would a bunch of Ogres have taken you prisoner?"

"I...I don't know," said Petra. Probably not the cleverest thing to say.

"Really? Well I think I do," replied the voice. "It wouldn't have anything to do with the rumours coming from the Human lands, would it?"

Petra stayed silent.

"If the rumours were true, the Ogres would no doubt be looking for a magic Pixie. They would try to capture her, or kill her. And of course, tie her hands so she couldn't use her powers."

A second later, she felt her blindfold being lifted.

It took her a few moments to take everything in. A light green face was staring at her. Long, white hair and pale eyes. She was a Goblin. Petra could tell that immediately.

She looked around and saw more Goblins standing there. They were all quite short and dressed in plain white robes. They seemed young, probably about her age. The wooden slingshots in their hands made them look even younger. How had they managed to defeat a group of fully grown Ogres?

"It is you, isn't it?" said the Goblin in front of her. "Don't worry, you're safe here. You don't harm us, and we won't harm you."

Petra didn't say a word.

"Okay then, Petrunia," continued the Goblin. "You don't have to tell us anything, but we'll tell you who we are. I am Larah, and this is Totalia, Soloma and Korjee. We are the last surviving members of the Great Enchanters."

Petra stared at her.

"That's right, we're the real Great Enchanters. The legends are true. You've found us!"

"Wow, really?" said Petra. "The Great Enchanters... that's amazing."

"You've never heard of us, have you?" said Larah.

"No," replied Petra.

"Well that's disappointing," said Larah. "What do they teach Pixies in schools? Anyway, it doesn't matter. Let's take those ropes off your hands and feet. Come with us, and we'll tell you all about it."

Chapter 15

King Wyndham sighed. Another group of soldiers had come back. He was glad they hadn't been killed obviously. But there was no sign of Petra.

He had thought about returning home, but he had decided against it. What good would it have done? Whoever had taken her, they were surely heading back to the Ogre Realm. Or even the Goblin Realm.

There was no chance of finding her if they just wandered around nowhere. They had to keep going to Lancha. It made sense. He had convinced himself of that.

Samorus had been in such a state. He was clearly devastated by the whole thing. The King had sent his travelling jester, Frittles, to try and cheer him up; even that didn't seem to help. And Frittles was one of the funniest jesters in the realm. His hat had bells on.

The old Pixie had stuck with the Humans. He couldn't leave until they found Petra. And he still believed they would.

At least they had finally made it to Lancha. The last couple of days hadn't been fun. It wasn't just Samorus – the mood around the whole party had been sombre. More scouts had gone out and searched the lands, but they had all come back empty handed. Alive, thankfully, but empty handed.

Wyndham wasn't just worried about Petra's wellbeing. He was worried about his own soldiers. Without the magic Pixie, they were weak. The troops he had sent for still hadn't arrived yet; hopefully they would make it here in a day or two.

The reception at Lancha hadn't been what the King had hoped. The Governor of the city had greeted them and seemed friendly enough. But there was a certain coldness to the way he talked. He hadn't seemed overly pleased to see them.

The city itself was almost entirely underground. The Goblins mainly used the surface for growing crops and grazing animals. That tended to be useful during wars, as people from the west of the Known World would often struggle to find the city.

In the 8th Age, the Royal General Bardier of the Human Army once declared a glorious victory over the Goblins, when he laid siege to the whole city of Lancha. For over three months, he guarded every possible entrance, and ensured that no food could make it inside.

He planted a great flag in the cornfields above and prepared to enter the city and accept the Goblins' surrender. It was only then that they realised the caves they were guarding didn't have any underground entrances. And Lancha was in fact 30 miles away.

The cornfields were just ordinary fields, with nobody living there. But at least they had conquered them. It was still a victory of sorts. And it was thanks to this victory that Royal General Bardier gloriously became Captain Bardier, and then even more impressively became Soldier Bardier soon after that. Very few generals had ever managed that many demotions in such a short space of time.

The Governor had asked King Wyndham why they had come. Wyndham said, of course, to help and support the Goblins. The Governor had asked whether the two Humans in prison were also there to help and support the Goblins. Wyndham admitted they probably weren't. Shooting their king in the face wasn't really very supportive.

Of course, King Wyndham had tried to distance himself from it. He had assured the Governor he had no knowledge of the incident at the time. He didn't even know who these two Humans were. It was the truth.

The Governor had said he believed him. But he probably didn't. There were clues which Wyndham picked up on. To start with, there was the accommodation they had put them in. The King and his Humans were honoured guests in the city. But they hadn't put them up in a castle or anything fancy; they were told they had been given one of the extra special guest buildings instead. So special that it didn't have proper bedding or armchairs. And the rooms were especially small.

Then there was the food. The Governor had invited them to a fabulous feast to celebrate their arrival. Goblin food was considered quite a delicacy in the Human realm; most people hadn't even tried it, but knew that it came from far away which presumably made it impressive.

But the food they had been given was very plain – just slow-cooked meats, which hadn't actually been cooked very slowly. There was no music, and very little wine. It was all over well before morning. Not a sign of a great party in the Goblin realm.

As dawn was finally breaking, Wyndham decided to go for a walk. The Goblins would all now be sleeping. But Wyndham wasn't sleepy. He needed to think.

The building he was staying in was very near the surface. He knew the way up. It was a short passage through a tunnel, and then a couple of flights of stairs. It was a crisp, cold dawn, but the King didn't mind it; he liked the feel of the cool wind against his cheeks.

There wasn't much to see around him. Just fields, and a few hills in the background. He wandered aimlessly around, trying to figure out his next move. They had to wait in Lancha until his reinforcements arrived. And then head to Nuberim. He had no idea what to expect when they arrived there. But he had to try.

He noticed a hooded figure about fifty yards away. The figure seemed to be on his own and staying completely still. Was it a monk? Maybe just a scarecrow. Did Goblins even have scarecrows?

Curiosity got the better of Wyndham. He walked over to the hooded figure. It was a person. He was kneeling down. Maybe praying? He seemed to be doing so in silence.

Wyndham coughed accidentally as he approached. The figure turned round.

"Wilfred?" said the King, taken aback.

The Lord of Science looked back. It was him all right. Many Humans had hairy brows and white beards. But the King knew his lords like they were his children. Though he often thought his children would probably do a better job.

"What are you doing here?" asked Wyndham.

Wilfred didn't reply.

"Can't sleep either?" continued the King. "I understand. It's not easy getting used to these underground chambers."

In the Human Realm, people tended to live in houses. A few wealthy Humans had recently taken to building underground homes, the way the Goblins did. It made them seem more cultured. They would invite people over and talk about their experiences in the Eastern lands, saying things like 'Oh you've never stayed in an underground Goblin chamber? It's a much more spiritual way of living'.

King Wyndham didn't understand this trend. He preferred to sleep above ground, the old-fashioned way.

Wilfred stared back at him. Wyndham got a proper look at his face. It looked red and forlorn.

"Wilfred...have you been crying?"

The Lord of Science nodded slowly. "Sire, I have something I need to confess."

The King frowned. "What is it?"

"Well," began Wilfred. "I told you I wanted to come on this trip to discuss recent developments in transport mechanisms. But the thing is…"

"There are no recent developments in transport mechanisms?"

"No, it's not that," said Wilfred. "Although you're right about that too. There haven't been any breakthroughs at all since the five-wheel carriage. And that was completely unnecessary – the extra wheel just got in the way."

Wyndham frowned. "So what is it then? Why did you come here?"

The Lord of Science sighed. "I know those two Humans. Ridley and Fulton. I'm the one who... sent them on their mission."

The King laughed. Then he saw Wilfred's face again and realised he wasn't joking.

"Why?" he said in shock. "Why in the Known World would you do a thing like that?"

"Well, it seemed like a good idea at the time." Wilfred couldn't think of anything better to say. "I wanted to bring about peace."

"By killing someone?" retorted the King.

"Yes, it umm... seemed like a good idea at the time."

Wyndham took a breath. He was beginning to see why there hadn't been any breakthroughs in transport mechanisms. Or any kind of mechanisms. When his Lord of Science was this stupid, it was surprising they weren't uninventing things they already had.

"So who are they? The two men you sent to kill him. Why did they agree to do it?"

"Well, partly because I paid them," said Wilfred. "But they believed in what they were doing too. They must have also thought it..."

"Seemed like a good idea at the time?" said King Wyndham.

Wilfred nodded. "I think I need some time off, sire," he said. "A break from everything. For my own mental health."

"Mental health?" snapped Wyndham. "What about the mental health of the Goblins whose king you had killed? Not to mention the King's physical health."

"Yes okay," said Wilfred. "I know it's bad. I guess I'll have plenty of time to take a break from everything while in prison."

Wyndham shook his head. "You killed a king, Wilfred," he said. "You know the rules of our realm. That's treason. They'll execute you!"

"You mean... you'll execute me?" replied Wilfred. "You're the king..."

"Yes, I'll execute you," replied Wyndham. "I'll have to Wilfred, it's not like I have a choice."

"You're the king…" said Wilfred again.

"Yes but it's not just up to me. I can't make an exception for lords of the realm. There would be outcry. Rioting!"

"What if we don't tell anyone?" suggested the Lord of Science, visibly trembling.

"Wilfred…"

"I can make it right," he said desperately. "I can make a formal apology. What if I save Ridley and Fulton? Pay a tribute to the Goblin realm? What if…"

They heard a rustling sound in the distance. Wilfred looked round and saw a beautiful white creature, proudly walking across the plains.

"What if I capture that unicorn?" he said.

King Wyndham looked at him, aghast.

"I could do it. It's really a unicorn!"

"Oh yes, I forgot about that rule," said Wyndham. "You're not allowed to kill a king, unless you also capture a unicorn afterwards."

"I know… but imagine if I did it!" replied Wilfred. He seemed almost hysterical. "Just one. That's all it would take. We could study it, learn its ways. Maybe one day we could ride them like horses. We would all be able to fly!"

Wyndham looked round at the creature. Its long wings sprung out at its sides. The silver horn was unmistakable. It was a real unicorn.

"What's it *doing* here?" asked Wyndham. He had never seen one so close.

"I don't know. But I can catch it," said Wilfred. "I could be the man who caught a unicorn!"

Wilfred suddenly rose to his feet. Then he crept slowly towards the beautiful beast. It was close. Maybe twenty yards away. Wyndham watched, baffled but also slightly intrigued.

The unicorn was chewing on grass with its head down. It had no idea a ridiculous old man was edging towards it.

Wilfred put his arms out. It looked like he was sleepwalking. He was still about ten yards away.

The creature looked up. It must have heard a noise. Wilfred froze. They stood there staring at each other. The unicorn let out a loud grunt, and instantly darted away.

As it ran, it flapped its wings and took off in a matter of moments. It was gone. The two Humans stared into the distance, but it was now so small they could barely see it.

"That went well," said King Wyndham sarcastically. The Lord of Science put his head down.

"At least we know unicorns can be spooked by old men creeping up on them," he continued. "That's a real breakthrough."

Wilfred looked at him. His face was red. His eyes were watering once more. He turned away and put his black hood over his head once more. And then he walked, without looking back.

"Wilfred," called out Wyndham. "Where are you going?"

He didn't turn round. He just kept on walking.

"Where are you going?" he shouted, louder.

As the figure started to fade into the distance, the King was still trying to comprehend what had happened. There was no doubting anymore – Humans were responsible for killing a Goblin king. At least one.

He had known the Lord of Science for over thirty years. The man had always seemed a little eccentric. Maybe even odd. But how could he have done something like this? So stupid. So… strange?

Wyndham could no longer see the figure, which had disappeared over the horizon. He wondered where Wilfred could possibly be going. And whether he would ever come back.

Deep down, he already knew the answer.

Chapter 16

Petra looked around as she walked. There wasn't much to look at. She could barely see. These people were taking her underground, deeper and deeper. The occasional torch lit up one of the walls, but that was about it. She was tempted to use her magic powers and create a flame, just so she could see a bit better.

"Here we are," said Larah.

They approached a large room. It looked quite fancy and well kept. The floor seemed to be made of marble, covered with a large rug in the middle. There were stone columns along the walls. And plenty of torches. Petra could actually see!

"What is this place?" she asked.

Larah smiled. "This," she began, "is the ancient headquarters of the Great Enchanters."

She paused, as if she was expecting some kind of reaction.

"Oh…wow," said Petra. "This is the headquarters?"

"That's right," said Larah, smiling. "This, quite literally, is where the magic happens. Come, take a seat, and we'll tell you our story."

"But there are no chairs?" said Petra.

"Oh really?" replied Larah.

She looked round again. A wooden table and chairs were in the middle of the room. How had she missed that before? Had they somehow made them appear from nowhere?

"Take a seat," said Larah, still smiling.

Petra walked over to the table and sat down. Her new Goblin friends all did the same.

"Drink?" offered Larah.

"Thanks," smiled Petra, as she was handed a glass of something clear.

Petra gulped it down. It tasted like water; she probably should have sipped it first, but she was so thirsty. She started to wonder why she trusted these Goblins so much. For all she knew they were going to keep her prisoner here.

"You're the Pixie, aren't you? You're THE Pixie," said Larah.

"I...I don't know," replied Petra. "I'm just a normal Pixie. Just like everyone else."

"Right," said Larah, laughing. "We know who you are, even if you don't."

Petra smiled. She couldn't help it.

"Have you really never heard of the Great Enchanters?" said one of the other Goblins. Petra thought it was Soloma, but she wasn't sure; they all looked pretty similar, quite young and dressed in the same white robes.

"Sorry I haven't," replied Petra. "But I'd love to learn about it!"

"Very well," said Larah. She cleared her throat. "In the beginning was the First Age. Before that, there was nothing. And before that, there were the Great Enchanters."

"Really?" asked Petra, confused.

"No, not really," replied Larah. "But we do go back a long way. Nobody really knows how far. Ancient secrets of sorcery and enchantment have been passed down the generations. Always hidden away from the rest of society. To most people, we're merely a legend. Or a myth. But we're real."

"What the Known World will never know," said one of the other Goblins. "But we will ever protect," said the whole group together.

"Our words. The words of the Great Enchanters," said Larah, catching Petra's eye.

The young Pixie looked around again. She had no idea what was going on, whether these people were wise wizards or just weirdos. But she was enjoying it.

"So what are these ancient secrets you protect?" she asked.

"Well we can't just tell you that," said Larah. "Only sorcerers may know about the secrets of our sorcery. Only a true wizard, can know about wizardry."

She looked at Petra. They all did.

"Only a true wizard," said Larah again.

Petra sighed. She knew exactly what they wanted her to do. They had hardly been subtle about it.

She paused for a minute to think. She still didn't know whether to trust them. But they were friendly. The had treated her well and had saved her from the Ogres. That had to count for something. She decided to go with her gut.

First, she looked up at the ceiling to check it was safe. Then she held her hand up and sent out a flame. It crashed against the stone ceiling, causing a minor shake. And lots of 'oooh' and 'ahhh' noises from the Goblins around her.

"So it's true!" remarked one of the Goblins excitedly.

"I knew it!" shouted Larah. "You're the Magic Pixie. You're THE Magic Pixie!"

"Yes, I suppose I am," said Petra.

"How do you do it?!" asked Larah. "Can you teach us?"

Petra shook her head.

"Sorry, I really can't," she said. "It just something I found out I could do one day. I just channel all my energy, all my anger, into my hands. I think about nothing else. And I let go."

"We could do that," said one of the Goblins.

"You could try," Petra sighed. "But many other people have, and no one has managed it. I've lost count of the number of times I've tried to teach people. They've stood there with their hands outstretched and their eyes screwed up. And nothing's happened. One person spent nearly a whole day doing it without stopping. He figured out how to get pins and needles in his feet, but that was about all."

Larah nodded.

"I still think we should try," said another Goblin.

"There's plenty of time for that," replied Larah. "But

first, you asked about our secrets. Secrets only wizards are allowed to know."

She turned to one of her friends. "Totalia, you can uncover the wall now."

One of the Goblins, apparently called Totalia, walked over to the back wall. Petra hadn't noticed the dark red curtains running across it.

The Goblin stretched both her arms out wide. Then she grabbed a rope on her right and pulled. The curtains opened. Magic.

They revealed a set of wooden shelves, running all the way across the wall. Some had cupboard doors, others were just open. There were random ornaments dotted about. Stones and statues, of different shapes and sizes. Petra didn't recognise any of them.

"Come," said Larah. They made their way to the shelves.

Petra looked at the objects again. Moving closer didn't help – they still just looked like a bunch of random shapes.

"What are they?" she whispered to Larah.

"Well, to your average person they're just a load of rocks. But to a wizard, they're a load of rocks that can do amazing things!"

She picked up one of stones next to her. It was grey and pear shaped, slightly bigger than her hand.

"This," she said, "is a Nutchen."

"What does it do?" asked Petra.

"Just watch," said Larah, smiling.

A silence followed. Petra stared as Larah turned the stone to the right and closed her eyes. She waited.

Suddenly a light layer of smoke appeared. The young Goblin seemed to disappear and then reappear about a yard to her right. What just happened? Petra stood there, open mouthed.

"Did you just…"

"Teleport? That's right," said Larah. "That's what a Nutchen does."

"But…" stammered Petra. "That's…that's incredible. How do you do it?"

"Only a real wizard can do it," said Larah.

"So…" said Petra, not sure what to say. "So what do you use it for? How far can you teleport?"

"Well actually, what you just saw…that is how far we can teleport," said Larah. "About a yard."

"One point two yards," added Soloma.

"Ah," said Petra.

A silence followed.

"So about as far as you could jump?" asked Petra.

Larah nodded. "We're working on it though. It was only half a yard a few hundred years ago."

"Slightly less than half," added Soloma, nodding.

"Try this," said Larah.

She tossed a small pebble to Petra. She flinched but caught it square in her hand.

"Another Nutchen?" she asked.

Larah laughed. "Nope. This is a Levela," she said.

"Wow!" said one of the other Goblins.

They seemed to start whispering to each other.

"Look, it's true!" said another.

Petra looked around. "What is it? What does it do?"

Larah looked at her. "It's doing it right now. Look down."

The young Pixie stared at the ground. It looked the same. Her feet looked the same. What were they talking about?

"How does it feel to be levitating?" asked the last Goblin. Petra couldn't remember her name.

"Lev…levitating?" asked Petra, puzzled.

She looked down again. It still looked the same. It felt the same, didn't it? Maybe not. The soles of her feet were slightly colder. They weren't touching anything!

"You really are a magic Pixie!" exclaimed Larah. "I don't know anyone else who could do it on the first try."

"I'm barely above the ground?" she said.

"You're still levitating!" replied Larah.

"Let me guess, this is about as high as it gets?" asked Petra.

The Enchanters all nodded. "Higher than it used to be," said Soloma. "And it still has its uses."

"Like what?"

"Well, if you have muddy feet. You hold one of those and you don't get any dirt on the floor."

"Right," said Petra.

"Or, for walking on water," said Larah. "Well, over water. It really works. You can hover over any surface."

"That's actually pretty cool," said Petra. These magical devices weren't exactly perfect, but she was beginning to see that they could still be useful.

"You think that's cool, how about this?" added Soloma. She picked up another rock, light blue this time. "It actually makes the air around you colder."

"How much colder?" asked Petra.

"Noticeably!" replied Soloma. "Well, sometimes noticeably. If you concentrate."

Petra smiled. She didn't notice it getting any colder.

"How about this one?" said Larah. She picked up a black rock from one of the lower shelves. "It's a breaker. It breaks stuff!"

"What kind of stuff?" asked Petra.

"Anything," said Larah. "Provided it's less than a quarter of an inch thick."

"Ah," said the Pixie. "You mean thin enough to break with your hands?"

"Not necessarily," said Larah. "What if it's something made of metal? Like chains. Or handcuffs."

Petra paused. "It can break handcuffs?"

It suddenly made her think about Fulton. That poor Human who had gone to the Goblin Realm who was now in a Goblin prison, probably in handcuffs right now.

She could save him. It didn't seem like a pipe dream anymore. These Goblins could help her.

She waited for an opportunity – once they had finished showing her a few more of these amazing devices. There was the stone that gave people 5% more strength sometimes. There was the stick that made you feel really hungry all of a sudden. And there was a shell that they were sure did something, but they couldn't remember what.

"Listen," said Petra at last, turning her face as she spoke to look each of the Goblins in the eye. "I need your help with something."

She paused for a second. "And if you help me, I'll do something for you in return. I'll try and teach you how to create flames".

Larah's eyes lit up. Everyone's did.

"What's the favour?" asked Soloma.

"I need you to help me break someone out of prison."

Chapter 17

In the history of the Known World, Humans had always found it hard to trust Goblins, who would generally side with the Ogres whatever the situation. In the past, people sometimes thought Ogres and Goblins were the same, but that was wrong and presumably offensive. The Goblins were smaller, a lighter shade of green, and a bit less aggressive than their Ogre counterparts.

The Elves used to say that if you ever encountered an Ogre you should run a mile. But for a Goblin, 500 yards was more than sufficient.

Given this, the 14th Age was quite a remarkable time. Goblins these days were considered friendly and civilised people. They wouldn't start a fight or kill a Human without good reason.

Unfortunately for Ridley and Fulton, they had given the Goblins a rather good reason to kill them. As they sat in their cell, they were trying not to think about whatever was coming next. Apparently, they were going to suffer a fate worse than death. Followed by actual death. It was hard not to think about it.

"It's time!"

A Goblin guard came bursting through the corridor, looking very excited and rather proud of himself. There were two guards sitting in front of the cell. They both shot up.

"It's time?" said one of them.

"Yes, it's time," repeated the first Goblin.

"It's really time?" said the third guard.

The first guard nodded again. Ridley turned towards his cell mate.

"Do you reckon it's time?" he said.

Fulton stared out of the cell.

"Excuse me," he said loudly. "Time for what?"

The guards stopped and turned. They looked at Fulton blankly. Then started laughing.

"You'll find out soon enough," said one of them, still sniggering.

Ridley didn't feel reassured. He had an idea what it was time for.

"Please just tell us. Is it time for our trial?" he asked, optimistically.

"Trial? Haha good one," replied a Goblin guard.

"Is that a 'no'?" said Ridley, dejectedly. "Are we even getting a trial?"

"Are you going to kill us?" asked Fulton slowly.

"Of course," smiled one of the guards. "But not right now."

He walked over, plucked a key from his pocket and unlocked the cell door.

"Right now, we're going to kill your souls."

He pulled both the prisoners out of the cell, and one of the other guards slipped a set of handcuffs around them. The two Humans didn't resist. They were too weak and tired. And they were hardly going to overpower three armed Goblins.

They were led up some steps. And then a few more steps. There were so many that Ridley lost count, and started trying to imagine a time when they weren't climbing steps.

Eventually they found themselves in a large tunnel. It was more than a tunnel really; it must have been fifty feet high. And its width was staggering. How long must it have taken to dig all this?

And there were people everywhere. Goblins, mostly. But a few Ogres. Maybe even one or two Humans, but it was hard to tell. There were torches dotted across the walls, some very high up. But it was still quite dark.

The Goblin guards stopped. So did Ridley and Fulton. A few passers-by also stopped and stared at them.

"Where's Bastian?" asked one of the guards.

"He said he'd meet us in Lybley Street," said another.

"Seriously?" asked the third guard. "There are

thousands of people here. How are we supposed to find him? What kind of idiot came up with this idea... oh wait, there he is."

He pointed to a group of Goblins. They were all dressed in the same way. They wore chain mail with metal helmets and swords at their sides. *More guards, presumably*, thought Ridley as the group walked over to them.

As they got closer, Ridley noticed they were dragging two large objects. They were big and wooden, almost like two small walls. Each one took two Goblins to pull them.

"What are those things?" asked Ridley to the nearest guard. He didn't respond. "What are you... going to do to us?" he continued. He could feel his heart beating quickly.

"I told you, we are going to kill your soul," snapped the guard.

He took Ridley's arm and unlocked the handcuffs. Ridley felt a relief as his wrists were able to breathe. But it didn't last long.

"Now, put your head through there."

Ridley flinched. The wooden objects were in front of them now. Both had a large hole in the middle, and smaller holes on either side. He looked around him, and then walked over to the first wooden object. He slowly stuck his head through the large hole. It only just fit.

"Now," bellowed the nearest guard. "Put your hands through the smaller holes."

Ridley did as he was told. He could feel himself shaking. His heart was still beating fast. What was this thing? He waited for a few moments. The guard seemed to be fastening his head and hands in place somehow.

He could barely move his neck, so he couldn't tell what was happening around him. But he heard the steps and rustling to his right. Presumably it was Fulton, going through the exact same thing in the device next to him.

Another pause. Ridley tried to tilt his head slightly to the right. He could just about see his companion.

"What do you think is happening?" whispered Fulton,

next to him. "Are they going to chop our heads off?"

"I don't know," replied Ridley. "But I have a feeling it's going to be something much worse."

"Excuse me!" bellowed a loud voice from behind him. "Gather round. Everybody! Everybody, gather round!"

People seemed to be listening. More and more were stopping and staring at them. A crowd was forming. Ridley could tell that, even with his limited view.

"I present to you," continued the Goblin loudly. "The two Humans! The Humans who killed Prince Nutrec."

There was a murmur among the crowd. Almost like a hissing sound.

"Shame on you!" shouted a voice among the hissing.

"Disgrace! Kill them both!" cried another.

"I also disagree with what they did," said a third.

"I know, I know, you all want to see these horrible Humans punished," continued the Goblin guard. "They will be brought to justice. Don't you worry. But now is not the time for death. Now is the time for suffering!"

The murmuring continued, and Ridley could hear a few cheers.

"And that's why they're both here in the stocks tonight," bellowed the guard. "For Civic Response!"

Now there were loud cheers and clapping. Some whoops. And even a few whistles.

"What's Civic Response?" whispered Fulton.

"How should I know?" snapped Ridley.

"The rules are, as always," continued the guard in a loud voice. "You may only throw mud from the designated buckets. One at a time. And stand behind the white line."

Ridley hadn't noticed that the crowd of people were all a few feet away. Now they started to cluster together, forming one long queue.

One of the Goblin guards came into view, carrying a large bucket on a stand. Another excited looking Goblin stood at the front of the queue. She was short with long silver hair. She must have been quite young. Her eyes were bright, her teeth even brighter.

She reached into the bucket and pulled out a handful of wet mud. She flung it straight at Ridley. It caught him square on his forehead. He closed his eyes and felt a drip start to run down his face.

"Try to smile," said a voice to Ridley's left. "Show a bit of emotion. Entertain the crowd, for the Gods' sake."

It was another one of the guards. Ridley could recognise the growling voice by now, even if he couldn't see him.

Splat. Another handful of mud hit the wooden board, this time missing his face by a few inches.

"How long do we have to do this?" asked Ridley.

"Just for the rest of the night," said the guard. "And then again tomorrow, and the next night."

Ridley took a deep breath. "Why?" he stammered.

"I told you, to kill your soul," replied the guard.

"By getting people to throw mud at us?"

"Exactly," said the guard. "The shame. The humiliation. Can you imagine anything more soul destroying than this?"

He has a point, thought Ridley as he heard another splat. This time the mud got him right on the chin.

Chapter 18

The Lord Protector stood still. He slowly raised his axe past his right ear.

Focus on the target, he told himself.

It was about twenty yards away, but it felt closer. Higarth was calm and confident. Hitting a still target with an axe. Easy. But he had to set an example to his troops; they couldn't watch their lord protector miss a simple throw. It would be a sign of weakness.

"Is everything okay, my Lord Protector?" It was Redmer, one of his assistants.

"Yes, fine," replied Higarth.

"It's just you seem to be taking your time," continued Redmer.

"I'm focussing!" hissed the Lord Protector.

A few of his soldiers had stopped practising. They had turned to watch their leader. Higarth bent his elbow and pulled the axe back further. He was poised and ready. Deep breath. And...

"Good luck, my Lord Protector!" said Redmer, just as Higarth was releasing the weapon.

He jumped, and the axe went flying off to his right. It hit a target, but not the one in front of him. It was several targets away. A few more of his soldiers turned to look at him.

"Back to work!" yelled Higarth. He turned to his assistant.

"Sorry, my Lord Protector," said Redmer dejectedly. "But well done on hitting the target. I mean *a* target..."

"Indeed, a fine throw," added General Chandimer.

A few of the nearby soldiers also started clapping, rather faintly, trying to seem sincere and not ironic.

Chandimer had accompanied Higarth down to the firing range – a large, open aired facility near the centre of Siglitz.

Higarth looked around. The soldiers had gone back to

work, and were busily throwing axes and spears at their targets. A few seemed to peer at him, but quickly turned away again to avoid eye contact.

Higarth rolled his eyes. *At least none of the Goblins are here to see this*, he thought to himself. It was nice of the Governor to let his Ogres use their facilities, especially without any supervision. It was a sign that she trusted them.

"How about another throw, my Lord Protector?" suggested Redmer, trying to dig himself out of the doghouse.

Higarth shook his head. No more axe throwing. The axe was an Ogre's best friend – Ogres were as young as five when they were given their first axe. They would sit there playing, chopping little bits of wood and throwing them. They weren't allowed to run with them obviously, that was too dangerous. But they did pretty much everything else.

It was an Ogre who invented the first throwing axe. The great Danduk back in the Fifth Age. Legend had it that while building a fence, he saw a squirrel in a nearby tree. Without thinking, he flung his tool in the direction of the ferocious creature. It missed, but only just. And the weapon stuck straight into the tree; he could hardly get it out again.

It made Danduk realise how much power he could generate from throwing the thing. It could be a weapon, stronger than any spear or arrow.

It soon caught on, and people across the Ogre realm started throwing the things. The army started using them, surprising their enemies who weren't prepared to deal with the fast and powerful weapons. They became very accurate. One day Danduk hoped to finally hit a squirrel. And those things were quick.

Higarth was as skilled with an axe as any in the Ogre realm. He could throw one a hundred yards if he needed to. On a good day. If a tailwind was behind him. But right now, there was no point; he wasn't going to risk humiliating himself any further in front of his troops.

He saw a couple of young Ogres approaching. Both were in black chainmail and carried daggers at their waists. They must have been in the army but probably very junior. Higarth had never met them before.

"Lord Protector," called one of them as they approached. "I am Cadet Gadri, and this is Cadet Buku. We have some news about the magic Pixie!"

"You found her?" exclaimed Higarth.

"Well, no," said Gadri. "But we think we found some people who found her."

"Dead people," added Buku. "We think they let her escape."

Higarth paused, then asked them what they were talking about.

"Well, we were out searching for the Pixie," began Gadri, "when we came across this cave, quite far south in the Goblin realm. Four of our soldiers were dead inside it, around a fire. There were ropes on the ground which had been cut."

"Four of our soldiers were killed?" shouted Higarth. "How? And what are you saying? That they captured the magic Pixie, but she escaped and killed them?"

"Maybe," replied the young soldier. "We don't know."

The Lord Protector nodded. "But what makes you think it was the Pixie who was captured? It could have been anyone!"

"We can't be sure," said Gadri. "But there were signs. Small footprints, they looked like Pixie feet."

"And they were Ogre soldiers," added Buku. "They must have gone out looking for the Pixie, so there's a fair chance it was her."

Higarth scratched his head. These two young soldiers may well be right. Maybe the Pixie really was out there somewhere. Maybe she was more dangerous than he thought.

"So do we get any of the reward?" asked Gadri.

"What? What for?" exclaimed Higarth.

"Well... you said there's a reward for finding the Pixie?" replied the soldier.

"For finding her and bringing her back to me!" retorted Higarth. "Not for finding people who may have found her, been killed by her and let her escape."

"Well we don't know it was her who killed them," added Buku, as if that helped their case.

Higarth sighed. "No reward," he replied. "But since I'm in a generous mood, you can have a silver each for your trouble."

He picked a couple of coins from his left pocket and flicked one to each of the soldiers. They nodded, thanked him and went on their way.

"Chandimer!" Higarth called out to his general, who walked up to the Lord Protector. "I'm going back to my quarters," he continued. "When they're done with training, tell the troops to prepare to leave the city. We head out to Nuberim tomorrow."

"Are you sure? What's happened?" asked the general.

Higarth was convinced it was the right move. They could probably get to Nuberim in a few nights. There was an excellent tunnel which ran between the two cities, wide enough for his entire army to use. The Goblins rarely used the tunnel themselves, but they had spent a lot of money building it, so they felt they should probably spend money maintaining it too. That meant they were spending even more money on it, which meant it was presumably even more important to maintain.

"It may be nothing," continued Higarth. "But four of our soldiers are dead. And if this magic Pixie exists, she might have had something to do with it. I'm not wasting time sitting around in Siglitz. We need to go to the capital and get the Goblins on our side. And we fight anyone who opposes us. Especially magic Pixies."

"Yes, Lord Protector," said General Chandimer. "I'll prepare the troops. Oh, and once again, that was a great axe throw you did just now, really excellent."

"Yes thank you Chandimer..." replied Higarth gruffly.

"Nobody could tell you hit the wrong target, the soldiers all– "

"Thank you Chandimer!" snapped Higarth again.

He turned and left, before his general could say anything else.

Chapter 19

"See those walls? We're already on the outskirts of Nuberim," said Larah.

"What's different about the walls?" asked Petra.

"Can't you tell?" replied Larah. "The rock in Nuberim is slightly lighter. And the torches are different."

"Ah of course," said Petra, even though she didn't notice any difference.

They hadn't been far from Nuberim to begin with. Larah reckoned they could make it there in three nights.

The other members of the enchanters had remained behind, but Petra was grateful that Larah and Soloma were helping her. Petra didn't know how she would have survived without them; she probably wouldn't have even made it this far.

It wasn't just that they knew the way. It was all the amazing devices that these Enchanters possessed. They had brought the Levela with them, in case they needed to walk above ground. They carried the Breaker too, in case they needed to break the Humans' chains. And the Nutchen, in case they needed to move very slightly to one side and couldn't be bothered to jump.

Aside from these magical objects, they were travelling light. Each of them carried one wolfskin bag, tied around their waists. They contained food, water and a few other necessary supplies.

"Wait, stop!" called Larah suddenly. "What's that up ahead?"

A crowd of people was beginning to form in the tunnel, about fifty yards ahead.. Petra could just about see a few Goblins in armour at the back.

"What's happening?" asked Larah.

"Border controls apparently," said a voice to her left. It

was a middle-aged Goblin man, with a long nose and short white hair.

"What? Why?"

"They need to protect the city. Have you heard what's been going on at Lancha? In Siglitz? There may be a war coming!"

"You mean they're sealing up Nuberim?" asked the young Goblin.

"You can't trust anyone right now," replied the stranger. "Ogres, Humans, Elves, Pixies…"

"Put your hood up," whispered Soloma in Petra's ear.

She did. And she kept her gaze on the floor, suddenly aware of the danger around her.

"Nice cloaks by the way," said the stranger to Larah. "I like how you all match. Are you some sort of sports team, or musicians?"

"Nope, just ordinary Goblins. Three ordinary Goblins," said Larah.

She started to move away from the crowd, and beckoned her two companions to follow her.

"What do we do now?" whispered Petra when they had made it a safe distance.

"We find another way in," replied Soloma. "There are over a hundred ways into Nuberim, surely they can't guard all of them."

"Well I think they do have over a hundred guards…" replied Larah. "We had better be quick. And find the weirdest, most unusual entrance possible."

"How about one of the Western tunnels?" said Soloma.

"No tunnels, too obvious," said Larah.

"An overground entrance up north?"

"Not obvious enough," said Larah.

"What? That doesn't make sense."

"Okay fine," said Larah. "But they'll still be guarding those entrances."

"What if we cross Gila Lake?"

Larah paused. "Too dangerous," she said. "You've heard the legends. The stories of people trying to cross that lake and their boats being swallowed whole by hideous monsters. And nobody has ever lived to tell the tale."

"Wait," said Petra. "If nobody has ever lived to tell the tale, then how does anyone know it's happened?"

Larah frowned. "Good point," she said. "Maybe it's worth a try."

The journey to the Gila Lake was long and involved lots of narrow and winding paths.

"Dawn must be breaking now," said Soloma, as they walked.

"We're so far underground, how can you tell? How can anyone tell?" asked Petra.

"Because it gets quieter," said Soloma. "People go home to sleep when the day breaks."

"Right," said Petra, even though that didn't make any sense.

Many people believed that the Goblins first originated underground. They were built for the dark. Their eyes were sensitive to light, which meant they could see in areas that were almost pitch black. They had excellent hearing, which they could use to navigate when they needed to. They even liked the smell of dirt.

As ages passed, the first Goblins ventured to the surface. They rather enjoyed it for a few hours, until a terrifying ball of light appeared in the sky. It nearly blinded them. So they went back underground and prayed to their Gods, asking them to make the nasty light go away.

A few hours later it did, and they could enjoy life on the surface once again. Temporarily.

They soon realised that if they prayed to the Gods, the light would eventually disappear. But the prayer didn't last long, as the ball of light always came back. So once again they would have to pray, and then wait for it to go again.

That happened every night for years. They tried praying for the Gods to keep the light down permanently, but it never seemed to work. Then one night, one of the cleverest minds in the Goblin realm came up with an idea: they could pray that the Gods continually bring the light up and then down again, without the need to pray every time. Somehow, that seemed to work. Thank the Gods!

These days the Goblins were a lot more sophisticated. They realised this ball of light, or 'sun' as pretentious people called it, was useful to them. It could help them to grow food above ground and raise certain animals. Modern Goblins still slept during the daytime but could handle the sunlight when they needed to. Of course, some people continued to pray every night that the sun would go down again, but some people are idiots.

As Petra looked around, she realised how quiet it was. They hadn't seen any other Goblins for hours. She could hear the echo of her footsteps as she walked. This didn't feel like the edge of the city. It felt like the edge of civilisation.

"We're close," whispered Larah.

It was so dark that Petra could barely navigate – she was using the sounds of her companions to guide her forward. Then she started to see a glimmer of green light as the tunnel opened in front of them. The light seemed to be coming from the water.

"Is this the Gila Lake?" she asked in amazement. "What makes it glow like that?"

"Probably all the monsters," retorted Soloma. "Maybe they somehow make the lake light up to entice people to enter."

"Enough talk about monsters," said Larah in a low voice. "We need to figure out how to cross."

A silence followed as they all realised something that should have been obvious from the start. They didn't have a boat. And swimming was surely out of the question; the water looked dangerous, and they couldn't even see the other side.

"Can we use the Levela?" asked Petra. "We could raise ourselves slightly, then walk over the water?"

"We could, but we only have one," replied Larah.

"How are we all supposed to get across?"

"What happens if we all hold it at once?" asked Petra.

The young Goblin frowned. She thought for a moment, and then seemed to nod.

"I think that could actually work," she said at last.

She took the hard object from a pocket in her cloak and held it out for the others. Petra and Soloma both put a hand on the Levela. They tried to get a firm hold, which was hard given there were three of them, and it was only about the size of an egg.

"It's working!" said Larah.

Petra looked down. She was right; none of their feet were touching the ground.

"Now, very slowly. Let's take this step by step," said Larah.

It must have been a strange sight – three people holding onto a small rock, trying to move in the same direction. It was far from graceful. And far from quick. But it just about worked.

Petra tried not to look down at the water as they stepped. If there really were monsters in this lake, the Pixie and her Goblin friends were about as easy a meal as they could ask for. There was no chance of escape.

"What's that sound?" gasped Soloma suddenly.

The three of them stopped, keeping a tight grip on the Levela. There it was again. A low vibrating noise deep below the water. It started to oscillate up and down as it repeated itself. Almost like a giant lute player tuning their lowest string. Not that such a thing existed.

"Stay calm," whispered Larah.

Petra looked at Soloma. She had frozen. Some kind of tentacle had grabbed hold of her leg. The slimy thing was wrapped tightly around the young Goblin. It was moving.

Without flinching, Petra held out her right hand. She focused hard on the tentacle just above the water. She could see nothing below the surface. There was no way of knowing what monstrous creature lay beneath.

She didn't have any time. She waited, trying to force a flame from her palm. Nothing came out.

The tentacle was wrapping itself higher around Soloma's body. It reached her chest. Any second now the monster could pull her straight under the water.

Focus! shouted Petra to herself. It wasn't working. Why couldn't she create a flame? She was breathing fast. Soloma was disappearing under the pulsating tentacle. It was grabbing her arm as she desperately clung on to the Levela.

Suddenly Petra heard a splash. She looked round. The tentacle had unwrapped itself from Soloma's body. It seemed to unravel and disappear below the surface of the water. Larah was holding up a small stone in her right hand, while keeping her left hand on the Levela.

Petra realised what had happened instantly. That small rock was the Breaker. Larah had managed to cut the tentacle, and it had somehow scared the creature away.

"Right. Keep going!" shouted Larah.

Soloma looked back. She might have appreciated a moment to wipe the hideous slime away from her body. But she couldn't argue. That thing could be back at any moment.

They picked up the pace. Larah started shouting "One, two, three," keeping them all in time.

The vibrating sound came again. It was even more terrifying now since they knew what was causing it. Petra didn't look back. None of them did. They could see the rocks at the other side of the water now. This gave them hope; never had rocks looked so appealing.

Soloma was struggling. Every step she took seemed to take a lot of effort. That tentacle had wrapped around her tightly; maybe it had caused her some damage.

"We're nearly there, don't worry," whispered Petra. "When we get to the other side, we'll take a break and find you some water. And there won't be any monsters in it."

Soloma tried to laugh, but nothing came out. She kept going though. They all did.

Another vibrating sound. Petra thought it seemed quieter than the others. Like a slightly smaller lute player tuning a slightly smaller lute. Whatever that monster thing was, maybe it was retreating.

Larah looked down. She could see her foot was now hovering over the rock at the other side of the water. She let out a loud sigh of relief. Petra and Soloma quickly joined her on the shore, and they all let go of the Levela.

They sat down and breathed, with the comforting feeling of the dry, hard rocks beneath them. Everything seemed still. There were no signs of people anywhere.

Soloma was the first to speak. "Why are we doing this again?" she said.

"We're saving two Humans' lives," replied Larah.

"Well I hope they appreciate that we've nearly died to rescue them."

"If we rescue them," said Larah. "We're not near the prison yet. It's only going to get harder."

"Great!" said Soloma, sarcastically.

"You know something," added Larah. "That tentacle was huge, and I must have barely scratched it with that breaker. It must have been quite a cowardly monster to get scared off by that!"

Soloma laughed. Then she turned to Petra, who hadn't said a thing. "You okay?"

"Why didn't it work?" she replied. "I was trying to force a flame at that tentacle. And nothing came out!"

"It didn't matter," said Larah. "It all turned out okay."

Petra nodded. "But it nearly didn't. And what if it happens again?"

She looked at the two Goblins. Then she gazed at the lake once again. The green glow lit up the ground around them. It had a haunting beauty to it – so still and inviting, if it wasn't for the monsters lying below it.

Then her eye caught something about twenty yards away. A small wooden vessel with two oars attached, lying peacefully on the bank by the lake.

"Is that a boat?" she asked.

Soloma then muttered some expletive words, which probably would have offended all their Gods at once.

Chapter 20

The trees looked like moss from up here. King Wyndham could see all the way to the mountains in the North. He must have been really high up. He grabbed his horse's mane. It was soft, and white. Just like the creature's wings.

Of course, it wasn't a horse. It was a unicorn. He was dreaming again. He felt the cool breeze around his beard. It must have been a dream, but it felt very real.

Wyndham looked around, trying to get a sense of his surroundings. It was no use; he had to get lower. He grabbed the unicorn's mane harder as it started to descend. He felt more confident riding it this time. And more importantly, he knew was dreaming. So he rode the unicorn quickly, feeling the adrenaline as the magnificent beast hurtled towards the ground like a lightning bolt.

He was closer to the ground in no time. The mountains had disappeared – he must have been about fifty yards up now. He tugged on the unicorn and brought it to an abrupt halt. Then he looked around again, as the creature hovered in the air.

He saw the buildings instantly below him. There were six of them. Just like his last dream. They were made of stone and looked quite new. They were a light grey colour. Maybe they were built by one of the great sculptors in Peria? Only the Humans could make buildings that fine. Elves would be too weak to lift the stone. And Goblins would probably give up and just start digging instead.

As he gazed at the stone structures, he realised they weren't grey at all. They were slightly green; in fact, they seemed to be turning greener. The pristine buildings now looked a little old, and almost diseased. Every stone had gone a slimy green colour.

He saw the buildings start to crumble. The hard stone was disintegrating in front of his eyes. All six of them were becoming soft green mounds. They weren't buildings anymore; they were just piles of earth. Nothing but remnants of what they once were.

Wyndham woke with a jolt. He looked around. Something was wrong. It was dark in his chamber; he couldn't see much. But he could hear shouting and screaming around him. He put on his robe and ran out of the room.

He hurried down the steps and out into the street. He was underground of course, most of Lancha was; it was a Goblin city after all. But now there were torches on both sides of the tunnel around him. People were everywhere. Mostly Humans from what he could tell – he recognised the armour of his soldiers. They seemed to be running round frantically in no particular direction.

He turned to the guard, who had been standing in front of his door. It was Robsun, one of his Royal Guard. The Royal Guard had a very similar job to any other guard, except they had a slightly nicer uniform.

"What's happened?" cried the King.

"Good evening sire," replied Robsun.

Wyndham stared at him blankly.

"It's Ogres, sire," he continued. "That's all I know. You had better stay safe and go back inside."

"How many Ogres? Why did they come here?" Wyndham didn't know what he was saying.

"I don't know, sire. But clearly there are enough of them to cause alarm."

"So are they gone now? Have we dealt with them?"

"I think so sire, but I don't know," continued Robsun. "I can't really see a lot when I'm stood here guarding you."

King Wyndham realised he was gasping for breath. He shouldn't be running down steps at his age.

"Sire!" called a voice from nearby.

It was Cecil. He wore his silver plated armour and carried a sword by his side. Both were purely for aesthetics, obviously – the Lord of War had never been in an actual battle. He was too important for that.

"What's happened, Cecil?" asked King Wyndham. "Is everyone okay?"

"Just about, sire," said the Lord of War. "The Ogres are gone now. From what we could tell, there were about ten of them. They ambushed us, caught us completely off guard."

"So how did we stop them?"

"Well there were people on guard."

Wyndham sighed. "So the guards awoke the other soldiers?"

Cecil nodded.

"Who sent them here? Were they operating under the Lord Protector's orders?"

"I don't think we know that, sire. The soldiers were probably too busy fighting to ask whether they were here on official business."

"Yes all right!" snapped Wyndham. "Any casualties?"

"A couple," replied Cecil. "And a few of the Ogres escaped. With two of our soldiers."

"They escaped with two of our soldiers? Why?"

"We don't know, sire," replied Cecil. "Again, we didn't ask while we were in the middle of fighting. Apparently they picked them up and carried them out the city."

Wyndham paused for a moment. "Which soldiers?"

"Carage and Metlook."

"Why those two? What do we know about them?"

Cecil thought for a moment. "Well Carage is from Stonem originally. Been in the army close to ten years. Now a captain."

King Wyndham nodded. "And Metlook?"

"He's young, in his early twenties. A recruit, from Peria I believe."

The King scratched his beard. He looked around and got the feeling that things were getting calmer. The shouting and screaming had subsided.

"So there's nothing that connects the two soldiers?" he asked. "Why would they take them?"

"Well..." added the Lord of War. "They are both quite small."

"You mean they're easy to carry?" replied the King. "So they took them because they were the easiest ones to take. Is that what you're saying?"

"Not just that," replied Cecil. "We know the Ogres are looking for the magic Pixie. Maybe they took Carage and Metlook, thinking they were Pixies?"

Wyndham put his hand over his face. As it happened, a few people were now gathering near him. These people included Samorus and Prince Vardie, who both looked confused by all the commotion.

"What about those two?" asked Wyndham, staring at his Lord of War. "Why wouldn't they just take two actual Pixies?"

"It's just a theory," replied Cecil, dejectedly.

"Sire!" cried an excited voice. It was Jensen, one of the captains.

"We caught one of the Ogres!"

"What? How?"

"Superior tactics!" replied the general. "We outsmarted him. Outmaneuvered him!"

"That's right," said another soldier, who stood next to the captain looking equally as excited.

"The Ogre tripped and fell. So we cunningly stabbed him while he was on the ground."

"Genius…" replied the King. "Is he still alive?"

"Yes, we stabbed him in the leg. Now we've taken him prisoner."

"Ah, well done," said King Wyndham.

"Have you managed to get any information out of him?" asked Cecil.

"He's not talking," said Jensen. "He's said he won't talk."

"Did he say why?"

"No. He said he won't talk about why he won't talk."

Cecil frowned. "Have you tried? Offered him a carrot?"

"He said he wasn't hungry," said Jensen.

Now it was the King's turn to frown. "Did you threaten him with torture?"

Jensen nodded. "Yes, but he told us it wouldn't work.

He said if we tortured him, he would talk even less."

"You mean less than not at all?" said Wyndham.

"Yes sire. And we didn't want to risk him talking less than not at all, so we thought it was best not to interrogate him any further."

The King closed his eyes for a moment. Of course, it was never easy to get a prisoner to talk. And torture was generally frowned upon these days.

The Trolls never really saw the point of torture. Why torture someone when you could just kill them? It was like making a sandwich and only eating the bread.

The Elves would never torture anyone. They wouldn't hurt a fly, so how could they hurt a person? Maybe if that person had hurt the fly. But even then, their form of torture would probably involve sitting the person down and telling them how disappointed they were. And making them apologise to the fly.

The Goblins considered torture a thing of the past. Maybe such barbaric practices were okay in the Eleventh Age, but this was the Fourteenth. Their form of torture generally involved public shaming or humiliation. Nothing would be hurt except feelings.

Ogres still used torture. But even they had limits. They only did it to get information. Or punishment. But they didn't enjoy it. Well some of them didn't enjoy it. Some of the time. And Pixies didn't use torture either. If they caught a prisoner they would just keep them in a cell. And considering Pixies were four foot tall, their prison cells were rather small. So that was torture enough for most people.

King Wyndham looked back at Jensen. "Okay, give it some time and try again," he said. "And well done for capturing him in the first place."

He raised his voice to the large crowd of soldiers who had now gathered around.

"And thank you everyone for handling this so bravely. We don't know what has happened here today, but we will find out. Please attend to the wounded and try to get some rest."

The crowd of Human soldiers began to disperse. Wyndham now turned to Cecil.

"I think we need to send a few scouts out. Two of our soldiers have been taken, and we have to bring them back."

The Lord of War nodded.

"And send for the Governor of this city. Maybe the Goblins will know something."

"Yes, sire," replied Cecil. "Oh and one more thing," said Wyndham. He came in close so nobody else could hear them. "I had a dream just now."

"Ah that's nice, sire," said Cecil.

"I think it meant something!" snapped the King. "Could you send for Captain Soder again? I need her advice."

Cecil nodded again and went on his way. King Wyndham stood and watched as he disappeared. He hoped the captain would come soon to analyse his dream. But he wasn't sure he needed her. It was pretty obvious what it meant.

Last time the buildings had caught fire. This time, they had turned green and crumbled. Maybe it wasn't Petra who was putting the fate of the Known World at risk. It was the Ogres. Or Goblins. It was hard to tell since they were both green.

Chapter 21

Nuberim. The capital city of the Goblins. One of the oldest cities in the Known World. It might have even been the oldest; nobody really knew.

People sometimes debated whether the remnants of old dwellings towards the top of Nuberim were older than the crumbling stone buildings on the outskirts of Orthica, or the stumps of palisades in the North of Lanthyn. Arguments would often get heated, until people generally accepted that there was simply no way of knowing, and it wasn't worth arguing about. And that it was a boring topic of conversation anyway.

Even if Nuberim wasn't the oldest city, it was certainly an impressive one. Petra was starting to notice some of the patterned walls, polished slate paths and even a few statues. They were clearly getting closer to the city itself.

It had been hard going. They had almost drowned and been attacked by a terrifying water monster. But they had made it. The first part of their journey was done. But getting into the city wasn't enough; now they had to find Fulton and Ridley.

"Why aren't we taking the Gansey Tunnel?" queried Soloma, as they walked.

The young Goblin seemed upbeat for someone who had nearly been strangled by a slimy tentacle a few hours ago. She hadn't washed, but the tunnels were dark, and the three of them had got used to the smell.

"I think we're better off getting to Mayne Street first," said Larah. "It may take a little longer, but it should be safer. We've done enough wandering through dark alleys."

"But how are we actually going to get to the prison? Or get inside it?"

"I haven't figured that out yet," said Larah. "Let's just get near it first."

"Well it's probably worth thinking about," continued Soloma. "Candor Prison is the largest in the realm. Apparently there are over five hundred prisoners there. Gates as high as houses. Walls as hard as stones. Windows which are completely opaque..."

"Yes all right," muttered Larah. "I'm sure we'll manage. We have made it this far."

"We made it into the city, yes," replied Soloma. "But this is going to be so much harder. Finding the two Humans will be close to impossible. How are we even supposed to get inside the prison? Some say it's guarded by demons who never sleep!"

"I think they actually do eight-hour shifts," replied Larah. "I had a cousin who used to work there."

"Well even if we get inside, we would get lost in the never-ending corridors, spiral staircases. We could be wandering round forever. With no chance of ever finding them."

"There they are," said Petra, suddenly. The two Goblins stopped and looked at her.

"I'm serious," she added. "Over there on the right. Those two Humans with their heads in the stocks. That face, that's Ridley. And there's Fulton. I'm sure of it!"

Larah and Soloma both turned and looked at where the young Pixie was pointing. There was a crowd of people gathered around the two prisoners. They were taking turns to throw mud into the prisoners' faces.

"What are they doing to them?" asked Petra, feeling both confused and excited.

"Public humiliation," replied Soloma. "They do it to the most hated prisoners. It's apparently soul destroying."

Petra frowned. "It's horrible," she added. Although, to be fair, it was far less horrible than anything else she could have imagined.

"This is a good thing. In fact it's a great thing!" said Larah. "Firstly, we've found them. They're safe and alive. Secondly, they're out in the open. Not hiding hundreds of miles below us. It's got to be much easier to rescue them now."

"So how are we going to do it?" asked Soloma.

Larah smiled. "With magic!"

There was a pause.

"What does that mean?" said Soloma. "You might need to elaborate."

"Yes okay," said Larah. "I need to think through the logistics. We're actually going to need a combination of magic and thorough planning."

"Sounds good," added Petra.

She checked her hood to make sure it was covering her face. There were people everywhere in this busy street. She didn't know if anyone would recognise her, but a Pixie wandering around here could easily arouse suspicion.

"I think we need to wait until morning is approaching," continued Larah. "There are too many people around here now. When it empties out, we strike."

"And what does 'strike' mean?" asked Soloma. "There are three guards around the Humans. They aren't just going to fall asleep when morning comes."

"No, they aren't," said Larah. "We'll need to distract them."

Petra and Soloma looked at her intently. She had a plan. Quite possibly an ingenious one.

"Here's what we need to do. Petra, you create a flame. Maybe a few flames. And send them far out that way."

Larah pointed to the left, where the street continued a long way, sloping slightly downwards.

"Is that going to work?" asked Soloma. "It might make them look up for a second, but we need to draw them out from this place."

"That's why we need a second distraction!" replied Larah, triumphantly.

Soloma raised an eyebrow. At least that's what it looked like – it was fairly dark in the street.

"After Petra sets off the flames, you run in the same direction as the fire."

"In the same direction as the fire?"

"Yes. It's perfectly safe obviously. Petra's flames will

129

just hit the roof of the tunnel, it won't cause any damage."

"Right," said Soloma. "So Petra sets off the flame, and then I run after it."

"Yes," said Larah. "And here's the brilliant part. You shout 'magic Pixie' as you run. You make the Goblins think she created the flame."

Soloma paused. "But she did? Well, she will have."

"Yes, but Petra won't be near it. The guards will have to run towards it. Well, one or two of them anyway. They know how valuable the magic Pixie is. Everyone is looking for her."

Petra smiled. It was still surreal having people talk about her like this.

"So, it's not really a second distraction," added Soloma. "It's more an extension of the first distraction?"

"Whatever," said Larah. "The point is, that will leave me and Petra here, with whatever guards remain. Then Petra reveals herself, and tells the guards to let the Humans go, or else."

"Reveals herself?" asked Soloma.

"Shows her face," clarified Larah. "And if there are any problems, I've got the Breaker. I can attack the guards with it. Or break the Humans out of the stocks."

Soloma thought for a second.

"Okay, suppose that all works. Then what? What do I do after I've created the distraction? Or part of the distraction?"

"Well, then we run. You let the guards run past you, then come back this way. Hopefully we'll be able to re-group. But if not, we meet back at the bank of Gila Lake."

Petra looked puzzled. "You mean we're going back the way we came? After we nearly died on that lake?"

"Yes."

"Oh, okay then," said Petra, sarcastically.

"We have to," replied Larah. "Once this happens, there will be outcry. There will be twice as many guards as before. We have to leave through a safe exit."

"Safe in terms of guards," said Petra. "Not so safe in terms of terrifying swamp monsters."

"True," said Larah. "But I don't think we have a choice."

Petra looked at Soloma, who had nearly been strangled by the monster. She was nodding. Not smiling, obviously. But she understood.

"Okay." said Soloma. "I think the plan is okay."

"Anything you think we should do differently?" asked Larah.

"Maybe a third distraction?" asked Petra.

Soloma smiled. "No, I think it's okay," she said. "It's not perfect, but it's never going to be."

"What happens if…" said Petra, pausing. "If we don't manage to regroup. What if one of us doesn't make it to the lake?"

Larah looked at her, and then at Soloma. They didn't have to say anything; all three of them knew the answer.

Chapter 22

In the realm of the Humans, only two things were certain: death, and compulsory payments to the Lord of Gold for financing the realm, otherwise known as taxes. (The Lord of Gold didn't like to use that word, because people didn't like the sound of it).

But they generally accepted that taxes had their benefits. They paid for people's safety and security in case the Ogres ever invaded. They paid for the roads, which were useful for travelling. And they paid for the king's palace, which admittedly didn't have many benefits unless you were the king.

Death, on the other hand, had very few benefits. It didn't pay for anything, and nobody really gained from it. Of course there was the afterlife to look forward to, but that depended on what you believed in. Some believed it was paradise, but others believed it was punishment. So, on balance, it was probably quite mediocre.

Over the last few nights, Ridley and Fulton had actually discovered quite a significant benefit to dying – you didn't have to stand with your head in stocks, getting mud thrown at you for ten hours a night.

At first it had felt like a relief, almost a nice change. Then fairly quickly it became unpleasant, but they tried to look on the bright side – at least people would laugh when they threw the mud. They were bringing joy to people, and that was something.

But then, soon after that, they started to find the laughter annoying. And by now, they would both have gladly ended laughter across the whole of the Known World if they could.

The Goblin guards had said the stocks would destroy their souls, and they weren't wrong. Fulton wasn't sure if he believed in an afterlife. But he convinced himself that if it existed, and it was paradise – there would be no mud, or stocks, or sarcastic Goblin guards.

And no matter how hard it was for him, he knew that it was even harder for his cell mate. Fulton was young and physically fit, and he was often finding his back aching and a stiffness in his legs. So for Ridley, who was probably 15 years older, it must have been twice as hard.

"Having fun?" asked one of the guards. "You'll be sad to hear that it's morning soon; time to go back to your cell."

Fulton shuddered. The guard had lowered his head to the side of his stocks. Fulton could feel the Goblin's breath against his skin; it wasn't a great feeling.

The guard got to his feet and started to unlock the stocks. It was a simple buckle which lifted up the top half so Fulton could lift his head and hands out. Then, obviously, the handcuffs would go back on and they would lead the two Humans back to their cell. It was the same thing every morning.

And then, in an instant, everything changed. From out of nowhere, Fulton heard a loud crash. And then another. It was followed by shrieking.

Fulton lifted his neck out of the stock, which had just been unbuckled. There was smoke in the distance to his right. People were gathering towards it in a panic.

Over the top of the murmuring he suddenly heard a loud voice.

"Magic Pixie!" Someone was crying from far away. "It's the magic Pixie!"

"What's going on?" shouted one of the guards. "Was that fire? Where did it come from?"

"The magic Pixie?" said another.

"You don't believe in that rubbish?" said the first guard.

"Well I'm starting to!" replied the other one. "Whatever it is, we should investigate it!"

"We're guards, not detectives!"

"The roof is smoking. Something crazy has happened. They may need us!"

"Let the city guards handle it."

"It's nearly morning. There probably aren't any city guards around."

"But they're supposed to patrol all night and all day. What are our taxes paying for?"

"Well it makes sense to have more around when there are more people."

"Yes but that's not the point. The principle…"

"Will you two shut up!" bellowed the third guard. "Something terrible has happened! Dorfen, go investigate. We'll look after the prisoners."

One of the guards immediately ran towards the crowd.

"Good luck, detective!" shouted the first guard.

"Enough," replied the other one, who was still standing there. Apparently the one in charge.

Fulton looked over at Ridley. He had also been released from his stocks, and stood there handcuffed. He wasn't even looking at the commotion to his right. He was staring straight ahead of him, almost frozen.

Two short figures appeared in front of them. Both wore white hoods, which covered their faces.

They pulled their hoods down in tandem, as if they had rehearsed it. Fulton looked at their faces. It was dark, but he could just about make them out.

They looked young. One was clearly a Goblin – green skinned and white eyed. But the other was pale, with dark hair which had been messed up from the hood. And those eyes. They looked familiar. The emerald green seemed to shine through the darkness, like some kind of magic.

"Petra!" he cried. A little too loudly.

The two guards turned round. "What?" hissed one of them, just as loudly.

Fulton looked up. The crowd were still gathered further away; no-one else was looking at them.

He turned back to the young Pixie. He didn't know if this was real, or if he had died and gone to the afterlife. But it was her. Somehow, she was standing in front of him right now.

She smiled at him, and then turned to the guard he was handcuffed to.

"Don't move," she said firmly.

The guard snorted. He was twice her size.

"Get lost," he growled.

"I would be nice to her if I were you," said the young Goblin to her side. "She can turn you into flame with a flick of her wrist."

The guard frowned. "I said GET LOST."

Petra let out a flame. She clearly didn't want to waste any time. It wasn't meant for the guard; it just shot at the ground in front of him, and disappeared in smoke without causing any damage. It was enough.

Both the guards jumped back. One of them yelped. The Humans, still handcuffed, were pulled back too.

"Now, please don't move," continued Petra, still smiling.

She didn't move either. But her Goblin companion walked up to Fulton, took out some kind of rock, and held it up to his wrist.

His cuff somehow seemed to split in two. The two guards were standing frozen behind him. They shared a glance as if to say 'I don't know what's going on either'.

Now it was Ridley's turn. The young Goblin seemed to break his handcuffs even quicker.

"Come with us," said Petra, beckoning the two Humans away. They both did.

The young Pixie turned back to the guards.

"And you two, please stay there. Don't try and follow us."

They walked quickly. Petra and Larah set the pace. The two Humans followed just behind.

"Petra," whispered Fulton as they walked. "It's really you, isn't it? This is real!"

"Yes it's me," she replied, barely turning her head.

"I've missed you!" replied Fulton.

"I've missed you too, but now is not the time," said Petra. "We need to get out of here."

"Oh okay," said Fulton. "I'm not quite sure what's happening but... shouldn't we be running?"

"No, not yet," said Larah mechanically. "We don't want to draw attention to ourselves."

Fulton nodded. He looked at Ridley, who seemed in a daze.

"We'll tell you when we need to run," continued Larah.

"Stop! Turn around!" came a loud, booming voice from behind. "Those are the prisoners!"

"Now," said Larah. "Now we run."

Chapter 23

"Quicker," shouted Larah. "Quicker. We have to get out of here!"

Ridley was wondering whether the young Goblin could give them any more instruction than just 'quicker'. It was fairly obvious that you need to go quickly when you're a prisoner on the run, getting chased by Goblin guards.

He looked across at Fulton, who seemed to be coping. For weeks they had either been sitting in a cell or crouching with their heads in stocks. It had taken a toll on their bodies; they were both surely stiff, and not used to running like this. Fulton was young and fit – it wasn't such a problem for him.

But Ridley felt like his muscles had turned to stone. Every step was a challenge, and it was taking all his strength to keep pushing. He could feel a sharp pain in his right leg. He had broken it, or at least heavily sprained it before he was captured. It still hadn't completely healed.

The tunnels were getting darker and narrower. Ridley had no idea where they were going, but he followed blindly. He couldn't tell how far behind the guards were. But he heard voices. And horns were sounding every few seconds.

"This way," said Larah, leading them down another dark passage to their right.

Ridley turned abruptly to follow and felt a click in his leg. The sharp pain turned even sharper. It was like a dagger cutting inside his shin.

Another horn came from behind him. It was deafening.

"Wait, there's a route through here," said Larah.

Before Ridley could ask what she was looking at, the young Goblin had disappeared down a small hole in the side of the wall.

He just about heard her say "This is a shortcut, trust me!"

Petra turned her head back, and then followed her companion down the hole.

"Are you okay?" panted Fulton, turning to Ridley.

He looked at the hole again. It was clearly going to be a tight squeeze; easy enough for a Pixie or a short Goblin, but a different story for two fully grown Humans.

"There's no time," replied Ridley, nodding. "Just go for it."

Fulton dived in, feet first, and then pushed himself through. It was a struggle but he managed. Once his whole body was in, it got easier. It was almost like a slide.

Ridley breathed. His sense of relief didn't last long as another horn filled the air around him.

He put his feet in the hole and pulled himself down. Something wasn't right. He wasn't moving. He must have been caught on something.

He reached down around his knees. He couldn't feel anything; maybe it was something stuck to his clothes. He tried to edge himself forward, but his body was motionless. His legs seemed to have frozen.

"What's happened?" whispered a voice at the other end of the hole. It didn't sound too far away, but he guessed Fulton wouldn't be able to reach him from here.

"Go!" Ridley snapped down the hole. "Run!"

He could see the lights of torches coming round the corner. He tugged again, but it was no use. He was stuck, half in and half out of the hole. His arms and head were sticking out, on display for anyone to see.

He heard a pattering nearby and felt something sniffing the side of his head. Then he heard a soft growl. It was a dog. Some sort of guard dog presumably. He had seen them before around the prison.

"Well, what do we have here?" said a voice.

"Hmmm," said another. "It seems to be a Human stuck in a hole. That's something you don't see every night."

Ridley desperately struggled to free himself, but it was too late. He felt a firm hand on his arm.

"What happened here then?" sniggered one of the

Goblins. "Trying to escape down a hole? Did your friends get through, but tubby here was too fat to make it? Is that what happened?"

Ridley felt tired and angry, but above all he just felt beaten. Everything had been such a whirlwind; he had been so close to freedom only minutes ago. But now he was right back where he started. Things would probably be much worse.

"I think little piggy has been eating too much prison food," said another Goblin. "If it wasn't for that, you might have made it."

Ridley was about to explain that he could have fitted through the hole if he hadn't been stuck on a rock. And that the prison food wasn't anywhere near enough, and he had never felt so skinny.

But he didn't see the point. There wasn't much point in anything right now. One of the guards pulled a set of iron handcuffs out of his pocket. He had only been free of them for a few minutes.

Suddenly he felt a tug on his leg. And then his other one. He couldn't tell what was happening – his wounded leg was in agony as someone, or something, pulled on it. The blinding pain was all he could think about. Before he knew it, he had been dragged down the hole, and landed on the other side with a thud.

He looked up and saw Fulton smiling down at him. Ridley had never been so pleased to see his young companion.

"How did you do that?" asked Ridley.

Fulton shrugged. "I just reached up and pulled. It's not actually that far."

"Next time, could you pull the leg that *isn't* broken?" Ridley replied, doing his best to feign a smile.

"Quickly!" said Larah from nearby. "We have to keep moving!"

Ridley shot to his feet, and they all started running. The pain in his leg was still agonising, but he pushed through with every ounce of strength he still had.

He heard the pattering of feet behind them. The dog

must have run down the hole after him. Maybe the guards were about to do the same.

The beast started snapping at Ridley's ankles. He could feel the sharp teeth trying to dig into his flesh – the creature was angrily trying to grab a hold of something and knock him off balance.

Luckily, Larah turned round at that moment. Without thinking, she threw something towards the dog. It must have been a piece of meat. And it worked.

Whoever had trained the guard dogs in the Goblin realm clearly didn't do a very good job. The dog went straight for the food, and Ridley didn't hear another thing from it.

The sound of horns seemed to get quieter. Hopefully the guards didn't risk going down the hole. Maybe one of them got stuck in it. Either way, if the guards were taking the long way round to catch them, they might just manage to escape.

Chapter 24

If the world ended, Ogres would still go on living. They would be too stubborn to die just because everybody else did.

Lord Protector Higarth was possibly the most stubborn of all. If the rest of the realm disagreed with him, it just meant they needed more convincing. Thankfully, people rarely disagreed with him. He was the leader of all the Ogres, and he was always right.

They had been walking every night, and most of the day. His advisers had suggested they should allow time for rest, but Higarth insisted they travelled throughout day and night.

This meant they had arrived in Nuberim very quickly. And now they were here, his troops had time to rest. So once again, he had been right.

Higarth, of course, didn't need to rest. It was a sign of weakness, and lord protectors were not weak. Only the strongest Ogres could ever become generals, and only the very strongest of all could become lord protector.

So while his soldiers were now settling on the outskirts of the city, Higarth was in a room deep underground, about to have a difficult conversation with the Goblin queen. Generals Lang and Chandimer were sitting either side of him. The Goblins were sitting opposite – Queen Niella with two of her warlords: Sepping and Uoro. This wasn't simply a discussion – it was a battle of wills, a staring contest. And Higarth wouldn't be the first to blink.

"What are you proposing?" asked the young queen.

"In ages past, Ogres and Goblins have always stood side by side," began General Chandimer, as if giving a pre-rehearsed speech. "In recent times, this relationship has been tested, but we should always stand firm against such tests. The two greatest civilisations are even greater together."

"Please," said the queen. "Would you mind just getting to the point?"

The general looked at his Lord Protector.

"We want you to join with us against the Humans," said Higarth. "Our armies must join together and march towards Siglitz."

"Yes, we agree," said the queen.

Higarth paused. "Excuse me?"

"I said we agree with you," repeated Queen Niella. "We had reached the same conclusion. We may never know the full story of what happened to our kings, but we do know that Humans killed one of them. It's time to pick a side. We're with you."

Higarth took a breath. That was a rather easier discussion than he had anticipated. "Well, that's great," he said. "When should we set off?"

"Let's give it a few nights," said the queen. "Allow some time to prepare, and give you some time to rest."

"Ogres don't need to rest," retorted Higarth. "We are always alert, always ready for anything. But we are happy to wait in the city for a few nights."

"Very well," replied Niella. "We can accommodate your troops here. And we'll give you a room in the citadel, Lord Protector, where you can remain alert and ready for anything, while the rest of us are resting."

Sepping gave a wry smile. Higarth glared at him.

"These are dangerous times after all," continued the queen. "Intruders everywhere, nobody can be trusted. Not to mention this magic Pixie who could be anywhere."

"Enough about the magic Pixie," replied Higarth, raising his voice slightly. "We have sent bands of Ogres out searching for her. If she exists, she'll be in our hands soon enough. She's nothing to worry about!"

"But you haven't found her yet?" remarked Niella.

Higarth answered with another glare.

"Well even if you don't find her…"

"We'll find her!" growled Higarth.

"Yes of course you will," continued Warlord Sepping. "But even if you don't, we won't have to worry about her coming near the city. As you know, every possible entrance to Nuberim is guarded. We're perfectly safe."

Higarth nodded slowly. "Is there anything else we need to discuss?" he said. "How are all the Goblin folk doing since the terrible tragedies?"

"Better, thank you," replied the queen. "It's been a tragic time, but everyone has pulled together."

"What about those two Humans? Are they still alive? I know they seem to have less than half a brain between them, but they could still come in useful. They might give us some insights into Wyndham's military plans."

"We haven't killed them yet," said Queen Niella. "I agree we may need them, so we're keeping them alive for now. Under close surveillance in the deepest dungeon in the city."

There was a sudden knock on the door. A Goblin messenger burst in, barely waiting for the queen to say 'enter'.

"Your majesty, great warriors," said the young Goblin, gasping for breath. "There's been a break in at the prison. The two Humans who killed the King. They've escaped!"

Queen Niella jumped to her feet. "How? How could this happen?"

"Maybe your guards should have been more alert and ready for anything," muttered Higarth under his breath.

"We don't know your majesty," said the messenger. "But there are rumours that it's the magic Pixie."

Lord Protector Higarth and Warlord Sepping exchanged a glance.

"It can't be the magic Pixie," said Higarth, glaring at Warlord Sepping. "There's no way she could get through Sepping and his guards."

"If it was the magic Pixie, surely Higarth and his soldiers would have caught her first," said Sepping in reply.

"Right, enough!" growled Higarth. "What are we waiting for? We have to stop her! Lang, Chandimer, assemble the troops. Tell them to circle the city. Nobody gets in or out!"

"Sepping, Uoro, do the same with the Goblin guards," said Niella. "They have to block every exit."

"They already are."

"Well tell them to do it better!" she snapped.

Chapter 25

The boat was still there. Thank the Gods. There was probably even room for all five of them in it! They could make it back across the water.

Petra stopped and caught her breath. Larah ran straight into the boat and grabbed both the oars. Fulton followed her, supporting Ridley, who was clearly in pain. They both sat down; the boat seemed to take their weight.

"She's not here!" gasped Petra. "Soloma should be here by now."

"Get in the boat!" cried Larah. "There's no time."

"At least give her a moment," replied Petra.

"The guards will come running around the corner in less than a moment. We've waited as long as we can!"

Petra looked behind her again, and then ran to join the others. She pushed it forward and jumped in, making it easier for Larah to start paddling.

It was a bit of a squeeze, even with four of them.

"Guys?" came a voice from the shore.

Soloma appeared. She must have been hiding in the shadows somewhere. Petra smiled.

"Come on, jump in!" shouted Larah.

Soloma hurtled towards them and took a heroic leap for the boat. She just about made it, falling into the water with a splash, but within reach of the vessel.

Fulton leant over and pulled her in. She collapsed on top of the four of them, breathing heavily.

"We need to go faster," said Larah, whilst straining to push through the water with as much force as possible.

"You're the one doing the rowing," replied Petra.

"Yes, thank you," said Larah, sarcastically. "I mean I need your help. Could you all paddle with your hands at the same time?"

They all reached over the sides of the boat. Petra

looked down. The water was still a shimmering green colour; amazing, but also potentially deadly. She knew what lurked beneath the surface, and she didn't want to put her hand anywhere near it.

But she didn't have a choice. She and Fulton both started paddling behind the young Goblin on the right of the boat, while Ridley and Soloma did the same on the left.

It didn't take them long to find a rhythm with Larah's oars. Petra wasn't sure how much of a difference it was making, but she kept going. At least the boat was moving forward.

"Are you sure they came this way?" came a voice from the bank. The guards had tracked them down.

Petra craned her neck to try and hear what they were saying. There was a lot of grumbling; she could hear a dog barking.

"I'm sure of it," said another voice.

"Don't listen to them," whispered Larah. "Just keep going."

Petra looked forward. She thought she could just about see the other side of the lake in the distance. Maybe they were far enough away now. Just maybe.

"Hey!" came a loud and piercing voice.

They had been spotted.

The young Pixie felt a chill run down her spine. She didn't know whether the guards had any way of catching them now. Did they have another boat? Anything that could swim? She couldn't look back. She just closed her eyes and kept paddling.

Petra could feel the tension in the group. Nobody said anything – they were all just paddling furiously.

Suddenly she heard a low-pitched scream from the other side of the boat. It was Ridley.

"Something's got me!" he shrieked.

Petra saw something long and thin protruding from the Human.

"I think it's an arrow," she said, "are you okay?"

"It doesn't matter if he's okay, keep paddling!" hissed Larah.

"Yes, it matters if I'm okay!" growled Ridley back.

Larah sighed, without looking round. "All right, where did the arrow get you?"

"My leg," said Ridley, panting.

"Well then it didn't affect your arm, so you can keep paddling," snapped Larah. "We'll look after you soon, but right now we just need to get to safety."

Ridley groaned. "Well is it all right with you if I cry out in pain?"

"Yes, provided you keep paddling," replied Larah mechanically.

Petra could feel vibrations behind the boat. She couldn't tell what was going on, but there could have been arrows landing all around them. She saw a few splashes up ahead. More were coming. Any second now, and one could find its way into her skull.

The young Pixie looked ahead. She could see the bank of the lake now; she was sure of it. Only a hundred yards or so now.

Her arm was aching. It was hard being surrounded by Goblins and Humans, and always the shortest one of the group. It was a strain to even reach the water, let alone generate enough power to keep pushing forward.

Ridley was still breathing heavily and letting out a scream every few seconds.

"Aaargh!"

That one wasn't Ridley.

"What happened?" she said, to no-one in particular.

"I felt something in the water!" said Soloma. "Something slimy, trying to grab my hand."

"Keep…"

"Yes I know, keep paddling!" snapped Soloma. "It's okay, it just brushed me. Hopefully it's nothing."

The shore was almost in reach now. Petra's heart started pumping fast.

"It may have just been the bed of the lake," she said. "I think it's getting shallower."

Thanks to the light from the lake, Petra had a clear view up ahead. She couldn't see anybody on the other side.

Petra looked back. The arrows might just have stopped. Surely there was no archer in the Known World who could shoot one this far.

The boat lodged itself as the water became too shallow. Larah instantly jumped out and waded for the shore. Petra and Fulton followed, while Soloma supported Ridley – she took his weight as he hobbled to the shore on one leg. He was clearly still in a lot of pain.

"We have to keep moving," panted Larah, once they were all together on dry land. "They know exactly where we are right now, and they could find a way to cross this lake at any minute."

"What about Ridley?" said Fulton, turning to his friend. "He clearly needs to rest."

"He needs someone to remove the arrow from his leg, that's what he needs!" said Soloma.

"I'll be okay," said Ridley, still panting. "You guys go on without me. I'll only slow you down."

Larah sighed. "There's no need for that," she said. "I know where we need to go, and it won't take long. We'll carry you."

They didn't say anything more. Everyone realised this had to happen, and it had to be a group effort. Fulton grabbed one of Ridley's arms, and Larah took the other. Soloma carefully lifted his good leg, while Petra positioned herself under his back. Paddling the boat was hard work, but this was even harder.

"It had to be the biggest person who got hit by the arrow, didn't it?" muttered Soloma, between breaths. "If only it had been Petra, this would have been so easy."

The young Pixie smiled. "I can only apologise that nobody shot me," she said.

Without the glow of the lake, it just got darker and darker. Petra felt like she was running blindly into nowhere, carrying a very heavy weight above her (with no disrespect to Ridley).

She didn't know how long they had been running for. Maybe an hour. Maybe a lot less. But finally, Larah told them all to stop.

They laid the wounded Human down, and then sat next to him. Petra could hear everyone panting for breath. She felt a nagging pain in each of her arms. She could see absolutely nothing.

"Where are we?" whispered Soloma.

"Exactly," replied Larah. "Nobody knows. We're in a cave, far from the city and nowhere near any pathways."

"How can you even tell that?" came Fulton's voice. "We can't see a thing!"

Larah seemed to snort. "Maybe you can't," she said. "I feel sorry for overground beings sometimes. You lot get so terrified as soon as you're out of the sun. How have you survived as civilisations?"

"By staying above ground!" replied Ridley between breaths. Petra could sense a slight indignance in his voice.

"Okay, sorry," replied Larah.

"But how about a little light, for us poor overground beings?" continued Fulton. "Maybe we could light a torch?"

"Oh great idea," added Soloma, sarcastically. "Let's make it easier for everyone to find us!"

Fulton didn't respond.

"What about Ridley?" said Petra. "We don't even know how badly he's hurt. He needs help!"

"Already on it," replied Soloma. "The Great Enchanters have many talents, as you know. A few ages ago, we developed a stone called a Naseth. It's capable of cutting and cauterising your skin without feeling any pain at all.

There was a snap, and Ridley let out a loud scream.

"Unfortunately I didn't bring it with me," continued the Goblin. "So I've just had to pull the arrow out by hand. Don't worry though, I still have something to cauterise it. You'll be fine, it's just going to be a little agonising for a few days, and then slightly less agonising for a few more weeks."

Petra heard Ridley mutter 'thanks' among the panting and groaning.

"Who are you, anyway?" asked Fulton. "Oh and thanks for saving us! But why…why did you?"

"She's Soloma, and I'm Larah. And we saved you because Petra asked us to."

"Petra?" said Fulton, turning to the Pixie. Or at least, where he thought she was sitting.

"You're welcome," she said, fully aware that he couldn't see her smiling.

"She also said that she would teach us her magic," added Soloma. "Although I don't think now would be the best time to create fire with our hands."

"Yeah about that," said Petra. "To be honest, I really don't know if I can teach it. But I'll try, I really will."

"It's okay," said Larah. "I don't think either of us expect it to work. That's not the reason we did this. We did it for you."

"What do you mean?" said Petra.

"The Great Enchanters follow the magic," said Soloma. "Your powers – they are the greatest any of us have ever seen, and we respect that more than anything. If there's something you need doing, then the Great Enchanters have to help. It's who we are."

The young Pixie didn't know what to say. She was a little relieved that there wasn't this pressure any more to teach them how to make fire. That had been weighing on her mind all this time.

But more than that, Soloma's words were hard to comprehend. These Goblins would do anything for her, simply because of her magic power. It made her feel like their leader. Or even more than that – like their God! Well that was probably going too far, but it was still a surreal feeling.

"I don't know what to say," was all she could muster in response.

"You saved our lives," said Fulton. "I'm the one who doesn't know what to say!"

Petra wasn't sure he was saying this to all of them, or just to her. But she smiled again, regardless.

"Best not to say anything," suggested Soloma. "That way nobody can hear us."

Ridley seemed to have gone quiet. Hopefully that was a

sign that his pain was becoming more bearable.

"I think this Human could use some water," said Soloma.

"I think we all could!" replied Fulton.

Petra reached into her bag and pulled out the waterskin. She took a large gulp, and then handed it in the direction Fulton's voice was coming from.

She held the waterskin there for a few seconds, waiting for Fulton to take it. She felt a large, warm hand around hers. She was still clutching the water carrier, but Fulton's hand didn't seem to want to take it.

It just stayed there and started to clasp hers even tighter. Petra closed her eyes. She didn't want the moment to end.

Chapter 26

Being king of all the Humans was surely the hardest job in the whole realm. Who in their right mind would want to do it?

There were a few benefits: living in palaces, being constantly waited on, and people obeying your every command. But aside from that, it really was a thankless job.

The most difficult part of all was the loneliness. King Wyndham was always surrounded by advisors and servants, and he had his family back home. But all the major decisions in the kingdom were ultimately his responsibility, and he had to live with them. That was true for all kings and queens, whatever their realm.

There was one exception back in the Fifth Age of the Known World, when twin girls were born to the reigning Human king. The oldest was supposed to inherit the throne, but nobody could remember which one was born first.

There was only one fair solution – they had to both become queen. And to save the cost of building a whole new throne, they simply agreed to share the role between them. Louisa was queen for three days a week, and Marabel for the other three days. They alternated on the seventh day.

It seemed to work well for the first few years, until they started to disagree on some fundamental things. Queen Louisa wanted peace with the Goblins, but Queen Marabel wanted war. This meant that the Human realm was at war with the Goblins on the first, second and fourth day of the week, and occasionally on the seventh day, but at peace the rest of the time.

Nobody was more confused by this than the Goblins. This was especially true when they captured one of the

Human villages, only to be told that it didn't count because it happened on a Wednesday.

Thankfully, one of the queens died before the other, which meant the whole system could go back to normal. The remaining queen, Louisa, then passed a law. It said that in future everyone had to try really hard to remember which of their children was born first.

King Wyndham couldn't help but wonder what it would be like to share his responsibility with someone else. And more to the point, to get a few days off each week. As he stood facing a fiery looking Ogre, he knew he had a big decision to make. And very little time in which to make it.

"Why did you bring me here?" he said to his Lord of War.

"We just wanted to try everything," replied his lord. "No matter what we do, the prisoner won't talk. We just thought it might make a difference if he saw the king. Maybe you're the only person he will talk to."

Wyndham sighed and looked at the prisoner.

"Are you willing to talk to me?" he growled.

The Ogre looked at him but said nothing.

"There we go," said Wyndham, "at least we tried."

"We'll keep trying, sire," said Cecil, as Wyndham started to leave.

The King made his way up the winding tunnels of Lancha towards the surface of the city. He needed some fresh air.

The decision was simple really: was it time to move his soldiers on to the Goblin capital, or should they stay in this city a while longer? He wasn't sure what they were achieving by staying here. The Goblins seemed so stand-offish. It didn't seem to be helping their relations. But at least his Humans could regroup here, and continue to recover from their journey.

Then there was the issue of safety. If they stayed here, they risked being attacked by Ogres again. On the other hand, if they marched onto Nuberim, there would be more Ogres, and once again they would be attacked. And if they retreated, they might be safe, but they would probably end up being attacked by Ogres. This decision wasn't easy.

Wyndham saw daylight up in front of him. Just as he was about to walk up the final steps, he heard someone running behind him. He turned round, and saw a young Human looking flustered. It was Wenda, one of his messengers.

"Sire!" called out Wenda.

"Yes, what is it?" said the King, slightly frustrated.

"I come with news," she continued. "From the East of the city. It's good news and bad news."

"Okay, what's the bad news?"

"The Governor of Lancha has left the city."

Wyndham frowned. "He's left the city? Why?"

"They are evacuating. He's taken a lot of the residents with him. They're heading east, to settle somewhere else for a while I guess."

Wyndham shook his head. "But why? Did he see us as some sort of threat? Or were there orders from elsewhere? We came here peacefully!"

"I don't know I'm afraid sire," said Wenda, "I'm just the messenger."

"Fine," said the King, closing his eyes. "What's the good news?"

"The Governor of Lancha has left the city."

Wyndham scowled at his messenger.

"Yes sire, it's the same news. It's just that it may be good news as well. The city belongs to you now. It's effectively under Human occupation."

"Right, so…"

"I'm sorry about the good news and bad news thing, sire," continued Wenda. "It's just that Tobey and I were debating whether it was good news or bad news. And we couldn't decide, but we didn't want to stand there any longer, so I suggested we tell you it's both. And Tobey thought that was a really good idea, but then…"

"Right!" growled Wyndham. "Is there anything else you know? How far away is the Governor now? Can we get in touch with him?"

"I think it would be difficult, sire," replied his messenger. "It would take us a while to reach them now. Our soldiers saw them leaving at the last dusk gone."

"Last dusk gone? Then why didn't you come to find me sooner?"

"That's exactly what I said to Tobey, sire!" said Wenda. "I said we needed to come to you right away, without delay. But then Tobey said we need to verify our sources and be clear about what the message is. So I told him that…"

"Enough!" snapped Wyndham.

This was unbelievable. His troops had come here peacefully. They had only meant to rest here for a while before moving onto Nuberim. They were here to help the Goblins, but had somehow ended up declaring war on them and capturing a city.

He took an apple from the pocket of his robe, and bit down on it hard.

"Go after the governor. Try and find him," he said to Wenda. "Tell him there has been a misunderstanding, and we are friends of him and his people."

She nodded.

"I'll also tell Tobey that next time we'll come straight to you without deliberating. No more delay. No more…"

She saw the King's face and immediately stopped talking. Then she shot off in the direction she came.

King Wyndham closed his eyes. A few moments ago, he had one decision to make: whether to stay or to keep moving. Now he had about a thousand. How could he fix this mess? They couldn't just leave the city now. Were any Goblins still here? How could they keep the city going? And what do they do when Ogres attack? Or Goblins for that matter?

And where could he find some better messengers?

He was about to climb the steps to the surface again when he heard someone else come up behind him. This time it was someone smaller, clad in soft white chainmail and a gold bracelet on his left arm.

It was Prince Vardie, the second in line to the Pixie throne, and a trusted companion.

"Everything all right, Wyndham?" he said.

"Not really," replied the King. "It seems we've captured this city."

Prince Vardie frowned. "I didn't think we were trying to?"

"We weren't," replied Wyndham. "But apparently we have anyway."

Vardie paused for a moment. "Anything else?" he asked. "I'm assuming the Ogre hasn't talked yet? Any news about Petra?"

King Wyndham shook his head.

"I don't understand what's happening," continued Vardie, who seemed surprisingly calm. "But I know it isn't good. You need help. And don't worry, it's coming."

Wyndham turned to him. Prince Vardie started walking up the steps to the light, and Wyndham followed him.

"I sent a message out days ago," said the Pixie. "Our soldiers will be here soon."

"Pixie soldiers are coming?" replied Wyndham in shock.

"Hundreds of them," said Vardie, nodding. "It's pretty clear that we haven't seen the worst of this yet. There will be more attacks, and we're here to help. We'll stand side by side until we've sorted this out. And until Petra is back with her people!"

Wyndham started to smile. This was surely good news, even Wenda would admit that.

Of course, Pixies were small and generally didn't do too well in battle. People used to say that they had the fifth strongest army of all the six civilisations in the Known World, if you didn't count the Elves. If you didn't count the Goblins, they had the fourth strongest. And if you didn't count any of the other civilisations, they almost certainly had the strongest.

That didn't matter. More soldiers meant more strength. And at least they would be better prepared to deal with anything that may come their way.

As they reached the surface, the air started to feel fresher. King Wyndham turned to his right and wondered if he could see the white armour of Pixie soldiers over the horizon. The gentle movement as they marched towards the city. The gleam of steel daggers reflecting the sunlight.

Or maybe it was just rocks in the distance. It was hard to tell – Pixies really were rather small.

Chapter 27

A night had passed. Maybe two. It was hard to tell when you were deep underground in Goblin land.

They had been doing a lot of walking, but also taking a lot of breaks. Poor Ridley was doing well for someone who had busted their leg, and then had an arrow shot through it.

They had been taking turns to support him while he walked. It was impressive that he was able to walk at all, even with their help. But it was slow going.

Petra didn't know where she was, or where they were trying to get to. Or how close they were to getting there. She didn't really know anything. Larah said they were trying to get towards the surface of the land. The higher up they got, the less likely they were to run into any other Goblins. And thankfully, they hadn't so far.

Life was full of surprises. But it was even more full of dull and predictable things. Most of the time Petra had just been walking through tunnel after tunnel with no respite. She had become accustomed to the dark, but it was still difficult to find her way anywhere. Any glimpse of light was welcome, but it didn't happen often.

Suddenly Petra saw a red glow in the distance, which seemed to be getting bigger. It rose out of the tunnel like a small flame, lighting up the walls as it moved.

"What's that?" whispered Petra.

"I'm sure it's nothing," replied Larah, behind her. "Probably just a nymph or a rock fairy. These tunnels are so desolate, I bet a lot of them live around here."

As Petra looked ahead, the glow seemed larger than before. It was a sort of red orb, and probably nothing to worry about. But it was getting closer.

In fact, it was coming towards them fast. Petra could

hear a fluttering. She saw webbed wings beating. And legs. Or were they claws?

It made a loud hissing sound. Petra jumped. Everyone did.

"That's no rock fairy!" gasped Soloma.

"Just keep walking," said Larah. "Whatever it is, it won't harm us if we don't harm it."

Larah was proven wrong almost immediately. The creature swooped down and hissed again, even louder. It sunk its teeth straight into Larah's arm. She started screaming uncontrollably.

Petra was about to react but saw Soloma jump in front of her. She took out her dagger and sank it straight into the ghastly animal.

It was enough. The creature fell to the floor, shrieking in agony. It wrestled and jumped, flapping its wings in vain until the last ounce of energy left it.

They all surrounded the animal's lifeless body. It was almost like a crab with wings, but bigger and more fierce. Its white eyes made it seem like it was still staring directly at them, even though it was no longer alive.

And the glow. It was still glowing bright red, even in death.

Soloma took a cloak from her bag and wrapped it tightly around Larah's arm, trying to contain the wound. Petra reached forward cautiously and pulled the dagger out from the animal's shell. She handed it back to Soloma.

"Seriously, what is that thing?" said Fulton, who was supporting Ridley to stand up.

There was a moment of silence.

"I think it might be a happy bat," said Larah at last.

Another silence. Nobody asked her what that was, as if they didn't want to appear stupid.

"They're ancient creatures, who haven't existed for ages and ages," continued the Goblin.

"Well clearly they have…"

"Yes all right, obviously they still do exist!" she retorted, "assuming that is what this is."

"Well what do you know about them?" asked Petra.

"They are dangerous," said Larah, rubbing her arm. She was clearly in pain, but the blood didn't seem to be getting through the cloak yet. "They're unpredictable, and they're ruthless. According to legend, they let out a red glow to give a warning to their prey, just so they have a chance to escape."

"Why would they do that?" said Petra.

Larah shrugged. "To make it a fair fight. It would be boring if it were too easy for them. Or so the legend goes…"

Petra frowned.

"They used to terrorise whole villages in the deepest parts of the Goblin realm. Luckily they never ventured too close to the surface, so people just moved away from the creatures and left them alone. The Goblins hoped that if they just went about their lives and never talked about happy bats again, eventually they would stop existing. And thankfully they did, or at least they thought they did."

"But nobody knew why they stopped existing? Did anyone even try looking for them?"

Larah shook her head. "I doubt it. It was too troubling to think about. Much more comforting just to believe that they no longer existed, and not worry about why, or how, or whether it was true."

"And why did they call them happy bats?" asked Petra.

Larah shrugged. "It's a comforting name, I suppose. Better than calling them 'death bats' or something".

"Anything else?" asked Petra, frowning.

"They were vengeful and fierce. And they would hunt in packs. In fact, the legend said they would send one happy bat out to explore, and hopefully it would come back with food. But if it didn't come back, the rest of the pack would track it down. And kill anyone who had harmed it."

"Anyone who had harmed it?" said Soloma instantly. "Great, you mean me. You mean there's going to be a whole pack of those things coming to kill me?"

"It's just a legend," said Larah. "And besides, I'm probably wrong. That thing could be something else."

"Don't worry," said Petra. "We're all here with you if anything happens. But I'm sure we won't see any more of those creatures," she added, based on absolutely nothing.

"Besides," added Fulton. "How would they know you were the one who killed it?"

"They do. They always know," said Larah. "Or so the legend goes."

"But how?"

"Nobody knows," replied Larah. "They're just scary little things. Maybe they can smell the blood of the victim, or they can just tell when someone looks shifty."

"Or so the legend goes…" added Fulton unhelpfully.

Larah nodded. "It will be okay. We should get out of here though."

They picked up the pace, following the tunnel up a gentle incline. They still must have been deep underground, in the middle of nowhere. But at least they were getting gradually closer to the surface.

Ridley seemed to be making every effort to keep up with the rest of them, putting more weight on his leg than before.

They were more alert now. Petra kept looking either side of her for any more signs of light.

It didn't take long. The tunnel suddenly lit up in front of them. It was almost blinding, making the glow from before seem like a tiny firefly.

And the noise. First the flapping, and then the shrieking. It was deafening. Petra didn't know how many of the things were coming towards them, but there were a lot.

They all stopped and braced themselves. Larah and Soloma both grabbed their daggers. Petra stood ready to shoot flames from her hands. Ridley and Fulton just crouched down. They had no weapons and were frankly going to be completely useless.

The creatures swooped down on them like locusts. Petra shot flame after flame at the moving red targets.

But they were too quick. They kept avoiding the fire.

She managed to hit one in the abdomen as it flew. It fell instantly to the floor.

Larah was slashing about with her dagger, but the happy bats weren't coming close enough. In fact, they were only targeting one person.

"Soloma!" cried Larah.

Petra could barely see her Goblin friend amongst the crowd of happy bats that had thrown themselves on top of her. But she could hear the screaming.

In an instant, the creatures had risen into the air again. Petra could just about see one of Soloma's legs among the swarm of animals. A few of the happy bats had picked her up with their teeth and were carrying her away.

Petra started shooting flames at the red mass of creatures, desperately trying to hit some of them. She managed to get one or two, but there were just too many of them – she barely made a dent in the red, glowing sea. She could no longer catch a glimpse of Soloma.

The happy bats were too quick. The red mass started disappearing down the tunnel. Larah chucked her dagger in vain. Fulton shouted 'stop' and 'come back', presumably to make it seem like he was helping.

Petra kept firing, but the target was getting smaller and smaller. And she was struggling to create more flames. She didn't know why, but her hands were losing strength. She was thrusting them forward and hardly any fire was coming out.

Petra and Larah ran down the tunnel, but they both knew it was no use. They could never run anywhere near as quickly as those things could fly. They stopped and turned to each other.

"What can we do?" cried Petra.

Larah didn't say anything. Even in the darkness, Petra could see the tears rolling down her cheeks.

"We can find her," continued the Pixie. "Wherever they have taken her, we'll find them!"

Larah was shaking her head. "You saw what was

happening. Those things don't just capture people and then give them back. They kill them!"

"We don't know she's dead…" added Petra. But as she said it, she realised it was inevitable. She had heard the screams, and she had seen what those creatures were doing. Soloma was gone.

She turned to Larah once again. This time she didn't say anything, and just put her arms round the Goblin. Petra closed her eyes as she could feel them welling up. And she had only known Soloma for a few weeks. She could only imagine what Larah was going through.

"She was a real hero," whispered Petra at last. "She saved us. She saved all of us."

Larah nodded, wiping the tears from her eyes. "She was always there for me, even when we were children. She was always…there."

Petra hugged her again. "I'm so sorry," she said.

They stood there, holding each other closely like a mother and child. Neither one of them wanted to let go.

Ridley and Fulton joined them, walking slowly down the tunnel. They stood there in silence, trying to process what had happened.

"Are you okay?" asked Ridley eventually.

Larah nodded. "No, not at all," she sniffed, drying her eyes. "But I will be."

"What are we going to do?" asked Ridley.

"One night, sometime in the future," began Larah. "I'm going to come back to this very place, with hundreds of people, and weapons. And I'm going to kill every last one of those evil creatures."

Petra nodded.

"But not tonight. Right now, we need to get out of here."

Nobody needed to say anything more. They just turned back up the hill and started walking.

Ridley could feel the pain in his leg getting stronger again. But he kept pushing through it; he could hardly complain about leg pain when he had just seen someone getting eaten alive by furious monsters.

Fulton was still helping him. They were making progress, and every step brought them a little closer to safety. They had to believe that.

Petra and Larah walked further ahead. Despite everything, Larah knew that the group needed her right now. She had to find the route out of these tunnels, and now wasn't the time to grieve.

"You know that I'll come back with you, don't you?" said Petra. "Whenever you return here to kill those creatures, I'll be with you. We'll turn those happy bats into dead bats."

Larah managed to force a smile.

"It will be me and you, and hundreds of soldiers," continued Petra. "With swords and spears, arrows, and much more."

"That sounds good to me," replied Larah. "Happy bats are vicious and terrifying creatures. But if they have one weakness, it's hundreds of fully armed soldiers."

"Is that right?" said Petra, smiling.

"So the legend goes," replied Larah.

Chapter 28

Queen Niella sat on her horse, wondering how it had come to this. A few nights ago, the Human prisoners had escaped. There was panic in the city and talk of a magic Pixie. Everybody had frantically searched high and low for the prisoners.

But they hadn't found them. It was a mystery, really. They had guarded every entrance and exit to the city. Except for the one they escaped from apparently. And perhaps several others.

She was told they had disappeared across a lake, in one of the western borders of Nuberim. And now they were nowhere to be seen.

The queen's immediate response had been to place more soldiers at each exit, to make sure this didn't happen again. The warlords had all agreed that was an excellent idea.

Then one of the warlords had questioned whether there was much point in ensuring it didn't happen again, when the prisoners had already escaped. They were already outside the city, so presumably the chances of them coming back to the jail and escaping a second time were unlikely.

She took a couple of nights to think about it, and then decided to call a lot of them back. The warlords had all agreed that was an excellent idea.

After that, they had continued searching near the city. Then one of the Ogres suggested the prisoners were probably a long way from the city by now. And maybe it would make more sense to think about where they would have gone.

Queen Niella had then gathered a group of intelligent people to try and figure out where they might have been heading. The warlords had all agreed that was an excellent idea.

But the problem with intelligent people is that they're often not very intelligent. They came up with many possible theories as to where the Human prisoners could have gone. The obvious answer would have been the Human realm, maybe Stonem or Peria. But that was probably too obvious – they would get caught.

So they might have gone somewhere completely different, where nobody would expect them to go. Like the Ogre realm, or even somewhere in Troll lands. That was unlikely, but then the Humans probably knew that they would think it was unlikely, so maybe that's exactly where they went.

This intelligent logic meant that the Humans must have gone to either the most obvious places in the Known World, the least obvious places in the Known World, or somewhere in between. In other words, they could have been anywhere.

This meant there was really no point in trying to find them. But they did know where some other Humans were. The governor of Lancha had recently fled the city, which had apparently been taken over by King Wyndham and his soldiers.

So the queen had decided to go to Lancha. Maybe the king of the Humans knew where the prisoners were hiding. Maybe he was hiding them himself. Or maybe it was time to forget about the prisoners, and just attack them. The warlords weren't so sure, but the Ogres all agreed this was an excellent idea. Especially Lord Protector Higarth. In his view, attacking Humans was always an excellent idea.

That's how Queen Niella now found herself riding on a horse to Lancha, accompanied by a thousand Goblin soldiers. And alongside them, another two thousand Ogre soldiers marched in unison.

The queen surveyed her surroundings. It was quite a sight; archers, sword and spear soldiers, mounted soldiers, really any kind of soldier she could think of. And it wasn't just the soldiers. There were torch holders on all sides of her, lighting up the night sky, and reacting with the moisture in the air to create a thick layer of smoke around them.

To her left, the Goblin drummers were beating in unison, creating a low thud every second. Horn blowers would occasionally join in, just to make a bit more noise. She could hear some general chatter, and even laughter amongst the troops. It almost felt like a party, not a march to battle.

Every so often a chant would start amongst the Goblin foot soldiers. They were famous for them across the Known World. In ages past, people would quiver and hide in fear whenever they heard a Goblin war chant. She heard another one start:

The Known World will always know the Goblins,
As the greatest, fiercest and the best,
The Known World will always fear the Goblins,
As the Goblins are better than the rest

The Known World will marvel at the Goblins,
As they see the strength of Goblin hands,
The Known World will tremble at the Goblins,
As we're the greatest soldiers in the land

Terrifying stuff. Niella could only imagine the sense of dread that Humans, Elves and Pixies must have when hearing these words in the distance.

She adjusted the silver plating around her shoulders, to let a bit of air in through her neck. She wasn't used to wearing armour, and it was always uncomfortable.

While her staff were dressing her, they had insisted that she wear a thick, woolly robe underneath. Apparently, it was a substance called 'cotton wool' and it would make her extra safe, just like all the blankets she had been given before. She had agreed, since everyone seemed so sure. But wearing it did make her feel rather hot.

Another chant started further behind her:

Who are the greatest soldiers?
The Goblins! The Goblins!
Who are the weakest soldiers?
Everyone else! Everyone else!

Who are the fiercest soldiers?
The Goblins! The Goblins!
Who are the least fierce soldiers?
Everyone else! Everyone else!

The queen nodded. She looked across to her right, where she could see the Ogre soldiers a few hundred yards away. Their troops were taller and stockier, but they made very little noise.

They had no drummers, and hardly any horn blowers. They didn't even start any chants and made no attempt to try to correct the Goblins as to which soldiers were in fact the best. They just kept their heads down and marched.

The queen still didn't trust the Ogres and was worried about how this was all going to play out. But she couldn't help feeling inspired to see Goblins and Ogres marching side by side. She knew this hadn't happened in a long time.

They were making good progress, travelling above the ground each night to make use of the space. The dry plains to the south of Nuberim continued for miles and miles. They were almost flat, with a slight downward slope making it even easier to travel across.

They would probably make it to Lancha in another two nights. That was easy enough. But Niella had no idea what was going to happen when they got there. It wasn't just the prisoners, or the fact that Humans were occupying a Goblin city. Or even the death of their kings.

It was about the magic Pixie. The queen was getting more and more convinced that she was real. And this one Pixie had the potential to destroy the whole of the Known World. Another chant was breaking out.

What do we think of Elves?
Rubbish!
What do we think of Humans?
Rubbish!
What do we think of Goblins?
Awesome!

We are the Goblins, the mighty Goblins,
We are awesome, and we are green,
We are the strongest, we are the greatest,
That the Known World has ever seen

The queen smiled. The Humans were probably going to turn and flee as soon as they heard the Goblins singing.

Chapter 29

King Wyndham looked to his left, and then his right. A beautiful starry night. He could hear the howl of the wind around him. The air felt fresh and cool, somehow different than usual. There was no ground beneath his feet – he was somehow high in the sky.

Of course. He was on a unicorn again. It hardly seemed strange anymore. Wyndham smiled as he stroked the soft, white mane in front of him, while gripping it tightly with his other hand.

He studied the animal carefully. It seemed the same as the one in his previous dreams. He wondered if he should give it a name, but then shook his head. There was no time for messing around; it may have been a dream, but he had to get down to business. He needed to find those houses again – the ones from his previous dreams.

The unicorn seemed to swoop downwards without any instruction. Wyndham held the mane tightly, but he wasn't afraid. He was used to this by now, and you don't tend to worry about dying if you know it's a dream.

As the animal brought him closer to the ground, he surveyed the landscape once more. It looked quite bare this time, nothing but flat plains as far as he could see. The moon lit up the dull brown land below him. Wyndham thought he recognised this place. Maybe he had been here before.

Something was different. The unicorn was slowing down, but it didn't seem to be stopping. The land was getting closer and closer towards him.

He felt a thud as the animal touched the ground. He let out a slight scream at the same time; he knew it was a dream, but it was starting to feel more real now. The unicorn turned its head indignantly, as if to say 'you stupid Human'.

"Sorry," he said to the animal.

It turned its head and started walking forwards. King Wyndham looked around, barely holding onto the unicorn anymore.

The plains around him were so vast. He could see the horizon in every direction. This was no Human land – he was probably somewhere East. The Goblin realm? That was it. These must have been the plains to the north of Lancha; he had been here a few times on the way to visit King Grieber, back when the Goblin was still alive.

But he had never come here on a unicorn, obviously. Why would his dreams take him to this place? There was nothing here. That was why the Goblin plains were famous – because there was nothing interesting about them whatsoever.

The unicorn started trotting, gradually picking up the pace. Wyndham wasn't giving it any instruction – it seemed to know exactly where it was going.

The stone buildings appeared at a distance. Then the unicorn started to sprint. Wyndham held on tightly. He could see the structures getting bigger and bigger. In no time at all, they were right in front of him.

The animal stopped abruptly. There were three buildings on one side of them, and three on the other. Every one of them was identical – square, two stories high, with holes for windows on each side. And they were all empty. It was quite a chilling scene – so quiet, except for the howl of the wind.

"Come on," he whispered to no-one.

He didn't know what he was waiting for, but something was going to happen to these buildings. He dismounted the unicorn and started to pace across the land, in the stone structures on either side of him.

He felt a rumbling below. The ground seemed to be vibrating, almost like an earthquake. He had to catch himself as something sprang up in front of his eyes. A wall of stone was rising from the ground, running straight between the two sets of buildings.

In no time at all, it towered above him, blocking his

sight. He couldn't even see the tops of the three buildings ahead of him anymore – they had completely disappeared. The wall was now so high that he couldn't see the top of it. He couldn't even tell if it was still growing.

Where was the unicorn? It must have been on the other side of the wall. He thought he could hear the patter of its hooves. Wyndham tried to call out to it, but he didn't know what to say. He realised that it might have been a good idea to give it a name after all.

"Unicorn? Unicorn!" he cried.

But it was no use, and he felt ridiculous. This was only a dream...wasn't it?

He peered behind at the three buildings he could still see. They looked the same as before. None of them were setting alight, or turning green, like in his previous dreams. They just stood there, minding their own business.

Wyndham felt something below his feet. The ground seemed to be crumbling as if it were struggling to take his weight. The land was opening up below him. He tried to catch his footing, but everything was moving too fast. He suddenly felt himself falling into the void that was eating away at the ground.

He cried out in vain for the unicorn once more. But he could no longer hear anything. The view of moonlit sky above became smaller and smaller, as he fell deeper into this endless hole. It was just darkness. He could no longer see anything. Or do anything. He just braced himself, knowing he could hit something hard at any moment.

King Wyndham awoke with a jolt. He saw the posts of his bed, and the mirror in front of him. The tunnel lit torches through the window. The streets of Lancha. He was back in the real world.

"Sire?" called Cecil, as he burst through the door. "Is everything okay?"

"Yes, fine," snapped Wyndham. "Why would you enter my bedroom without knocking?"

"Well I was outside, and I overheard you saying

'unicorn, unicorn, I should have named my unicorn'. And I thought that was a little strange, so I came in to check if you were all right."

"I am fine," repeated King Wyndham. "I was just having a dream. Another very vivid dream."

Cecil frowned. "What was it about? Did it mean anything?"

Wyndham thought for a moment. "I saw the buildings again. This time they were separated by a wall. And then a hole appeared."

"I see," replied Cecil. "What do you think that signifies?"

"I have no idea. But if we ever figure out how to tame unicorns, and I get the chance to ride one, make sure I give it a name."

Cecil nodded, not knowing what else to say. He had been the Lord of War in the Human realm for many years. And his vast experience had taught him that if he didn't know what to do, it was best just to agree with whatever the King said.

"I need some water," said King Wyndham.

"Yes, I agree, good idea," replied Cecil. "I'll ask Robsun to send you some."

"Thanks," replied Wyndham. "Before you go, how are all the troops doing? I haven't visited the barracks in days. Are they coping okay with the death of those soldiers?"

Cecil nodded. "They are doing fine, sire. They're not commiserating anymore – they're celebrating!"

"Celebrating what?"

"Well, the capture of this city!" replied the Lord of War.

King Wyndham frowned. "Are you serious?" he said. "Cecil, we've talked about this. The Governor fled the city, but he wasn't supposed to. It's all been a big misunderstanding."

"Well yes, sire," replied Cecil. "But you've still captured the city."

"I didn't want to capture the city!" growled King

Wyndham. "It's not something to celebrate!"

"Yes, sire," said Cecil again. "But see the soldiers disagree. They would much prefer to celebrate something than not to celebrate something. Celebrating is much more fun."

The King sighed.

"So we thought it made sense to treat is as a victory, for the sake of their morale," continued Cecil. "A tremendous victory really. Very few casualties, and nobody even lost their weapons."

"But we didn't do anything!" said Wyndham. "We just turned up and all the Goblins left."

"Exactly. We've captured a city whilst doing very little actual fighting. It's quite impressive when you think about it. One of the most efficient battles we've ever fought."

Wyndham put his hands over his head. "Cecil, I've sent messengers to try and find the governor of Lancha. If he comes back, I'll explain what's happened and tell him the city belongs to the Goblins."

"It's up to you sire, but if you do that, it's best not to tell the troops. Better just to let them keep celebrating, and pretending the city is still ours. Otherwise it might seem like we lost after all. And the troops don't like losing, it's not good for morale."

The Lord of War left, with King Wyndham still scratching his head. A few moments later, Robsun knocked and opened the door. He was a young guard, whose job mainly consisted of standing still.

"Your water, sire," said Robsun.

As he opened the door, a servant stepped through it and handed the King a goblet.

"We'll be bringing your food in shortly sire," said the servant. "And if I might say, many congratulations on your tremendous victory."

"Perhaps we should call you 'Governor of Lancha' from now on, sire," added Robsun.

Wyndham nodded and forced a smile.

Chapter 30

Petra sat and stared out of the entrance to their cave, trying to spot where the walls ended and the outside world began. It was too dark to tell the difference. It was her turn to be lookout while the rest of the group slept, and there was nothing to do but sit and think.

She was finding it hard to remember the daylight. She had lost track of how long they had been underground, wandering through endless tunnels. It was very disorientating. The Goblins could have at least put up a few signposts or something.

The young Pixie felt permanently tired. Morale was low across the whole group. They continued to trundle through tunnels, taking breaks to sleep and eat whatever little provisions they still had. Most of the time they just walked in silence.

Since Soloma was gone, it meant they had to carry all her stuff. Petra could hardly complain in the circumstances, but it was still an extra burden. Soloma had carried more than her share – they had to divide it between them, and Ridley was still injured so couldn't really help. It meant that Petra had saddled a lot of the load herself.

Larah seemed to be struggling most of all. The bright eyes and toothy smile had all but disappeared. She had seen one of her closest friends snatched away by a swarm of hideous creatures, never to be seen again. That kind of thing can really wipe the smile off someone's face.

Petra had started to wonder if Larah even knew where they were going anymore. And that was quite important, since none of the rest of them had any idea. They could have been going round and round in circles for all Petra knew.

She closed her eyes, just for a second. It would all be

over soon. One day she would be back in the open air. She would be somewhere safe. She would see Samorus again, and maybe even make a few more vials of healing potion for old time's sake. The wars and conflict would all be over, and she could use her powers to help people however she needed to. She didn't know how soon, but it would happen.

She felt her eyes start to water and wiped them both with her hand. Everything had been so hard, but she knew she just had to keep going. Her mum used to say that the worst thing you can do is give up, unless of course you're a murderer, in which case it was the best thing you could do.

She thought she could hear a rustling noise nearby, coming from inside the cave. It was probably fine, just one of the group moving about. But in total darkness it was hard to tell. Then she heard a whisper.

"Petra? Are you there?"

It was Fulton. She could recognise his voice by now – slightly smoother and higher pitched than Ridley's.

Petra nodded. Then realised he obviously couldn't see her and replied softly "I'm here."

"Is it okay if I sit with you?" whispered the young Human.

"Of course," replied Petra, drying her eyes.

She heard him moving nearby and could just about make out his silhouette in the blackness.

"Couldn't sleep?" she asked.

Fulton shook his head, although Petra couldn't see it.

"No," he replied, still in a whisper. "I'm just finding it hard to do anything right now – eat, sleep, even breathing is a struggle in some of these tunnels."

"I know how you feel," replied the Pixie.

"Still," continued Fulton. "It's still better than in the prison. At least I can move around when I want to, and I'm not stuck in one place all the time."

"Yes it must be nice having a change of scenery, from one dark tunnel to another slightly lighter one every now and again."

Fulton laughed quietly.

"I don't think I ever properly thanked you for saving me," he said.

Now Petra laughed. "You definitely have. You must have thanked me at least ten times since we've left the city."

"Well maybe," he replied. "But you never really told me why. Why did you do it? You're the most magical and powerful person in the whole of the Known World. You could have done anything. What made you go to a dangerous prison in the middle of the Goblin kingdom, to save a couple of Humans?"

Petra took a breath.

"Because it was the right thing to do. And...because one of those Humans was you," she said.

Fulton paused.

"You mean you didn't want to save Ridley?" he asked.

"Of course I did, that's not what I meant. I wanted to save him too, but he wasn't the person I kept thinking about. He wasn't the person who gave me strength every time I thought about giving up. He wasn't the person who I travelled across half of the Known World for. You were."

Petra took another breath. She could feel herself blushing, even though there was no way the young Human could see it.

"I had a lot of time to think about things when I was stuck in prison," said Fulton, still whispering. "But back in Peria, I don't have a family. I don't really have a lot of friends, just a few close ones. Most of the time I wasn't wishing to be back in my cottage, or the local Tavern. I was just...wishing I would see you again."

Petra reached out to the young Human, and fumbled a bit until she found his hand. He grabbed hers back, tightly. His hands were so much bigger than hers, so he was practically covering it.

Fulton looked up at Petra. She could make out his pale blue eyes, even in the dark.

"You travelled across half of the Known World for

me," continued Fulton. "Just so you know...I would travel from one side to the other, and then back again, and circle all the way round it three times, for you."

"I would rather you didn't," said Petra, smiling. "But thank you."

She edged closer and put her other hand on Fulton's shoulder. She felt the warmth of his body beneath the cotton top he was wearing.

She leaned her head forward slowly, and her cheek came in contact with Fulton's soft beard. She brought her head up and started to kiss him. The young Human put his hand around her neck and brought her in even closer. Petra wasn't sure how long it lasted, or what was going to happen next. But she knew she wasn't going to forget this moment.

When the kissing came to an end, she wrapped both her arms around Fulton and held them there. She could feel the young Human's breath on her neck.

People would often say that love was the strongest force in the whole of the Known World. Those people had probably never seen an Ogre scorpion – a deadly weapon which could break stone walls in a matter of seconds. Admittedly, love wasn't strong enough to do that.

But to Petra, right now, it was all that mattered. She wasn't thinking about war, or dark tunnels, or even how lonely she had felt just a few moments ago. She was just trying to savour every second.

Eventually she let go and crouched back again in front of the young Human.

"Maybe one day," said Fulton, "we could circle around the Known World together?"

"Maybe," said Petra, smiling. "Let's stay above the ground though. I feel like I've seen enough tunnels to last a lifetime."

Fulton laughed. "Yes, definitely," he replied. "And I wouldn't mind taking a break before doing any more travelling. But one day, I would love to see the Elves in the north, and the Lonergan mountains. I've heard there's a lake up there which is so clear you can't even see it. You just walk into a hole and suddenly find yourself swimming."

Petra laughed.

"And I'd love to see more of the Pixie realm too. Visit the White Castle in the south."

"The White Castle is amazing, you really would love it," said Petra, still beaming. "I'd love to see some of the castles in the Human realm too."

Fulton nodded. "They're building round ones these days, in the north of the realm. Apparently it's the latest fashion amongst the lords; square castles are getting too old and boring. Buildings with corners are considered 'so 13th Age'."

Petra heard another rustling behind her, and then a loud groan.

"What's going on?" came Larah's voice, sounding slightly panicked.

"Don't worry," replied Ridley's voice from behind her. "It's just Petra and Fulton kissing."

"Kissing? Oh for the gods' sake," said Larah. "Guys, if you're going to be all romantic, please do it a bit more quietly. I'm trying to sleep!"

Fulton chuckled.

"And could you try and keep guard at the same time, so we don't all get killed by monsters?" added Larah.

"Sorry," replied Petra, still smiling, and keeping her eyes on the young Human.

Chapter 31

War isn't a game. Or at least it isn't a very fun one. It's only fun for the winners, and even then, only the ones who manage to stay alive at the end of it. In fact, whether there are winners in war is somewhat debatable. The High Elf of Lanthyn once claimed that there were only ever losers, and other losers who didn't lose quite as badly.

This theory was widely discredited during the 7th Age when the Lord of the People famously declared war on poverty. After that, a famine began in the realm, which was followed by a series of crime waves. Ten miserable years later it was generally accepted that poverty had actually won.

But even though war wasn't fun, or enjoyable, and there were very few winners, it still happened a lot in the Known World. There were a few benefits of wars, obviously. They helped to solve problems of overpopulation, gave soldiers something to do, and people often got interesting stories out of them. Occasionally they served a purpose in tackling injustices or solving conflicts. But most of the time, they were completely and utterly pointless.

King Wyndham didn't know how they had got here, but here they were. A few hours ago, a scout had spotted a few Goblins and Ogres on their way to the city. A short while later, another scout came back and reported that there were a few more Goblins and Ogres than they previously expected.

And a short while later still, a third scout had confirmed that there were a rather a lot more Goblins and Ogres than they previously expected. And in fact, there were thousands of fully armed soldiers on their way to Lancha.

"We'll straighten this out," the Lord of Peace had said. "There is clearly a misunderstanding. The army will arrive and we'll explain that we never meant to capture this city. We'll just give it back."

"We can't just give it back," the Lord of War had replied. "What kind of message would that send? The troops would be devastated. And the Goblins will think they can just turn up and we'll give them what they want."

He had a point. Although he was missing something; in fact, both lords were. It wasn't just Goblins coming here – it was Ogres. And these Ogres had already attacked them twice; they had killed some of his soldiers and kidnapped the magic Pixie. Petra was lost somewhere, and presumably in trouble.

The Lord of War was right, for once, but for the wrong reasons; they couldn't just abandon Lancha and retreat. They had to stand and fight, but not just for the city. For Petra.

Wyndham looked over at Prince Vardie, who had a stern look on his face. Not surprising really – he had hundreds of Pixie soldiers prepared for a battle, which was looking more and more likely to happen.

The leader of the Humans and the prince of the Pixies sat on their horses, surveying the troops around them. Vardie was on a smaller pony, since he was too short to ride a fully grown horse. But that didn't make him any less important, as the Prince was always keen to point out – what Pixies lacked in size, they made up for in other ways, presumably.

The land around them was too flat. It made it difficult to make any kind of tactical planning at all – they couldn't try to use altitude or divert the enemy troops into a bottleneck. They just had to stand there and fight each other.

"Do you think there's any chance that the Goblins and Ogres will go underground?" said Prince Vardie.

"Definitely," replied Wyndham. "But I think we need to keep our army above the ground, where it's safest."

"What if they tunnel underground, then come back up behind us?"

"We'll just have to turn round," said Wyndham.

Vardie didn't even smile. There was nothing to smile about. He looked at the rows of Pixie soldiers in front of him. There were about a hundred mounted fighters, all sitting on white ponies, clad in silver chainmail and cream-coloured cloaks.

Then there were the four foot soldiers. There were hundreds of them, but they were only four feet tall. They weren't huge fans of the nickname, but it had somehow stuck. And behind them stood the galciers – the Pixies' secret weapon. They were soldiers too but experienced in the arts of alchemy. They carried orbs of a mysterious powder, only recently developed, which could create sparks and white light when thrown.

The galciers wore white chainmail too but covered themselves in dark red cloaks. Just to make themselves look even more mysterious.

Prince Vardie sighed. All these soldiers were highly trained, but hardly any of them had fought in a real battle. The only real way to practice fighting an Ogre was to actually fight one; they were almost twice the size of an average Pixie, so just practicing amongst themselves didn't really help.

And there was only so much progress they could make with dummies. Ages ago, Arpola, one of the Pixie captains, once suggested they try and get a volunteer Ogre to practice on. Everyone agreed this was a great idea in principle, but there was surely no chance they would ever find one.

Arpola thought it was worth a try, so he had travelled to the Ogre realm and asked the Lord Protector if he could spare one of their soldiers to practice on. And thereby get better at fighting Ogres in case they ever needed to.

"I'll bring an Ogre to the Pixie realm, don't you worry," he had said.

Arpola never came back, but a few days later a large army of Ogres came to the Pixie realm and slaughtered quite a few of their soldiers. It wasn't a great outcome, although technically the captain did succeed in getting an Ogre to the realm. And those Pixies who survived did get some good practice.

They never tried it again.

King Wyndham looked to his left, surveying the Human army. The Lord of War was in his usual position – towards the back, so he could oversee the troops, and not do any fighting himself. Then there were the archers, the sword fighters and the spearmen.

And in front of them, nothing but barren, flat land.

At first, Wyndham could hear a lot of chat amongst the soldiers, and even some laughter. But gradually it had all died down, and now he could barely hear a word. Everyone seemed to be standing in silence. Just waiting for the enemy to appear.

As Wyndham squinted, he thought he could see something moving on the horizon. A distant grey line started to growth thicker, and darker. Soon he was able to make out a few shields and spears. And then the sound of drums and footsteps – faint at first, but getting ever louder, and more menacing.

There was no doubting it now. The Goblins and Ogres were coming.

They made their way quickly towards his soldiers in a steady march. Horns were blowing, and Wyndham could soon hear orders being shouted in the distance.

The soldiers at the front came to a halt, leaving a gap of about 50 yards. This was the line which separated his own troops from the Ogres and Goblins. The thin line between peace and war. Between heroes and villains. Between one group of people who had certain views about the world, and another group of people who had slightly different views about the world. And they were about to kill each other over it.

Wyndham could see two figures emerging from among his army, making their way towards the middle of the action. He sighed. Wenda was not used to this. Delivering messages was never an easy job, but she didn't usually have thousands of Ogre soldiers glaring at her while she was doing it.

Right now she was in the most dangerous place in the Known World. Fully armed troops stood in two long lines facing each other, and she was standing right in the middle of them.

Diggins was beside her. He was there to represent the Pixies – dark haired, dressed in a white cloak, and obviously the smaller of the two. The King could only just about make out the two figures from his vantage point, so he couldn't see or hear what was going on. But he imagined they both looked rather worried.

"What if they don't send anyone?" whispered Prince Vardie. "What if they just shoot them?"

"It won't happen. You don't shoot the messenger; everyone in the Known World follows that rule. Remember the wars that happened back in the Seventh Age, when the messengers kept getting killed when they arrived? And that meant nobody knew why they were fighting, or if the war was even happening anymore."

As he spoke, he could see two figures walking towards their messengers: a tall, fierce looking Ogre, and a slightly smaller, slightly less fierce looking Goblin.

Wyndham could feel himself shaking. Thousands of lives rested on what was going to happen next.

The four figures stopped, standing opposite each other. Nobody seemed to be moving a muscle.

"What are they saying?" whispered Wyndham to Prince Vardie. "What can you hear with your Pixie ears?"

"Nothing more than your Human ears, Wyndham," replied the Prince. "Just because we have slightly larger ears doesn't mean we can hear any better. It's just a stereotype!"

"Sorry," whispered the King.

The figures moved away from each other. He could see Wenda and Diggins make their way back to their troops. The discussions didn't last long. Probably not a good sign.

The soldiers parted in two, making a path for the

messengers to come through. The Ogres and Goblins were doing the same on their side.

The messengers started to walk briskly, back towards their leaders. They seemed to be hurrying.

"Can you see their faces yet?" said King Wyndham. "Do they look happy with the outcome?"

"I don't know, what do you see with your Human eyes?" retorted Vardie.

Wyndham didn't respond. He waited silently until the messengers were right in front of them.

"Sire," said Wenda, panting slightly.

"My Prince," added Diggins, straight afterwards.

"What happened?" said the King and the Prince simultaneously.

Wenda shared a glance with her fellow messenger before responding.

"Well the Ogre messenger started straight away. He said that the Lord Protector and Queen of the Goblins demand we leave the city."

"They weren't wasting any time. They didn't even say their names," added Diggins. "A little rude if I'm honest."

"Well, that's not surprising."

Wenda nodded.

"And then the Goblin told us to give back the two Human prisoners who killed their king."

Wyndham frowned.

"But we don't have them; they're in prison in the Goblin realm?"

"Apparently they escaped," continued Wenda. "We told the messengers we knew nothing about it. We said we would promise to keep an eye out for them."

"And they also demanded that we give them Petra," added Diggins.

"But we were demanding that they give *us* Petra!" growled Vardie.

"They don't have her," continued the Pixie messenger.

"But neither do we!" added Vardie. "So where is she?"

King Wyndham paused. "They may be lying to us. But

if the Ogres really don't have Petra, then it's a good thing. She could be anywhere, but at least she's not in the hands of the enemy."

"Yes, but even leaving that aside, we demanded that they give her to us," said Prince Vardie. "And they're demanding we give her to them. Neither side can agree to these demands. So the fight has to happen, it's inevitable."

King Wyndham nodded. "It was going to happen anyway." He turned back to Wenda. "Did you tell the Ogres about our final demand?"

"Yes sire," said Wenda. "I said that we demand they go back to the Ogre realm and leave the Goblins alone."

"And what happened?"

"The Ogre messenger laughed in our faces. The Goblin messenger seemed to feign a smile."

"And that was the end," added Diggins. "They went back to tell their leaders and ask them whether they can agree to the terms."

"They won't agree to our terms," said Vardie.

"And we don't agree to theirs!" bellowed Wyndham, letting his voice echo loudly across the troops standing all around him.

Vardie nodded, raising his sword in the air. King Wyndham did the same. He could just about make out Higarth and Queen Niella raising their swords on the other side of the battlefield. This was the symbolic gesture to show that they were not happy with the negotiation.

That was it. Shouts and cries echoed all around them. The front-line Ogre and Goblin soldiers started charging towards the Humans and Pixies.

It had begun.

Chapter 32

"Push! Harder! Faster!" shouted Lord Protector Higarth.

He had a decent view of the battlefield from the rock he stood on. But it was difficult to tell what was happening.

His Ogre pike soldiers had rushed forward, and dust covered the air. The Humans were keeping them at bay, but surely they wouldn't hold on for long.

As the dust started to clear he saw one Ogre stab his pike through two Humans at once. But as he tried to take out his weapon, it seemed to get stuck. Another Human came from behind them and slashed his sword across the Ogre's neck. That was bad luck, nothing more than that.

Higarth ducked as an arrow came close to his head. Probably some stupid Human trying to be a hero. There was no chance of that – even the Gods couldn't pierce his armour with an arrow from that distance.

"Lang!" he shouted to his general. "Where are the flaming axe soldiers?"

"On it, Lord Protector," he called back.

Higarth looked to his left and saw a line of flames moving forward from the back. Each Ogre carrying an axe which had been doused in oil and set alight. They stopped just behind the front line, about ten feet away from the Humans.

"Fire," came a call from further back.

The axes all flew up at once, lighting up the sky before crashing down among the Human swordsmen. Higarth thought he could hear shrieking, even from such a distance.

Some of the Human soldiers at the front line seemed to turn round at the commotion. That just made it easier for the Ogres to pounce.

Another round of flaming axes was already in place, as the Ogres who had thrown their weapons moved to the back of the line. They had got this system running perfectly.

"Fire!" came the call again, and another wave of flames shot up in the air.

Higarth smiled. "Is this it?" he muttered to himself. "Surely you can do better than this, Wyndham."

Unfortunately for the Lord Protector, Wyndham could do better than this. As soon as he spoke, he saw the Human sword fighters start to part in two, leaving a gap right in the middle. And then came the rumbling of hooves.

The mounted knights galloped forward, taking the Ogre pike soldiers by surprise. They couldn't get in position in time, and were knocked back like leaves caught in a gale. The flash of steel swords shone through the dust they were creating.

It was over as soon as it began. Someone must have shouted something as the horses rushed back in the direction they came from. The foot soldiers came together to close the gap, and once again held their line against the Ogres. This was the cavalry's first charge. And there would be more.

The Ogre axe throwers didn't seem phased. Higarth could see another round of flaming weapons moving forward. Once again they hurled them at the shrieking crowd of Humans.

The pike soldiers continued to hold their ground, trying to fend off the Human swords. But they were now alerted to the cavalry and were ready for another charge. Sure enough, the Human troops started to move apart again, forming a gap down the middle.

This time the Ogres didn't wait. Those nearest the gap started to run straight for it, trying to breach the lines before the horsemen had a chance to charge. There were probably fifty Ogres who managed to break through.

But no horsemen came. The Human sword fighters seemed to close the gap again, stopping any further Ogres coming through. And the ones who did were now trapped, fighting Humans on all sides. Those Ogres were courageous, but now completely helpless. It didn't take the Humans long to slaughter them, with their bodies disappearing beneath the swarm of soldiers.

Higarth looked around and caught Chandimer's eye just below him.

"Tell them to hold their ground!" he bellowed. "They move forward as a unit, or not at all!"

"Yes, Lord Protector," said Chandimer. "Although I think they know that now! Well the ones who are still alive do…"

"Hey!" cried Queen Niella, who was standing to the left of the Lord Protector and looking completely the other way. She was clad in magnificent silver armour from head to toe, with her white hair tucked into her helmet. She looked unusually large, as if she had some sort of padding beneath the armour.

The queen's focus was on her Goblins, who were fighting it out on the left of the battlefield.

It was mostly Pixies on that side, just as they had planned. Let the Goblins take on the weaker opposition. Surely even Goblins could defeat the Pixies.

Except, apparently, they couldn't. Figures dressed in white were gaining ground on them. Quickly. The queen jumped off the rock and rushed towards one of her warlords. Hopefully they would be able to clean up this mess without the Ogres' help.

There didn't seem to be many Goblin soldiers fighting. Higarth frowned. Surely they hadn't lost that many people already. What was going on?

"Charge!" came a loud voice, forcing Higarth to turn back to the centre of the battlefield. It was the Human horsemen again, though this time there were more of them, and they seemed to be ploughing even further into the Ogre army.

"Surround them! Cut them off!" shouted Higarth to nobody in particular. He was hoping the Ogres could use the Humans' tactics against them. But it didn't work – once again the cavalry just seemed to run back again behind the foot soldiers. Only a handful of horses were taken down.

"Lord Protector!" cried Lang from the bottom of the rock. "Should we change formation? We have soldiers at the back who could form a pincer and attack the Humans and Pixies on both sides."

Higarth shook his head. "We don't have enough people for that. We risk thinning out the troops in the centre and letting the Humans run straight through."

"Yes, Lord Protector," replied Lang, nodding. "But we have to do something!"

Higarth felt a drop of rain on his arm. He looked up and saw black clouds taking over the sky. The flaming axes would soon be less effective. Lang was right; it was time to try something else.

"Pull the axe throwers back, and bring in another layer of pikemen instead," he began. "They need to hold a firm line, with pikes up at all times so no horses can get through."

It didn't take his general long. By the time the rain had started pouring down, the flaming axes had been replaced with a row of pikes. The fighting at the front line was still in full force, but a few rows behind them everyone was still. The pikemen all held their weapons firmly, blunt end in the ground, and sharp end facing forward. It was like a line of barbed wire facing the enemy. No horses were going to penetrate this without suffering serious casualties.

It worked. Higarth waited, feeling the rain battering his helmet, but no more charges came. The mounted soldiers must have seen the pikes and pulled back.

The Humans at the front line were losing momentum. Ogre troops were once again making strides against their counterparts. They seemed to be pushing forward and gaining a few yards on the enemy. But without the horses charging, King Wyndham was going to try something else. And it came in the form of arrows. Lots of them.

Throughout the battle Higarth had seen arrows flying all around. But now they were more focused – the Human archers were targeting one small part of the battlefield at a time. And it made a big impact.

Higarth saw a flood of arrows fall about a hundred yards in front of him. The Ogres were fully clad from head to toe in armour. But with such a barrage of arrows coming at once, the effects were devastating. Enough Ogres were killed that a gap appeared on the battlefield. Higarth thought he could even see the arrows piling up on top of the bodies.

He cursed that they were fighting above ground. If they were in tunnels the Human archers would have been less effective. But it did also give them one advantage. And it was time to use it.

"Chandimer!" he barked. "Get the scorpion within range."

His general gave a wide smile, and rushed towards the back of the battlefield.

Chapter 33

"Out of my way, please!" growled Queen Niella, as she made her way through the Goblin soldiers to the far left of the battlefield.

She took off her silver helmet to brush the water away from her face. The shouts of Goblin soldiers were deafening. She could see mounted Pixie soldiers far away to her right, making strides into their front line.

"My queen!" came a voice behind her. It was Warlord Sepping. He was standing strong but clearly had a cut on his arm. Even this far back from the front they were struggling.

"What happened?" she asked, looking at the arm.

"Oh this is nothing," he said. "Just an arrow. I think it came from the Humans."

The queen turned round to the other side of the battlefield. Arrows seemed to be falling like a waterfall onto a small group of Ogre soldiers.

"They can reach this far?" she gasped.

The warlord nodded. Niella put her helmet back on.

"It's okay, they're focusing on the Ogres," said Sepping. "We need to concentrate on these Pixies right now!"

The queen turned round again. Something was happening. She thought she could hear people murmuring around her. A few lights seemed to appear behind the Pixie ponies. They were circular, like orbs, flashing brighter than any flame. People must have been throwing them.

"What are those?" asked Niella.

"It must be the galciers," replied Sepping, as he stood frozen to the spot. "These Pixies don't just fight with weapons. They fight with the magic arts."

She gulped. This was something new. Anything could

be coming out of those terrifying orbs. Absolutely anything.

One of them exploded with a bang. A loud bang. A cloud of shiny dust shot upwards, lighting up the night sky. Even the rain didn't seem to get in the way.

The queen took a breath. This dazzling display was high up. But now the dust cloud was coming down. What was going to happen when they hit the ground? She heard another few bangs, as more of the things were bursting open.

As the shiny dust descended, the light seemed to fade. In fact, the dust seemed to disappear completely, maybe just dissolving in the air.

Niella looked around. The other soldiers seemed just as confused. The explosions were deafening and the lights were amazing, but they had all faded before reaching the ground.

It was an impressive display of lights, but nothing more. Some of the soldiers even started clapping. Probably not the reaction the Pixies were hoping for.

"Maybe they threw them too high," said the queen.

"Maybe it was just a distraction," added Sepping.

The clapping seemed to spur the galciers on. More and more of the mysterious orbs were being thrown into the sky.

Niella could feel the vibrations on the ground as a group of mounted Pixies seemed to burst through the crowd. If the lights were a distraction, it worked. The Goblin foot soldiers were slow to get their swords in position.

It took them a scarily long time to cut the ponies down. The last one must have come within about ten yards of the queen herself.

She shuddered.

"We're really struggling, my queen," panted Sepping, getting his breath back. "We can't wait much longer for the diggers."

Niella nodded. They had sent a lot of their soldiers below ground. Maybe too many.

"We just have to hold on," she replied. "The first of them should start to come back up soon."

It was the perfect plan. If anyone saw Goblins disappearing below ground, they would assume they were going to reappear behind the Humans and Pixies. Surround them on both sides.

But that wasn't the plan at all. The Goblin soldiers were tunnelling just below the surface. One by one they were creating a great chasm below the ground. The very ground that the Humans and Pixies were standing on.

"What do we do until then?" said Sepping.

The queen looked around. Another wave of arrows was piling on a group of soldiers. It wasn't just Ogres this time – Goblins were getting hit too.

"Where are the crows?" she replied.

The rain was easing. Niella could see the air around her clearing. A few of the birds were starting to circle above the crowds.

Crows had a special relationship with the Goblins. They were one of the few birds that often like to travel underground. They had a certain loyalty and trust which never seemed to falter. A bit like a dog for a Human, or General Chandimer for the Lord Protector of the Ogres.

When the birds saw hundreds of Goblins marching to war, they had followed. And now it was time for the Goblin army to make the most of that fact.

"Alert the slingers," Sepping called to one of his nearby captains.

"Right away," came the response. Sepping then started to barge through the Goblin foot soldiers in a hurry.

Most slingers in the army would hurl rocks at the enemy. Small, dense stones could be slung from a great distance and cause a lot of damage. But the Goblin warlords had other tricks up their grey, embroidered sleeves. A select few stones hidden in the slingers' bags were covered in something much more deadly. Worms.

It only took a few slings deep into the Pixie ranks. The crows started swooping towards them. A stone would land and a handful of crows would be flapping around it, causing chaos for all the Pixie soldiers who happened to be in the way.

The birds didn't just target the worms. They started to peck at the Pixies too. Black wings were everywhere, blocking their view. Niella saw a few mounted soldiers knocked off their ponies.

The Goblin foot soldiers pounced. They charged at the Pixies, gaining all the ground they lost in a matter of seconds. That is, until the Pixies realised they could just pick up the stones and throw them back again. They couldn't throw them as far, but some of them still made their way to the Goblin soldiers. And the crows followed. They didn't peck at the Goblins, of course, but they were getting confused. Some of them seemed dizzy and just flapped around in circles. They became a general nuisance.

Then came the galciers again. The rain had died down slightly, which meant the explosions from the orbs were even more magnificent. They lit up the sky with dazzling light. It confused the crows even more. And started to scare them. Most of the birds couldn't stand it anymore and flew away to safety. The few that remained were getting taken down by Pixie soldiers. So much for a secret weapon.

"Look out!" came a loud voice.

The queen turned her head and saw an orb flying towards her. The light was blinding, but she could tell it was getting close.

She ducked, breathing fast. A split second later she heard a loud crash behind her. And then a scream.

She turned round. The orb had hit one of the Goblin soldiers and exploded on impact. Niella could hardly see the body. What a terrible way to die, even if it was also spectacular – the remains of the body were covered in glittering dust. As the smoke cleared, the dust started to flood the air. The lights shone even brighter on the ground. There was no clapping this time.

Niella shook her head. They didn't have long. The Goblin queen started to make her way to the back of her army. But she kept an eye on the front line at the same time, in case any more orbs were going to try and kill her in a spectacular style. Thankfully most of them were still exploding high up in the air.

It was still a long way to get to the back of the soldiers, but Niella moved swiftly. The soldiers all knew who she was – they could tell from the armour, even with her helmet on. So they were making way.

"My queen!" came another voice.

It was a young and excited looking Goblin soldier. He was covered in mud, particularly around his arms. The queen didn't recognise him, but she knew exactly why this young soldier was calling her. He had been underground.

Chapter 34

Petra brushed a fly away from her face. There seemed to be quite a few of them in this tunnel. But that wasn't too bad compared to the terrifying monsters they had encountered so far on their journey.

In fact, these flies were the only creatures they had come across in days. There were no more happy bats trying to carry them away. No more swamp monsters trying to strangle them. And most importantly, no Goblin soldiers trying to arrest them.

Things weren't perfect. They were still under ground and were running low on food and water. Although at least that meant they had less stuff to carry.

And Ridley was walking now! Not perfectly, but he had come a long way. It was hard to overstate how much of a difference that made. They had probably covered more ground in the last two days than the rest of the time combined.

Petra turned round and saw him walking behind, chatting to Fulton. She smiled. Things could be a lot worse.

Larah suddenly seemed to stop in front of her.

"What's wrong?" asked Petra.

The young Goblin turned round. Her white eyes opened wider, gleaming for the first time in a while.

"I know where we are!" she beamed.

Petra frowned. "You've always known where we are," she replied. "You've been telling us that the whole time."

"Yes, but I was...sort of lying," said Larah. "At least not telling the complete the truth. I didn't want to worry anyone."

Ridley and Fulton joined them, both staring at the young Goblin.

"Well at least she's honest," smirked Ridley. "Well,

honest about the fact that she's been lying to us."

"Honest dishonesty," added Fulton.

"I knew it," said Petra. "Time and time again, I asked you if you knew what you were doing. You've kept saying we were on our way to the Human realm; that any night now we'll get to the surface. That was all just a lie?"

"Not exactly," said Larah. "Well, it might have been exactly a lie. But I did think there was a pretty good chance we were heading in the right direction. Even if we weren't quite going in as right a direction as I was implying."

Ridley frowned. "Were we in fact going in exactly the wrong direction?"

Larah laughed. Although she quickly stopped laughing as she realised everyone was staring at her in a very serious manner.

"Look, it's not like that," she said. "It's good news. We're not quite where I thought we were, but we're close."

"So we're right by the Human realm?" said Ridley.

"Okay, well we're not that close."

Petra put her hand over her face.

"We're still in the Goblin realm, but we're on the right side," continued Larah. "We're far from Nuberim. In the Southwest of the realm."

"Southwest? You mean we're near the Pixies?" asked Petra, suddenly brightening up.

"Sort of," said Larah. "In that direction. We're on the outskirts of a city called Lancha, if you've heard of it."

Ridley nodded. "Of course we've heard of it, we're not completely ignorant."

"I haven't," said Fulton.

Everyone suddenly turned to Petra, who had let out a loud gasp.

"It's where we were going," she began. "Before I got captured, I was with Samorus and the Humans. We were on our way to Lancha."

She explained everything to the rest of the group – how

King Wyndham wanted to go there as a diplomatic mission, but brought a lot of soldiers with him just in case. But then there seemed to be Ogres attacking them, and nobody really knew what was going on.

"So what you're saying," said Larah, "is that there could be lots of Humans there having a nice time with the Goblin hosts. Or there could be an all out battle?"

"Well, yes I suppose so," said Petra.

"Or a battle has already happened, and the place is now a mess," added Ridley. "Or maybe they decided not to go to Lancha after all, and just turned round and went home. So the city is just full of Goblins, who are fully aware that there are Human fugitives on the run."

Petra nodded. "It could be the way to safety, or we could be walking straight into the mouth of a predator."

The four of them all looked at each other.

"I think we should keep going," said Petra. "At least for now. We finally know where we are. We can try to bear south and head straight for the Pixie realm when we get the chance."

"But in the meantime, we're getting closer and closer to a possible death trap?" said Ridley. "We're on the run. Surely we need to go further away from people. Not towards them."

He turned to Fulton.

"I think he might be right actually," said Fulton. "But then Petra may be right too," he added, seeing the expression on her face.

"Great, very helpful," said Ridley, who now turned to Larah. "Well then, our great dishonest leader, I guess it's down to you!"

The young Goblin glared at him briefly before turning to the others.

"We can't go back," she began. "Going back is not an option. For all we know the soldiers from Nuberim are right on our tails. If we get the opportunity, we'll bear south. Maybe even take some upward sloping paths towards the surface. But for now, we head towards Lancha."

Ridley sighed. He knew when he was beaten.

They set off again at a quicker pace. There was the relief that they now knew where they were going, but at the same time, the fear that they could be going somewhere very dangerous. The two feelings sort of balanced each other out.

The tunnel did seem to climb a little as they walked. There was still hardly any light, apart from the glow worms and moths they encountered every so often.

"How far do you think we are from the surface?" Petra asked Larah.

"Not far," she replied.

"Is that an honest answer?" added Ridley, sarcastically.

Larah didn't respond.

"Wait, can you hear something?" she said.

"I can hear an annoying Goblin talking…" replied Ridley.

"I'm serious!" she said, "There's a rumbling sound. Listen!"

They slowed their pace, trying to stay quiet. As a Goblin, Larah had the sharpest ears of all of them. But soon, the others could hear it too.

It sounded like a thousand people playing the drums at once. But softly, and very badly. With no rhythm whatsoever. Maybe it was an Ogre percussion band – they were supposed to be rubbish.

"I think we're walking towards the sound," said Fulton, keeping his voice low. "Is that a good idea?"

Nobody responded, they just kept walking.

"As soon as we see a passage turning right, we'll take it," replied Larah eventually. "Otherwise, we keep going."

The path continued on a slight incline. Petra looked behind, and then ahead of her. It seemed like the tunnel was getting brighter in front of them.

And the sound was getting louder. It wasn't drums at all – it was more like metal hammering on stone. And was that…voices? Petra was sure she could hear people talking. Surely Larah could too.

The young Goblin looked alert, trying to take in every noise around her.

"The tunnel's flattening," she whispered. "I think we're getting close. We should stay off the centre of the path, just to be safe."

They split into two, with Petra walking behind Larah on the left side of the tunnel, and Fulton behind Ridley on the right.

The path was definitely flattening, and even started to slope downhill. It meant they could now see quite far in front of them as they looked downwards.

And what they saw was terrifying. The tunnel opened up into an enormous hallway. It must have been fifty feet deep, and a hundred feet wide. Torches lit up the place on all sides.

They were Goblin soldiers. Petra could tell that, even from this distance. There were hundreds of them.

"What are they doing?" whispered Petra, slowly.

"They're...digging," replied Larah slowly, without looking back. "This used to be a simple set of tunnels. They've hollowed out this entire area."

"Why would they do that? Are they building something?"

"Maybe. But they're soldiers – all of them are wearing armour. How strange!"

Many were also carrying torches. It meant Petra could see what they were doing, even from this distance. Larah was right – they were digging. Picks and axes seemed to be hammering away at the rocks on every side.

"I think we're pretty near the surface too," continued Larah, still whispering. "If they're not careful, the whole ground could collapse!"

Petra shuddered. The path in front now had a steep downward slope, leading straight to this huge pit full of Goblins below them. Along with the digging, she could hear general laughter and chatter. It made them sound even more intimidating.

And for all they knew, guards from Nuberim were still on their tail. They couldn't go back, and now they couldn't go forward either. They were trapped.

"So what do we do now?" she whispered to Larah.

"We go sideways," she replied.

The young Goblin was looking to the right, beyond the two Humans. There was a tunnel on the other side. It was dark, as there were no torches anywhere near it, which hopefully meant there weren't any Goblins. But there was also no way of getting to it.

Larah beckoned to Petra, and they made their way towards the two Humans on the other side of the tunnel.

"We're going to shimmy round the wall," said Larah, keeping her voice low.

"Excuse me?" replied Ridley. "We're going to shimmy? I don't...I don't even know what that means!"

"It's the only way to make it to that tunnel. Once we're there, it's a straight path to Lancha. And there will be hundreds of other paths we can take if we need to."

"Yes but how are we supposed to walk across a vertical wall?"

"Grab onto it," said Larah. "It's possible. Even a Human can do it."

"Are you confusing Humans with lizards?" replied Ridley.

"You can do it!" continued Larah, indignantly. "Besides it's not vertical, there's a slight slope. And there are plenty of rocks to hold onto."

"I don't know..." added Fulton.

He was looking down at the chasm full of Goblin soldiers below them. If they didn't die from the fall, they would surely get slaughtered as soon as they hit the bottom.

They could feel vibrations from the picks and shovels. Just as Fulton finished speaking, several rocks seemed to break from the cliff, and came crashing down on the ground below.

If they weren't careful, that could soon happen to their bodies.

Chapter 35

Petra thought for a moment, then dipped her hand into one of the bags.

"What about this?" she whispered, pulling out a small rock. "We could use the Levela?"

Larah shook her head. "You need to be a wizard to make it work. The Humans won't be able to do it. No offence," she added, catching Ridley's eye.

"Have we got anything else in those sacks that might help?" asked Fulton.

"Any wings?" added Ridley sarcastically.

"No, but we do have rope!" replied Petra, beginning to feel a bit more positive about this whole idea.

They all paused for a minute, trying to think about what to do next.

Larah broke the silence. "The first person carries one end of the rope. When they get to the tunnel, hopefully they can find something to tie it to. Then the others come one by one, with a hand on the rope."

The others looked at her. It wasn't the best plan, but none of them had anything better.

"I'll go first," said Larah.

"Why do you get to go first?" said Fulton.

"Well, do you want to go first?" replied Larah.

"No, not really," said Fulton, who then went quiet.

"All right then," said Larah, picking up the length of rope from one of the bags. It was about 25 feet long in total, which should be more than enough.

"Take this as well, just in case. You'll need it more than me," said Petra. She shoved the Levela into Larah's pocket, before she had the chance to argue.

The young Goblin tied the rope around her waist with a double knot. Then she started to get her footing on the right-hand wall. A few moments later, she took her second foot off the ground, and was already on her way.

The others watched with bated breath. She was making it look so easy – her hands and feet were almost sticking to the rocky surface as she moved.

Fulton grabbed the rest of the rope. He held it up, letting it slip through his hand slowly as Larah continued to make progress.

The young Goblin disappeared behind the gap in the wall. She had made it already.

Petra and the two Humans stood still. The end of the rope seemed to be flickering around below them, which probably meant Larah was still holding it. She hadn't found anything to tie it to.

When the rope stopped moving, they didn't know what it meant. Maybe it was now firmly tied to something, or under a heavy rock. Or maybe Larah was just holding it still, hoping for the best.

Petra looked at Ridley and Fulton. She was up next. She picked up one of the bags, realising somebody had to carry them, and hoisted it around her shoulder. She took Fulton's free hand and gave it a hard squeeze, just for a moment, before setting off.

The wall seemed completely vertical. Her feet managed to find a few jagged rocks as she slowly made her way across. It was hard work, and the bag made it even harder. She couldn't hold the rope at the same time – she didn't have enough hands. But she kept it between her body and the wall, so that if she did happen to slip, she should be able to reach out and grab it in time.

She was breathing hard but tried to remain quiet. And most importantly, she didn't look down. She could hear the banging of hundreds of shovels far below, and general murmur of the Goblins soldiers. She just hoped they hadn't been spotted.

Eventually, her foot felt the firm ground below her, and she felt instantly relieved. Larah grabbed her, and pulled her in. Petra looked down. Larah had found a rock, which was lying on top of the rope. But it didn't look particularly heavy. The young Goblin also had her foot on the rope, hoping to anchor it down.

"Need some help?" whispered Petra, half smiling. She stood on the rope in front of Larah, but also crouched down and held it.

Petra peered round to her left and could see the silhouette of a large, clumsy looking man, struggling to find his feet on the wall. It was Ridley's turn.

He had tied a bag around his shoulders, so he could use both hands to grab hold of the wall. Even then, he was clearly struggling. He seemed to stop still a couple of times, desperately trying to find a firm hold on the rocks. Petra resisted the urge to shout 'keep moving', in case any of the Goblins below heard them.

When Ridley was eventually within reach, Petra held her hand out and pulled him in. Even in the dark tunnel, his look of relief was clear for all of them to see. He sat down on top of the rock which was anchoring the rope. He held it in both hands, still breathing heavily.

Petra looked round again, waiting for Fulton's shadow to appear. He seemed to take even longer than Ridley. Eventually he emerged with the end of the rope tied around his waist, and the last of the bags over his shoulder.

He pulled his foot off the floor and onto the wall. Every step forward seemed to take an age, as Fulton carefully felt the surface of the wall with his toes before making any movements.

Suddenly, a rock seemed to break off below Fulton's left foot. He flinched and lost his balance. He was left hanging by his arms, while both his legs were flailing around, desperately trying to find solid ground. "Come on" said Petra, under her breath, "you can do this!"

Unfortunately, he couldn't. A few seconds later his arms gave way, and he started falling fast. The other three reacted in a flash, each of them grabbing the rope with both hands, while Ridley wrapped his body around it.

Fulton swung round below them. A small length of rope was now the only thing keeping him from certain death. And he knew it. His hands were clasped around it like a vice.

The others pulled as hard as they could, but the rope was too long. Or more to the point, Fulton was too heavy.

"Drop the bag," whispered Petra, still aware of the army of Goblins below them.

The bag was tied around Fulton's neck. He had to take his hands off the rope to release it.

He was shaking. The rope was shaking. Petra couldn't see Larah and Ridley behind her. But she reckoned they were probably shaking.

Fulton took one hand off slowly. And then the second. He was now relying solely on the knot around his waist. He took a breath and tugged at the sack. Thankfully, it wasn't too tight. But the knot that mattered, around his waist, was holding.

He untied the bag and let it drop. He instantly brought his hands straight back onto the rope.

They heard a thud on the ground a second later. The Goblin soldiers below them must have heard too – there was no doubt about that.

The bag probably only carried a fraction of the weight, but it seemed to make a big difference. Now when they tugged, they could feel themselves gradually moving back. Fulton was stronger too, and able to pull himself up as they pulled.

When his hand made it over the edge, they gave him one final pull and he collapsed on the floor. The man was in tears. Petra ran over, crouched down and hugged him tight. The others came over too, both of them breathing heavily.

Nobody said a word for a long time.

"You should probably go back and get that bag," said Ridley eventually. Fulton managed a smile.

"Well, what now?" he asked, still panting slightly.

"The Goblins below know we're here," said Petra. "Or at least, they know someone's here. I think we need to get going, quickly."

Larah nodded. "Yes, we do. But we're nearly at the city now." She was untying the rope around Fulton as she spoke. "We keep going and head towards the surface. I still have no idea what we're going to find when we get there. Maybe there will be more Goblins, Humans, Ogres, who knows."

"And what then?" asked Ridley.

"Whoever it is, if they try and kill us, we keep running," continued Larah. "But if they're on our side, hopefully they'll be nice to us. Maybe even give us food."

"That would be good!" said Fulton. "I think most of our food was in that bag. Sorry it's now…wasted."

"Don't worry," replied Ridley sarcastically. "I'm sure it won't be wasted. A few of the Goblin soldiers will probably eat it. It will give them more energy before they come to kill us."

Chapter 36

Prince Vardie was the first in line to the Pixie throne. He had waited forty-two years for that crown. He didn't want his mother to die, obviously, but there would certainly be a silver lining if she did.

The Marelta family had ruled over the Pixie realm for nearly four ages. In all that time, nobody had ever contested the throne; there had barely been any rival claims, riots or even protests.

There were a few reasons for that. Firstly, a lot of Pixies lived in the countryside and kept to themselves. They were more interested in creating potions than they were in who was governing the realm. Provided they were still allowed to forage food and make shiny objects, they didn't care who was in charge.

Secondly, people never seemed to take the initiative to change things. Thousands of Pixies sometimes wondered whether they should challenge the system and bring about improvements. But each of them was just one person, so they assumed it wouldn't make a difference.

The final reason was that most people were happy enough with the system, provided things were going well. So the Marelta family tried to do a good job. In fact, 'we try to do a good job' was their family motto. It wasn't perfect, but it did the job.

'Doing a good job' meant working hard, and they shared responsibilities across the family. The queen had overall responsibility for the realm, and that meant she had to sit in her luxury castle and sometimes make decisions. The princes and princesses were responsible for practical things like keeping order, diplomacy, and in Vardie's case, defence of the realm.

As he ducked to avoid another onslaught of flaming axes, he made a mental note to renegotiate responsibilities with the queen. The battle was raging on. It was still the dead of night, and dawn didn't seem to be breaking any time soon.

The mounted Pixies charged once again. It felt like they were doing it for the hundredth time. More sparks from the galciers lit up above him. There was no doubt it was working; he saw two Goblins getting trampled by a single pony. The Goblins were dying, but for some reason their army never seemed to get any smaller. Where were they all coming from?

The Pixies were gaining ground. He was sure of that. He walked his pony a couple of yards forward as a gap opened in front of him. The rock he was initially standing on was at least twenty yards behind him now.

"Show them no fear! Show them no mercy!" came a voice to his left.

It was probably one of his soldiers trying to keep everyone going. Vardie was so proud of them for maintaining this level of energy during the most gruelling battle they had ever experienced.

He knew the Pixies' reputation across the Known World. But from now on, anyone who said 'a Pixie couldn't fight an ear infection' would surely have to think twice. It was a silly expression anyway – some ear infections were very hard to fight.

They were doing well. If they kept their discipline, they could keep the Goblins and Ogres at bay. Then, the Prince saw something which made his royal blood run cold. At the back of the Ogre ranks, a huge wooden device was coming into view. Vardie had never seen one before, but he instantly knew what it was. A scorpion.

He had heard the rumours. It was taller than trees. Heavier than buildings. Wider than trees that had been chopped down and laid on their side. The Ogres had apparently spent years developing this technology. It was essentially a giant crossbow, with arrows capable of obliterating anyone in their path.

As the Ogres wheeled the massive weapon closer, it certainly seemed to live up to the hype. He could see the steel arrowhead in the centre, which was probably bigger than his whole body. A thick rope lay behind it, tightly strung on both sides. It was poised and ready to shoot.

A hush descended around the soldiers. Some people seemed to be staring, open mouthed at this terrifying monster.

"Get back! Get out of its line of sight!" cried Vardie. He wasn't the only one shouting.

Humans and Pixies were darting frantically around, trying to find space either side of the field – as far as possible from the weapon's line of sight. But they only had a few seconds.

An Ogre must have released the rope, or whatever was holding the giant arrow in place. It shot forward in a flash, crashing into the ground and taking a pile of soldiers with it. The impact was devastating. The Ogres had positioned it perfectly so that it sailed right over their ranks, straight into the Humans on the other side of the field.

Vardie was a safe enough distance from the carnage, but still close enough to see it all unfold. Soldiers seemed to have disappeared beneath the arrow, whilst dead bodies lay on either side.

He wondered if King Wyndham was okay. He had lost sight of the Human leader a long time ago, and now he could be anywhere. Maybe even buried in the wreckage.

The Prince looked up. Something astonishing had just appeared in the sky. It looked like a unicorn – its white wings were flapping, and it was moving quickly through the air. As it came into view, Vardie saw there was someone riding it! He rubbed his eyes – surely this wasn't possible. He knew the Humans had been trying to ride unicorns for years, but nobody had even come close!

Voices came from nearby: "It's him!" "It's the Lord of Science!" "How has he managed to tame a unicorn?"

The Goblins and Ogres seemed to be looking up in shock. Everyone was simply amazed as the unicorn darted through the skies. Vardie wasn't sure where the lord was leading it, if he even had any control over the creature. It seemed to be flying around in circles, flapping its wings unnecessarily quickly.

The Lord of Science didn't actually have any control – in fact he clearly hadn't mastered the science of sitting on the creatures. He seemed to be desperately holding on to the unicorn's back, while his legs trailed behind it.

And a few moments later, lost his grip completely. The soldiers watched as he plummeted to the ground, landing deep within the Ogre lines. The fall must have killed him, but even if it hadn't, the Ogres certainly would have.

The unicorn just flew away without looking back, clearly glad to be rid of the Human. Vardie put his head in his hands. That had been a nice distraction for a few moments, but nothing more. His gaze turned back to the battle, and the deadly scorpion they were facing.

The Ogres were already loading another arrow onto the device. This would surely take them a while – it had taken about a dozen Ogres just to push the thing. But there was no time to wait. Another couple of arrows and their armies would be decimated. There would be no way back.

There was only one way out of this: they needed to destroy the scorpion. Vardie saw a flurry of Human arrows heading straight for it, but they hardly made a dent. The frame was too strong. The wood must have been reinforced. But it was still…wood.

"Fire!" shouted Vardie. A few Pixies also shot their arrows in response. The Prince shook his head. "No, we need fire. Now!"

He called to one of the galciers and told her to gather the whole group. They were to get as close as possible to the device, and all throw their orbs at once. Vardie wasn't sure the scorpion was within throwing range, but it was worth a try.

"This would be a lot easier if we had a magic Pixie who could shoot fire from her hands," he muttered to himself.

His army had oil. Not much, but enough to light their torches. If enough people could sneak behind the enemy lines and pour it onto the scorpion, maybe they could get it to erupt in flames.

"You there!" he called to a random foot soldier.

The soldier looked up, realised it was the Prince and looked slightly in shock. He was very young – this was probably his first ever battle.

"I need a handful of people to go on an incredibly risky mission," said Vardie. The foot soldier nodded, looking dazed and confused. "Get the oil from one of our camps. Go round the back of our troops – as far away as you need to until you can find a passage that leads in behind the Ogres. Then get close enough to the scorpion to cover it with oil and set it alight."

The Pixie soldier's eyes widened.

"You want me to lead a group of people to do that, sire?" he said, still in shock.

"If you're feeling up to it," replied Vardie, taking some pity on the boy. "Or if not, find someone more senior who is."

The soldier nodded. "Yes sire, I'll certainly do one of those things."

He ran off straight away towards the back of the army, as quickly as his white chainmail would allow.

"Don't forget to get a group of people," shouted Vardie as he went. "At least five of you!"

The Prince shuddered, wondering if there was any chance of him succeeding. He felt like he was sending a group of soldiers to their death. But then, they would all be dead soon enough if they couldn't stop the scorpion.

He thought for a second. Flaming arrows – that was the only other option. The Humans could find some fire for their archers to use. As he looked to his left, he could see some of them had already had that idea – there were a few of the Ogre axes that were still alight, which had dug into the ground amongst their ranks. That was a start.

Vardie took a breath. It was times like these that he wished he had faith in the gods. The Pixies worshipped two gods of course, but hardly anyone believed they existed. They were more symbolic – all the other civilisations had gods, so the Pixies thought they should too.

Symbolic or not, Prince Vardie still muttered their names under his breath. Just in case it helped.

Chapter 37

Lord Protector Higarth grinned. His yellow teeth glistened as the stars shone from above. The rain had beaten down on his army for hours, but now the night was clear. Not a cloud in the sky.

A few of his generals had doubted him. They had questioned whether it made sense to bring heavy artillery half way across the Known World, just in case they needed it in a battle.

"Isn't it going to be very expensive to transport it all that way?" General Hurgen had said. The fool. Everyone knew you couldn't put a price on smashing your enemies to pieces.

"What if it breaks down? What if the troops can't assemble it in time?" General Gorac had asked. Higarth had snorted at this suggestion. To be fair, the rain had set them back a while, but it didn't matter now. The scorpion was working incredibly well.

Higarth looked on as another arrow shot from the huge machine, landing with force on a group of mounted Human soldiers. There were not many horses left now – the Ogre axe-throwers had seen to that. His troops had sustained heavy casualties too, but surely not as many.

He saw another wave of arrows fly above him, clearly aimed towards the scorpion. A few seemed to be on fire. Higarth laughed – even the Humans couldn't be dumb enough to think they could destroy their prized weapon with a few puny arrows.

One or two of them hit the thing, but any flames had disappeared before they had even reached it. The arrows barely scratched the scorpion.

Finally, Higarth felt that things were going to plan. His only regret was that he hadn't done enough fighting himself – he was too busy commanding the army.

As he thought that, he suddenly felt a sharp pain in his thigh. He looked down. Something had penetrated through his armour. It was a Human dagger – Higarth could tell that from the leather handle alone. The cold steel cut against his muscle, but it hadn't reached the bone. He pulled it out with a quick tug. One of his guards wrapped a piece of cloth tightly around his leg. It helped to slow the blood, which was starting to ouze out.

"Are you all right, my Lord Protector?" asked the guard.

"Of course I'm all right," he snapped. "Did you see the Human who did it?"

As he spoke, another Ogre soldier came towards him, dragging a Human by the cloth around his neck.

"I was about to finish him, my Lord Protector, when he pulled out a dagger and slung it at you," said the soldier. "I don't know why he did it."

"I was trying to hit him!" snapped the Human, who could evidently still talk despite being heavily wounded.

Higarth nodded. "Thanks," he said to his soldier, before grabbing hold of the Human. He held him up with his left hand and thrust the same dagger deep into his chest. He didn't even look at the Human as he dropped him to the ground.

Higarth lifted his injured leg, and gently put weight on it. He felt a throbbing pain, but he didn't show it in his face. He didn't want to show any weakness in front of his soldiers.

"How is it going?" he asked the soldier who had brought him this Human.

"Very well, my Lord Protector," he replied. "The Human mounted soldiers are depleted. The few of them that are left seem to be leaving the battlefield to regroup. We haven't breached the archers yet, but we're not far away."

Higarth smiled again. The archers were the Humans' last remaining asset. Once the Ogres could get them in close range, they didn't stand a chance.

The soldier nodded and ran back into the battle. Higarth

rearranged the armour plating on his thigh – he didn't know how that dagger had got through, but he wasn't going to let it happen again.

Blood was still seeping out and covering his leg in a crimson colour. Higarth didn't mind. In fact he liked it – the Ogres always used to say that you hadn't truly fought in a battle unless you had shed blood. It made them feel alive. In fact, the more blood they shed, the more alive they felt. Until they shed so much blood that they died. That was the exception to the rule.

Higarth looked to his right. The Ogre axe throwers clearly outnumbered the Human foot soldiers. They seemed to be spreading out as well, trying to make use of their greater numbers by surrounding the enemy. The pincer tactic – his generals had ordered it.

It was a good idea, but it had its risks. If his soldiers spread themselves too thinly, the Humans might be able to penetrate through.

And that's exactly what happened. A bunch of mounted soldiers galloped through, trampling over the Ogres in their path. The Humans must have been holding back, waiting for their time to pounce.

It wasn't just that though; every one of these horse soldiers carried a lit torch. It didn't take a genius to figure out what they were doing – they were heading for the scorpion. They were a couple of hundred yards away but moving fast. His troops were scrambling to get their pikes in position while others were trying to stop the horses from behind. They weren't quick enough.

The Humans didn't quite reach the huge weapon, but many of them had made it within throwing range. And that was all that mattered – they started hurling the torches at the scorpion. At least twenty of them seemed to land.

The huge weapon suddenly erupted in flames. Fire covered every inch of it. Higarth didn't understand it – there had been so much rain, how could it burn so quickly?

A few Ogres were chucking buckets of water on the

scorpion, but it made no difference.

"We shouldn't make the scorpion entirely out of wood," General Lang had said a while ago. "Shouldn't we use a metal frame?" The idiot. Although Higarth had to admit that in hindsight, his suggestion was completely right.

Higarth shook his head in anger. He wanted to end this battle once and for all. The Goblins had come up with an idea the other night – and now was the time to put it into action.

He saw the back of his general's head and called him over.

"Lang," he said. "See if the Goblins are ready with the chasm. And if so, pull the troops back and get the two catapults into position."

The general nodded. "Yes, my Lord Protector. I'll get those *wooden* catapults into position."

Higarth glared back at him.

Chapter 38

"I don't understand it," said Larah. "We're near the centre of Lancha – where is everybody?"

Petra looked at the wide tunnel and empty buildings. Torches lit up the walls around them, but there wasn't a single person in sight. It was creepy – she almost wished it were teeming with Goblin soldiers to make it seem more normal.

"What do you think happened?" she whispered to Fulton. "Some kind of mass evacuation?"

"Seems unlikely," he replied. "Besides, it's not like Goblins to flee from danger. Aren't they too tough and proud for that?"

"You're thinking of Ogres," said Petra. "Goblins flee all the time."

Fulton laughed.

"I don't know what's going on here…but it can't be good," said Larah to the group. "We need to get to the surface."

She led them towards a partially concealed turning on their right. It started as a small tunnel and became a set of stone steps leading upwards. It was darker in there, and Petra had to feel each step with her feet.

It was slow going, and they kept their eyes peeled for any sign of life around them. The steps just went on and on, winding slightly to the left. Petra kept telling herself that every step they took brought them closer to the surface. After weeks spent underground, that was an exciting thought, no matter what was waiting for them at the top.

"Hang on," whispered Larah. "I think I can hear something. Or someone."

They all stopped.

"It's coming from further up," she continued. "Sounds like someone is breathing heavily."

Larah started walking again, more slowly than before. Petra was always amazed by the power of these Goblins. How could she hear breathing?

Before she knew it, Larah had found a door a few steps above her, and had pushed it open. The others followed. The door led to a small room, lit by a single candle.

"Get back!" came a low voice, suddenly.

Petra looked up. A Human was standing there, dressed in light armour. He was tall, with long hair and a dark, bushy beard. He held out a long blade which flashed against the candle's flame.

His voice sounded panicked. "Don't move," he continued. "And tell me who you are."

"Technically we can't do both," replied Fulton.

"Look we don't want any trouble," said Larah quickly. "We're just passing through."

The Human soldier looked at her, and then at the others in turn. He now seemed confused as well as panicked.

"You're a Goblin," he said to Larah. "And then you two look like Humans. And a... Pixie?" he said, turning his gaze to Petra.

"That's right," she replied.

"So you're not here to attack me, or to discipline me for hiding?"

Now it was their turn to look confused.

"We're just passing through," said Larah again. "We're perfectly harmless. I'm Larah, and this is Petra, Ridley and Fulton. We just want to get out of here."

The Human seemed a bit more at ease after they had introduced themselves.

"Now...lower your weapon and we can talk," continued Larah. "Who is trying to attack you?"

"You don't know, do you?" he said, lowering his sword. "You don't even know we're at war?"

The Human told them everything that had happened – the journey they had been on, the attacks by the Ogres, the Pixies coming to join them. Everything.

"So right now, there's a huge battle going on?" asked Ridley, once he had finished.

The Human nodded.

"So why are you hiding?"

"Because there's a huge battle going on!" said the Human. "I got scared. I'm not afraid to admit it – it was just too much. I saw people dying right in front of me!"

"That's what usually happens in battles," replied Ridley. "Why did you join the foot soldiers in the first place if you were too afraid to fight?"

"The money, I suppose," he replied. "And the prestige. They say there's no greater honour in the Known World than fighting for your realm!"

"How about hiding in a tiny room underground while you let others do the fighting?" continued Ridley. "There's not a lot of honour in that."

Petra nodded. There was an old Pixie saying: *you should never walk away from a fight. It's much better to run, otherwise they might catch you.*

"You're not going to tell anyone, are you?" asked the Human, nervously.

"Relax," said Larah. "We have more important things to worry about. Besides, we can't tell anyone when we don't even know your name."

"It's Fordham," replied the Human, before realising what he had said. "I mean, it's not that, it's something else."

Ridley put his hand over his face.

"I don't understand," piped in Petra. "If the Goblins are fighting an all-out battle right now, why did we just see hundreds of them digging underground?"

"Digging?" replied Fordham.

"There may have been thousands of them actually," continued Larah. "It was like they were hollowing out the whole area near the city."

"But why would they do that?" asked Fordham.

"Maybe they're tunnelling, so they can attack from the other side?" suggested Larah.

"They didn't seem to be though," said Petra. "Some of them were going back the way they came."

"Hang on…" interrupted Fulton. "What if it's…something else."

"Thanks for that," said Ridley. "Very helpful."

"No, listen," Fulton continued. "Remember the story of the fox and the tortoise? My parents used to tell me that one when I was a child."

"The fox and the tortoise?" asked Petra.

"Yes!" said Fulton excitedly. "The tortoise is running away from the fox. But it's too slow, it realises it's not going to outrun the fox forever."

"Can tortoises even run at all?"

"That's not the point. It's a snowy day, and the tortoise knows the fox is going to kill it. The tortoise is too small and weak – it's going to lose if it gets caught. So it has to use its cunning."

"Aren't foxes the ones who are supposed to be cunning?" said Ridley.

"Please just let me finish," continued Fulton. "It runs onto a lake, which is frozen over. It cracks the ice, but only a little, so it can still make it across to the other side. And then it stops. The fox thinks the tortoise has given up, so it runs straight onto the ice."

"And then the ice breaks?" asked Petra.

"Exactly!" said Fulton. "It's a trap. The ice can't take the weight of the fox, so it falls into the lake and drowns."

"I think foxes can swim…" added Larah.

"That's not the point," said Petra. "He might be right. It's a manoeuvre. The Goblins are hollowing out the ground, so when the Humans and Pixies walk over it, the land collapses beneath them."

"Making them fall to their deaths," added Ridley.

"That's right!" beamed Fulton, triumphantly.

"That's very clever," added Larah.

Petra smiled at him. "You're not just a pretty face, are you?" she added, clutching his hand.

Ridley rolled his eyes.

"We have to stop this from happening," continued the young Pixie. "Fordham, can you take us to one of the leaders? Prince Vardie or King Wyndham?"

"Wait," added Larah. "We're going to save the Humans

and Pixies, but then what? Are we going to let the Goblins die instead?"

"Nobody else needs to die," replied Petra. "If we stop this, maybe it can end the whole battle."

Fordham paused. "I can take you to King Wyndham," he began. "At least, I think I can."

"You can find him amongst the thousands of soldiers?"

"Oh, I know exactly where he is," replied Fordham. "I'm just worried someone will kill me before we get there."

Chapter 39

The sun was starting to rise. The Elves used to say a red sunrise showed that blood had been shed the previous night. And the sky today would have been bright red, if it wasn't for the fact that the saying was complete hogwash.

King Wyndham felt sick. He was tired, hungry and had no energy left. He couldn't remember being in a battle that had lasted this long.

His soldiers were still fighting bravely. There was no chanting or shouting any more. They were just doing their jobs. A few rows of sword fighters still guarded the archers, who were shooting whatever arrows they had left.

The huge scorpion was still burning in the distance, and they had managed to strike a significant blow to the Ogres by destroying it. Wyndham was just praying they didn't have another one of those things. Thankfully there was no sign of one so far.

The Human and Pixie soldiers seemed to be gaining ground quickly. As he looked around the rock he was standing on, the troops were moving forward – almost at a walking pace. Were the Ogres retreating?

He peered out towards the front line. He could see Ogre pike and axe soldiers moving further away, but they didn't seem to be running. In fact, they seemed to be stepping backwards in unison. Almost like they were getting ready to flee.

Surely the Lord Protector of the Ogres hadn't ordered his army to surrender. An Ogre would chop both their arms off before they even considered waving a white flag. And that would make it very tricky to do afterwards. But maybe the Goblin queen had ordered it?

Wyndham felt a tap on his shoulder. It was Prince Vardie. He hadn't seen the Pixie in hours, and he certainly looked different now. His dazzling white armour was now a dull grey, covered with a generous helping of mud.

"The Goblins are falling back," said Vardie, slightly out of breath.

"So are the Ogres," replied Wyndham. "I think we may be about to declare victory!"

He kept his voice low, so the soldiers nearby didn't hear him. It wasn't time to announce it to everyone yet. Both he and Prince Vardie had to be sure.

The Prince was nodding. "How do you want to do it? We could both raise our swords in the air?"

It was a good question. Everybody in the Known World knew the white flag was a signal for surrender. But there wasn't really a way of signalling victory – people just generally took it as given once they had killed everyone, or the other side surrendered. And 'declaring victory' wasn't something Pixie soldiers had to worry about very often.

"I like that idea," said Wyndham. "We put our swords in the air and order one final charge. And we let the Ogres and Goblins run like frightened children."

Prince Vardie smiled. He beckoned to his bodyguards who were standing nearby. Wyndham called for the Lord of War, who was presumably in his usual position towards the back.

A few of the nearest foot soldiers turned to look at their two leaders. They could sense something was happening. Cecil wasn't actually too far away; he joined them a few moments later. The lord, two Pixie captains and a couple of bodyguards stood around Wyndham and Vardie. They waited for their instructions.

"Sire! Sire!" came a cry from behind them.

The King looked up. A small group of soldiers were hurrying towards him. Although he wasn't even sure they were soldiers – most of them weren't wearing any armour, and a couple seemed very small. Almost like children.

"What is it? What's happened?" asked King Wyndham. He recognised the woman at the front – it was Rayda, one of his captains.

"One of my soldiers has found something," she said, making her way quickly to the inner circle. "Or should I say...someone!"

Wyndham looked at the others in the group, who all now stood either side of Rayda. There was a young foot soldier looking very nervous, and two other Humans who the King didn't recognise. They both looked tired and thin. They wore dull cotton clothes.

Then there was a short girl with white hair and a bright green face. Clearly a Goblin – what was she doing there? She looked young and smiled at the King.

He couldn't make sense of this at all, until he saw the final member of the group. She looked a little different from when he last saw her, but he would have recognised those bright green eyes anywhere.

"Petra?"

He couldn't believe it. He looked across at Prince Vardie, who was open mouthed.

"What...what happened to you?" asked Wyndham.

"It's a long story," she replied. "I can tell you all about it. But right now, there's something more important."

Larah then told Wyndham and Vardie about the Goblin soldiers they had seen digging under the city. She then turned to Fulton, who nervously took over. He told them about the Goblins' likely plan to make the ground collapse – just like the story of the tortoise who cracked the ice, making the fox drown.

"I thought foxes could swim," said the Lord of War, once he had finished.

King Wyndham frowned, trying to take it all in. He thought back to his dreams, which had been on his mind a lot lately. Six buildings coming apart. Crumbling. Turning green. And then...the ground cracking and disappearing below him. The huge gaping hole in the ground! It couldn't be a coincidence...could it?

He looked at Vardie for a moment. He could tell what the leader of the Pixies was thinking.

"Fall back!" shouted Wyndham. His booming voice travelled across the battle. He kept repeating it.

Vardie told his captains to spread the word among the Pixie ranks. Within moments, shouts of 'fall back' echoed far and wide.

The order made its way to the front line. Wyndham saw a gap starting to appear between the armies. His soldiers had stopped advancing, but the Ogres were still moving backwards.

He looked across at the Pixies and the Goblins. The same thing was happening. There was a huge partition between the armies as far as he could see. And it kept growing bigger.

They were now moving backwards at pace. And their enemy were doing the same; a lot of the soldiers presumably quite baffled by what was going on. Wyndham and Vardie started to move their horses backward along with everyone else.

"How far back do we need to go, sire?" asked Cecil.

It was a fair question, and the King had no idea. The gap must have been a couple of hundred yards by now. Was that enough? It all depended on what was happening underground. How far had the Goblins tunnelled?

It turned out he didn't need an answer. A few moments later, he heard a murmur in the crowd. People were talking and shouting, some even seemed to be screaming. He heard cries of "LOOK OUT!"

And then he saw it. A huge crack was appearing in the middle of the open space. It seemed to come from nowhere, and instantly grew bigger. And wider. It felt like an underground god was coming to the surface and parting the Known World in two. Although as far as Wyndham knew, no such god existed.

The soldiers on both sides kept edging backwards. Those at the front must have been panicking. A chasm now existed between Humans and Pixies, and Ogres and Goblins. And it was still growing.

Wyndham heard screams and looked to his left. The hole had almost caught up with some of his soldiers at the front – it was like they were standing on the edge of the cliff. He saw at least a couple fall from the ground and out of sight, probably plummeting to their deaths hundreds of yards below. He shuddered, thankful that he was a king and nowhere near the front line.

Vardie cried for his army to keep moving back. Wyndham did the same. Luckily, the chasm finally seemed to stop growing. He could no longer hear the ground cracking, or any rocks falling. In a way, that was even more unsettling.

King Wyndham looked from one side of the battlefield to the other. This hole in the ground stretched as wide as he could see.

He had no idea what the Goblins had planned to do next, but from the look of it neither did they. There wasn't a single soldier trying to scale down the edges or run around it somehow. Everyone just stood still.

He breathed a huge sigh of relief when he realised there was only one explanation. The Goblins had meant to collapse the ground with the Humans and Pixies above it, and they had failed. Now, the two armies just stood there staring at each other.

"Have we done it, sire? Is the fight over?" asked Cecil eventually.

"I... don't know," replied Wyndham. "I think it might be. I mean... there's no way they can get to us now."

"There must be a way round this huge hole, it can't go on forever," added Vardie.

Wyndham looked across at the Ogres. Some of them were just staring down at the chasm below them, and a few others seemed to have put down their swords and spears in frustration. Two catapults had appeared among the Ogre ranks, but even they wouldn't be able to reach this far. For the first time in the whole battle, they looked depleted. So did the Goblins.

But then, the same was true of his own army. And Vardie's.

"I don't think anyone's going to be doing that," said the King. "Something tells me the fight is over, at least for now."

Cecil nodded. "So shall I order the troops to stand down, and regroup at the city?"

"Not yet," replied Wyndham. "We can't be the first to turn our backs. We need to wait for the Ogres and Goblins to do that first."

"I agree," added Vardie.

There was a long silence. A very long silence. Both armies were just staring at each other, too tired and too confused to do anything else.

"Do you reckon Higarth and that Goblin queen are saying the same thing?" asked one of the Pixie guards eventually.

"Almost certainly," said Wyndham, sighing. "But we can't turn round first, it will look like we're giving up. We have to stand here as long as it takes."

Another silence followed.

"Of course that's an excellent plan, sire," began Cecil. "Although I think the soldiers are rather tired and hungry."

"I'm actually quite tired and hungry as well," added Larah. They were still standing near the two leaders, also not sure what to do next. "Maybe just...a few of us could turn around and go?"

"Nobody turns around!" growled Wyndham, keeping his eyes fixed on the Ogres.

"So we're just going to stand here forever?" piped in Petra.

"Do you have a better idea?"

"What if we all slowly walk backwards?" suggested Cecil. "Really slowly, but keep looking forward, so it doesn't seem like we're surrendering?"

Wyndham paused for a moment. He looked at Prince Vardie who simply shrugged.

"That's actually not a terrible idea..." replied Wyndham.

And that's how the battle ended – with hundreds of soldiers staring their enemies in the face, while gradually shuffling backwards. The Humans and Pixies all followed their orders. The horses and ponies must have been especially confused, but even they did as their riders instructed.

Wyndham continued the delicate task of guiding his horse backwards whilst keeping his gaze at the enemy. As he did so, he thought he could see the Ogres and Goblins doing the same.

When Wyndham was sure the enemy could no longer see them, he finally told everyone they could turn around. Prince Vardie did the same.

The city was empty, just as they had expected. King Wyndham asked Cecil to keep patrols around the borders, but he was pretty sure there would be no attack. The Goblins and Ogres would need to go back and re-group, just as they did.

Chapter 40

Samorus opened his eyes. He could see the light seeping in from the surface, as his room was only a few feet deep. For the thousandth time, he wondered what he was doing, sitting in a room in the middle of a Goblin city.

He had told Prince Vardie that he wanted to fight with his fellow Pixies. The Prince had said no, which was just as well, since he was lying; he hadn't really wanted to fight anyway. So he had stayed in this room, in a bed he could only just about climb up to, and waited to see what happened.

He was able to make himself useful now that the soldiers had come back. He had managed to forage some grassroot and red hyde from the surface above. It wasn't perfect, but it was enough for a makeshift 'healing potion' for the wounded soldiers. He had spent a lot of the night handing it round as the Pixies had come in and found places to sleep.

Admittedly, many had said they didn't want it. Some had questioned whether there was any evidence that healing potion worked. Samorus never really understood why people needed evidence to justify taking it. Besides, everyone knew that laughter was the best medicine, even though there was no scientific basis for that at all.

Amidst all the chaos, he kept hearing rumours about Petra. One or two of the soldiers thought they saw her, or spoke to someone who had. But Samorus didn't know what to believe.

Then came the knock on the door that changed all that. Petra flung it open and ran to the old Pixie, wrapping her arms around him tightly.

"I'm sorry I took so long to come find you," she said, beaming. "Prince Vardie and King Wyndham told me to stay with them for a while – tell them everything that happened to me."

Samorus just smiled and shook his head, he was struggling to say anything through the tears.

"What... what did happen to you?" he said at last.

The two Pixies both climbed up to the oversized bed, and Petra told him all about it: being kidnapped by Ogres, meeting a friendly group of Goblins, saving the Human prisoners. Everything.

Samorus listened, open mouthed. He was in awe really; it was a lot more impressive than what he had done, which was basically sitting around hoping she would return.

Once she had got to the part about crossing the water in a boat, a young blonde Human knocked and opened the door.

"Hope you don't mind if I join you?" said Fulton, smiling. He looked healthy; just one proper night's sleep and a decent meal had really helped him.

He jumped on the bed and put his arm around Petra, who kissed him on the cheek.

Samorus was even more amazed. He had met Fulton before a long time ago, back in his hovel in Madesco.

"Well it's nice to see you again," said the old Pixie. "But you're... an escaped prisoner?"

Petra laughed. "He's perfectly safe, don't worry."

"But what was he in prison for?" asked Samorus.

"For killing a king," she replied. "One of the Goblin kings, but he did it for a good reason."

"Well technically I didn't kill anyone," added Fulton. "It was Ridley who actually did it."

As chance would have it, his partner in crime happened to open the door just at that moment.

"Here, it was this guy," continued Fulton, laughing.

Samorus looked shocked.

"He's perfectly safe too," said Petra.

Ridley smiled. The word 'safe' echoed in his ears. For the first time in a long time, he really did feel safe. No more running and hiding; at least for the moment, until the Human soldiers figured out who he was.

Ridley said hello to Samorus and told him it was nice to see a familiar face. He didn't try and join the others on the bed, but just leaned against the wall instead.

"Is there a party going on in here?" came another voice. Before they knew it, Larah had also opened the door and entered.

"Apparently!" replied Petra, smiling.

Samorus tried not to look too alarmed that a Goblin had now joined them. He didn't bother to ask this time; he just took it for granted that Petra would say she was also 'safe'.

They all talked and laughed together. Petra took Samorus through the rest of the story, all the way to the point where they found King Wyndham and Prince Vardie, and Fulton figured out the Goblins' plan.

"Don't tortoises hibernate in the winter?" asked Samorus. "Why would it be walking over ice?"

Fulton ignored that comment.

A while later, Samorus asked a question that none of them had properly thought through: "So what are you all going to do next?"

He turned to the two Humans. "You two are from Peria, aren't you?"

"Yes, but I don't know if we can go back there," replied Fulton. "We are prisoners after all – we're on the run!"

Petra nodded. "I suppose I'm on the run too," she said. "I can't just go back home; it would only be a few days before Ogres tried to kill me again."

Samorus looked down for a second. He had expected that, but it was hard to hear. A part of him still hoped that the young Pixie would join him back home, and they could spend the days making healing potion. Just like before.

What he really cared about though, was that Petra was safe. And she didn't need him to protect her – it would be like asking a dog to look after a dragon.

"You'll still come to visit though, won't you?" he

asked. "When… when everything has calmed down?"

"Of course," replied Petra, hugging him again.

"All I know is, wherever Petra's going, that's where I'll be going too," said Fulton.

Ridley rolled his eyes.

"Come back with me!" piped in Larah. "It's perfect; we're so well hidden, nobody really knows where we live. And besides, everyone in the group will be happy to have the magic Pixie joining us! And… her friends," she added, looking at Ridley and Fulton.

Petra raised an eyebrow. Fulton beamed. Ridley looked somewhat less excited.

"Thanks for the offer, but I'm going back to Peria," he said. "I know it's a huge risk, and I'll have to watch my back wherever I go. But I don't belong in a secret hideout with an enchanted group. I just want to be back home."

The others looked at him in silence.

"And I do have a wife, who I should probably go back to at some point."

Fulton smiled. Over the last few months, he had travelled across half of the Known World and been through such crazy and terrifying things. And through all that time, Ridley had been with him.

"Are you sure we can't change your mind?" said Fulton. "I mean… we would be on opposite sides of the world. It would be the end of our brotherhood if you go!"

"I think it might be about time it ended," replied Ridley, laughing. "At least for now… but not forever."

"If you're ever caught and sent to prison again, we'll come and get you out," added Petra.

They all laughed at that. Even Samorus let out a little chuckle.

Chapter 41

For the first time in a long while, King Wyndham slept through the night. Of course, in the Goblin realm, people didn't tend to sleep at night. But the Goblin city of Lancha was now full of Humans and Pixies, so he didn't really see the need to observe their customs anymore.

The sun was shining as he climbed to the surface. It had been a couple of weeks now, and there had been no more attacks. Many scouts had gone back to the battlefield again in the days after it ended and looked down at the gaping hole below them. They had all said the same thing: there was no sign of any danger.

People had seen a few Goblins down in the gap, digging sideways. They weren't trying to get to the other side – they seemed to be making the trench longer and harder to get round.

Yesterday, the Goblin messengers had come. They had said that neither Lord Protector Higarth or Queen Niella wanted any more fighting for now. They had included the words 'for now' in the message.

It had continued, saying that they simply asked for three things: firstly, the Humans and Pixies weren't to come the other side of the trench. Or hole, or whatever it was called. Secondly, any Goblins who wanted to return to Lancha would be allowed back, to live freely in their homes. But they could remain governors of the city, for now. And finally, could they try their best to find the escaped prisoners, and the magic Pixie, and hand them over if they did.

Wyndham and Vardie had laughed at the message, but readily agreed to the terms.

"Shame there's been no sign of the prisoners, or the magic Pixie," Prince Vardie had said.

He and Vardie had spoken to Petra at great length. Of

247

course, they had seen Ridley and Fulton with their own eyes. Those two idiots had committed treason! But they had also helped a great deal in the battle, and most likely saved a lot of lives.

He had agreed to turn a blind eye if Ridley and Fulton disappeared. Provided they never showed their faces again, he wouldn't need to arrest them. Petra said she was going into hiding too – that was harder to agree to, but Wyndham accepted it in the end. So did Prince Vardie. It probably made more sense than her staying in one of their cities, where she would be easier for the enemy to find.

They had both asked for the same thing in return: that once enough time had passed, she send them a message (or give them a sign) to let them know where she was. And that if the Human or Pixie realms ever get attacked, she come to help them if she can.

Petra had agreed. Wyndham had also offered her thirty gold coins, but she said money wasn't important to her. She had only accepted twenty of them.

The King smiled as he looked around. The situation wasn't perfect, but at least the war was over. 'For now'. Many of his soldiers were gathering and chatting, looking in a far better mood than a couple of weeks ago. Cecil, Lord of War, came and joined him.

"Ready to go home today, sire?" he asked.

"Are you sure I'm leaving you enough people?" asked Wyndham in response. Roughly a third of his army had agreed to stay behind; they would need them to keep order in the city. Prince Vardie had made a similar arrangement for his Pixie soldiers.

"We'll be fine," replied Cecil. "Although as I said before, 'keeping order' is not really in my job description. It's something the Lord of Peace should be covering."

The King grinned. "We're not at peace yet," he added. "We're just... not at war either."

There was a lot of work to be done. They needed to recuperate, to rebuild this city, to govern it, and somehow to repair relations with the Goblins. Wyndham wasn't thrilled with the idea of Cecil being in charge for a lot of this, but it was the best thing for the moment. The Lord of Peace was needed elsewhere. Besides, if it went wrong, at least he could just blame it all on this man's incompetence.

"Do you think we need a 'lord of the uncertain period where you're not really at war but also not at peace'?" asked Cecil.

"I'll think about it," replied Wyndham. He felt a strong wind push against him; it almost knocked him over. The weather in the Goblin realm was much fiercer than it was back in Peria.

Wyndham thought about his Palace, with its grand arches ready to welcome him home. He thought about Queen Leila and his children who would be excited to see him. He thought about the peasant folk of the city, who might also be happy to see him. Well some of them. To an extent. He was ready to go home.

Lord Protector Higarth wasn't tired. Ogres never admitted to being tired – it was a sign of weakness. They never actually needed to rest, they just sometimes felt they could benefit from doing so.

Now was one of those times. Higarth sat on a wooden chair in Queen Niella's temporary hall. They had been camped near the site of the battle for two weeks now, and the place was beginning to feel like a permanent home.

He was thankful when their messengers arrived. It was about time. They apologised for taking so long; they blamed it on the fact that they had to walk all the way around the trench, which was getting rather wide.

But it was good news. The Humans and Pixies had agreed to all their demands. Apparently, they had even said they were impressed by the Goblins' strategy and offered commiserations that it had failed so miserably. There would be no more bloodshed for the moment.

Queen Niella smiled as she looked at the two messengers. She thanked them both, then turned to Warlord Sepping, who was sitting to her left.

"Well that's that then," she said. "Get the soldiers prepared to escort everyone who wants to return to Lancha. Those who want to come back with us can do that too."

Warlord Sepping nodded and walked quickly out of the hall. He started shaking his head once Niella could no longer see him. It was hard to feel content about everything that had happened. The war was far from over, and the city of Lancha was now under Human control.

Building a trench from one end of the realm to another was surely a temporary solution. And he wasn't even sure what it was solving. Still, he was trying to stay positive. At least their queen was still alive! He had ordered his staff to prepare additional cotton wool blankets for her journey back to Nuberim. Just in case.

Back in the hall, Lord Protector Higarth was feeling much happier. There was no doubt about it anymore – the Ogres and Goblins were allies, fighting side by side against the Humans. They hadn't defeated them yet, but there was plenty of time.

Next time, the fight would be bigger. They would bring more soldiers, catapults and scorpions. Ones that weren't even flammable.

Non-flammable wood hadn't existed in the Known World for ages, ever since the hardwood tree became extinct in the Troll realm. There had been a forest fire in the 10th age which killed them all. They hadn't burned, obviously, but the Trolls didn't want to risk another forest fire, so they chopped down all the trees that had survived.

But Higarth knew there were other ways of making their weapons safe from fire. Or from any possible attack.

"We'll keep a couple of hundred soldiers here, as agreed," continued Higarth. "No Humans will set foot on this land, you can be sure of that."

The queen nodded. "And the wall? Do you really think that's worth doing?"

"Definitely," replied Higarth. "It's a symbol as much as

anything else. If we build a wall next to the trench, there's no way they're getting through."

"But if it's next to the trench," continued Niella. "Couldn't they just tunnel underneath it?"

Higarth smiled. "You could do that," he began. "But the Humans couldn't. They're too afraid of the dark."

A group of Ogre soldiers suddenly appeared at the door. There were five of them, all wearing black chainmail. They looked very excited.

"Lord Protector!" one of them began. "Are you still offering a reward of a thousand silvers for the people who find the magic Pixie?"

Higarth got to his feet. Everyone around him stopped and stared at the group of Ogres.

"You've found her?" exclaimed Higarth.

"Yes!" replied the Ogre. "Well at least, we think we might have done. We took these two people from the Human camp weeks ago, in the south of the Goblin realm."

The group of Ogres revealed two small and dishevelled people, who they had been carrying. They both dropped down to the ground in front of the group.

"We're not sure if one of them is the magic Pixie," continued the same Ogre. "In fact, they might not actually be Pixies..."

Higarth got a proper look at the faces of the two people. He saw their dark eyes, and small ears. Their comically oversized hands.

"These are Humans!" he growled. "They're obviously Humans, what's wrong with you?"

A silence followed.

"Why did you think they were the magic Pixie?" he continued. "Did they do anything unusual?"

The Ogre at the front turned to the rest of his group. They had all suddenly become fascinated by their shoes and didn't want to look up.

"Well no," replied the Ogre. "But they're both quite small... So we thought there was a chance... they were actually Pixies?"

251

Higarth glared at him. The Ogre tried to avert his eyes but couldn't.

"Get out!" bellowed the Lord Protector. "And take those two small Humans with you!"

The group of Ogres gladly obliged and started to walk away. The spokesperson turned round just as he was leaving.

"I expect the answer's no, but…" he began. "Do we get any of the reward?"

Higarth put his head in his hands. When he looked up again, the Ogre had disappeared.

Petra finally loosened her arms from around Samorus. It was probably the longest hug she had ever given. The old Pixie wiped the tears from his face as she moved away.

"I'll see you again, very soon," she said, with a slightly broken voice.

Ridley and Fulton shared a much quicker hug, and then stood there slightly awkwardly as the Pixies embraced each other.

"I'll see you again soon too," said Ridley.

Fulton smiled. "Stay under cover," he replied.

"And look after this guy," Petra added, gesturing to Samorus.

When the goodbyes were finally over, Ridley and Samorus turned and started to make their way west. Samorus was heading to join the Pixie soldiers, who would hopefully be able to escort him all the way back to Madesco – to his small, cosy hovel, where he would be able to sit and make healing potion for as long as he wanted.

Ridley was planning to follow the Human soldiers, but not too closely; he could be recognised at any minute. But if he was careful and kept his wits about him, he would eventually end up in Peria. He put his hood over his head and kept it there.

Petra looked back a couple of times as the two of them walked away. Fulton grabbed her hand.

"We had better get moving," said Larah. "It could take us a few nights to get back to the Enchanters."

Petra soaked in the surroundings. There wasn't a cloud in the sky – it was as blue as she had ever seen it.

"Larah," she said. "Can we travel above ground? At least for now?"

The young Goblin laughed. "Sure, why not."

They started to walk over the open and grassy land. They kept an eye out for any danger – despite all the possible risks, they felt safe. They could see for miles around; if any soldiers, thieves or dangerous beasts approached they would have sufficient warning.

Petra wasn't even worried. She was just enjoying the journey. The hard part was now over, and they knew exactly where they were going this time.

"Hey Larah," she said. "You do know the way back, don't you?"

THE END

Acknowledgements

I would like to thank my friends, family and partner Catherine for all their support as always. In particular, thanks to my brother Adam for his ideas and suggestions as I was developing it.

And a huge thank you to Peter, Sofia, Alison and everyone at Elsewhen Press for all their hard work throughout the editing, proof-reading and publication.

Finally, thank you to everybody who read or reviewed *The Magic Fix* and decided to come back and read the sequel. I really hope you enjoyed it!

Elsewhen Press

delivering outstanding new talents in speculative fiction

Visit the Elsewhen Press website at elsewhen.press for the latest
information on all of our titles, authors and events; to read our blog;
find out where to buy our books and ebooks; or to place an order.

Sign up for the Elsewhen Press InFlight Newsletter at
elsewhen.press/newsletter

The Magic Fix

Mark Montanaro

The Known World needs a fix or things could get very ugly (even uglier than an Ogre!)

"Did we win the battle?" asked King Wyndham.
"Well it depends how you define winning," answered Longfield, one of the King's royal commanders.

In fact, the Humans are fighting a losing battle with the Trolls. Meanwhile the Ogres are up to something, which probably isn't good. Could one flying unicorn bring about peace in the Known World? No, obviously not.

But maybe a group of rebels have the answer. Or perhaps the answer lies with a young Pixie with one remarkable gift. Does the Elvish Oracle have the answer? Who knows? And, even if she did, would anyone understand her cryptic answers (we all know what Oracles are like!)

The Known World is in danger of being rent in twain, and twain-rending is never good!

Did I mention the dragon? No? Ah… well… there's also a dragon.

ISBN: 9781911409731 (epub, kindle) / 9781911409632 (240pp paperback)

Visit bit.ly/TheMagicFix

HOWUL

A LIFE'S JOURNEY

DAVID SHANNON

"Un-put-down-able! A classic hero's journey, deftly handled. I was surprised by every twist and turn, the plotting was superb, and the engagement of all the senses – I could smell those flowers and herbs. A tour de force"

– LINDSAY NICHOLSON MBE

Books are dangerous

People in Blanow think that books are dangerous: they fill your head with drivel, make poor firewood and cannot be eaten (even in an emergency).

This book is about Howul. He sees things differently: fires are dangerous; people are dangerous; books are just books.

Howul secretly writes down what goes on around him in Blanow. How its people treat foreigners, treat his daughter, treat him. None of it is pretty. Worse still, everything here keeps trying to kill him: rats, snakes, diseases, roof slates, the weather, the sea. That he survives must mean something. He wants to find out what. By trying to do this, he gets himself thrown out of Blanow... and so his journey begins.

Like all gripping stories, *HOWUL* is about the bad things people do to each other and what to do if they happen to you. Some people use sticks to stay safe. Some use guns. Words are the weapons that Howul uses most. He makes them sharp. He makes them hurt.

Of course books are dangerous.

ISBN: 9781911409908 (epub, kindle) / 9781911409809 (200pp paperback)

Visit bit.ly/HOWUL

Life on Mars
The Vikings are coming

Hugh Duncan

Racing against time, Jade and her friends must hide evidence of Life on Mars to stop the probes from Earth finding them

Jade is on her way to meet up with her dad, Elvis, for her sixteen-millionth birthday (tortles live a long time in spite of the harsh conditions on Mars), when she gets side-tracked by a strange object that appears to have fallen from the sky. Elvis' travelling companion Starkwood, an electrostatic plant, is hearing voices, claiming that "The Vikings Are Coming", while their football-pitch-sized flying friend Fionix confirms the rumour: the Earth has sent two craft to look for life on Mars.

It then becomes a race against time to hide any evidence of such life before Earth destroys it for good. Can Jade and her friends succeed, with help from a Lung Whale, a liquid horse, some flying cats, the Hellas Angels, the Pyrites and a couple of House Martins from the South of France? Oh, and a quantum tunnelling worm – all while avoiding Zombie Vegetables and trouble with a Gravity Artist and the Physics Police?! A gentle and lightly humorous science fantasy adventure.

Cover artwork and illustrations: Natascha Booth

ISBN: 9781915304124 (epub, kindle) / 9781915304025 (400pp paperback)

Visit https://bit.ly/LifeOnMars-Vikings

You might also like

SIMON KEWIN'S WITCHFINDER SERIES
"Think *Dirk Gently* meets *Good Omens*!"

THE EYE COLLECTORS
A STORY OF
HER MAJESTY'S OFFICE OF THE WITCHFINDER GENERAL
PROTECTING THE PUBLIC FROM THE UNNATURAL SINCE 1645

When Danesh Shahzan gets called to a crime scene, it's usually because the police suspect not just foul play but unnatural forces at play.

Danesh is an Acolyte in Her Majesty's Office of the Witchfinder General, a shadowy arm of the British government fighting supernatural threats to the realm. This time, he's been called in by Detective Inspector Nikola Zubrasky to investigate a murder in Cardiff. The victim had been placed inside a runic circle and their eyes carefully removed from their head. Danesh soon confirms that magical forces are at work. Concerned that there may be more victims to come, he and DI Zubrasky establish a wary collaboration as they each pursue the investigation within the constraints of their respective organisations. Soon Danesh learns that there may be much wider implications to what is taking place and that somehow he has an unexpected connection. He also realises something about himself that he can never admit to the people with whom he works…

ISBN: 9781911409748 (epub, kindle) / 9781911409649 (288pp paperback)
Visit bit.ly/TheEyeCollectors

THE SEVEN SUCCUBI
THE SECOND STORY OF
HER MAJESTY'S OFFICE OF THE WITCHFINDER GENERAL

Of all the denizens of the circles of Hell, perhaps none is more feared among those of a high-minded sensibility than the succubi.

The Assizes of Suffolk in the eighteenth century granted the Office of the Witchfinder General the power to employ 'demonic powers' so long as their use is 'reasonable' and 'made only to defeat some yet greater supernatural threat'. No attempt was made in the wording of the assizes to measure or grade such threats, however – making the question of whether it is acceptable to fight fire with fire a troublingly subjective one.

Now, in the twenty-first century, Danesh Shahzan, Acolyte in Her Majesty's Office of the Witchfinder General, had been struggling with that very question ever since the events of The Eye Collectors. An unexpected evening visit from his boss, the Crow, was alarming enough – but when it turned out to be to discuss his thesis on succubi, Danesh was surprised yet intrigued. Clearly, another investigation beckoned.

ISBN: 9781915304117 (epub, kindle) / 9781915304018 (334pp paperback)
Visit bit.ly/TheSevenSuccubi

The Vanished Mage

Penelope Hill and J. A. Mortimore

A vanished mage…
A missing diamond…
The game is afoot.

"*From Broderick, Prince of Asconar, Earl of Carlshore and Thorn, Duke of Wicksborough, Baron of Highbury and Warden of Dershanmoor, to My Lady Parisan, King's Investigator, greetings. It has been brought to my attention that a certain Reinwald, Master Historian, noted Archmagus and tutor to our court in this city of Nemithia, has this day failed to report to the duties awaiting him. I do ask you, as my father's most loyal servant, to seek the cause of this laxity and bring word of the mage to me, so that my concerns as to his safety be allayed.*"

The herald delivered the message word-perfect to The Lady Parisan, Baroness of Orandy, Knight of the Diamond Circle and Sworn Paladin to Our Lady of the Sighs. Parisan's companion, Foorourow Miar Raar Ramoura, Prince of Ilsfacar, (Foo to his friends) thought it a rather mundane assignment, but nevertheless together they ventured to the Archmagus' imposing home to seek him. It turned out to be the start of an adventure to solve a mystery wrapped in an enigma bound by a conundrum and secured by a puzzle. All because of a missing diamond with a solar system at its core.

Authors Penelope Hill and J. A. Mortimore have effortlessly melded a Holmesian investigative duo, a richly detailed city where they encounter both nobility and seedier denizens, swashbuckling action, and magic that is palpable and, at times, awesome.

ISBN: 9781915304186 (epub, kindle) / 97819153041087 (212pp paperback)

Visit bit.ly/TheVanishedMage

FAR FAR BEYOND BERLIN

CRAIG MEIGHAN

Even geniuses need practice

Not everything goes to plan at the first attempt… In Da Vinci's downstairs loo hung his first, borderline insulting, versions of the Mona Lisa. Michelangelo's back garden was chock-a-block full of ugly lumps of misshapen marble. Even Einstein committed a great 'blunder' in his first go at General Relativity. God is no different, this universe may be his masterpiece, but there were many failed versions before it – and they're still out there.

Far Far Beyond Berlin is a fantasy novel, which tells the story of a lonely, disillusioned government worker's adventures after being stranded in a faraway universe – Joy World: God's first, disastrous attempt at creation.

God's previous universes, a chain of 6 now-abandoned worlds, are linked by a series of portals. Our jaded hero must travel back through them, past the remaining dangers and bizarre stragglers. He'll join forces with a jolly, eccentric and visually arresting, crew of sailors on a mysteriously flooded world. He'll battle killer robots and play parlour games against a clingy supercomputer, with his life hanging in the balance. He'll become a teleportation connoisseur; he will argue with a virtual goose – it sure beats photocopying.

Meanwhile, high above in the heavens, an increasingly flustered God tries to manage the situation with His best friend Satan; His less famous son, Jeff; and His ludicrously angry angel of death, a creature named Fate. They know that a human loose in the portal network is a calamity that could have apocalyptic consequences in seven different universes. Fate is dispatched to find and kill the poor man before the whole place goes up in a puff of smoke; if he can just control his temper…

ISBN: 9781911409922 (epub, kindle) / 9781911409823 (336pp paperback)

Visit bit.ly/FarFarBeyondBerlin

About Mark Montanaro

Mark has always been a man of many talents. He can count with both hands, get five letter words on Countdown and once solved a Rubik's cube in just 5 days, 13 hours and 59 minutes.

His creativity started at an early age, when he invented plenty of imaginary friends, and even more imaginary girlfriends.

As he got older, he started to use his talents to change the world for the better. World peace, poverty reduction, climate change; Mark imagined he had solutions to all of them.

He now lives in London with his Xbox, television and non-imaginary girlfriend. He recently embarked on his greatest and most creative project yet: a witty novel set in a fantasy world, *The Magic Fix*, Mark's debut book. *The Enchanting Tricks* is the sequel.

Printed in Great Britain
by Amazon